What's Under? Down Under

The Richard Jackson Saga, Volume 14

Ed Nelson

Published by Eastern Shore Publishing, 2024.

Table of Contents

Other books by Ed Nelson

The Richard Jackson Saga
Book 1 The Beginning
Book 2 Schooldays
Book 3 Hollywood
Book 4 In the Movies
Book 5 Star to Deckhand
Book 6 Surfing Dude
Book 7 Third Time is a Charm
Book 8 Oxford University
Book 9 Cold War
Book 10 Taking Care of Business
Book 11 Interesting Times
Book 12 Escape from Siberia
Book 13 Regicide
Book 14 What's Under, Down Under?
Book 15 The Lunar Kingdom
Book 16 First Steps
In the Richard Jackson World
Mary, Mary
Stand-Alone Story
Ever and Always
Cast in Time Series
Book 1: Baron
Book 2: Baron of the Middle Counties
Book 3: Count
Book 4: Earl
Book 5: Earl of the Marches

Dedication

This is dedicated to my wife Carol for her support and help as my first reader and editor.

Thanks to my Editors: Ernest Bywater, Lonelydad57, Old Rotorhead, and Antti.

Also, the Bellefontaine High School Class of 1962, just because.

Professionally edited by Janet E. Rupert

Quotation

That's the way it happened, give or take a lie or two.

James Garner as Wyatt Earp, describing the gunfight at the OK Corral in the movie *Sunset*.

ISBN 979-8-89434-018-0
Library of Congress Control Number: 2022911369

Chapter 1

I realized I was exhausted after all my running around the world, and then hiking in and out of Korea to kill Haoran. I decided to head back to the States to rest at Jackson House for a while.

It was fun coming home to my family. I hadn't gotten to spend time with any of them for months.

The biggest change was in Denny. He was now seventeen and looked all of it. He'd had a growth spurt and it looked like he might catch up with me. He was already six foot three.

Eddie and Mary had also grown but not that much. Mary seemed more mature all the time. Eddie was still waiting for puberty to hit, but it would be any day now.

Mum and Dad were still Mum and Dad. They both had a little grey in their hair but not much.

Mrs. Hernandez was getting married and would soon be moving out of the house. The way she had dated, I thought she would marry some highflier. Instead, he seemed to be a down-to-earth nice guy who owned his own insurance agency.

I loafed around for the first week, playing some golf and surfing.

I even stopped by the studio to see what was going on, but everyone was busy on sets. I did get roped into being an extra in a sword-fighting scene. I wasn't even fighting one of the main characters. It was a byplay in the background. I bet it ended up on the cutting room floor.

Mum was having one of her charity events. I was waiting for the shoe to drop and to be asked to escort some young lady. The shoe didn't drop. Is it possible to be disappointed and relieved at the same time?

I did make the time in my second week to go over to the new R&D campus. The buildings weren't all new, as some bold start-ups overreached themselves and lost it all. We picked it up for a song.

There would still be many additions made, but it was a good start. The building I was interested in was the "Desktop Computer" building. There they were prototyping and testing the first commercial computers which would sit on an office desk and maybe in homes in the future.

The hardware was working like a charm; that is, except for early burnout of components. They had to bring the supply chain up to expectations.

The real problem was the green screen of death. This would appear when the software locked up. The only way to get out of it was to reboot the computer, hoping the software problem wasn't in the rebooting sequence.

To fix this issue they had to run tests, thousands upon thousands of tests. The computer had to be run until the green screen popped up, and then the experts would take over and try to figure out where the conflict in the code was occurring.

They had a huge building with five hundred computers set up. These were run twenty-four hours a day, seven days a week. Anyone in the area who wanted to work had a job. There were men and women from ages sixteen to eighty-seven running the machines.

Even then we had problems getting enough people until a childcare center was set up and bus pickups arranged.

They were testing every program that we had. I was told that if we didn't do this, we could kill the industry before it ever started. The worst thing we could do was release a program that had errors and let the public debug it for us.

I agreed with the concept but had to wonder what would be found when we went from thousands of tests to millions, every day.

My life had gotten very quiet. It was almost to the point of boring if playing golf, surfing, and cruising ever got boring.

That came to a crashing halt the next afternoon. I was at home reading in the library when the phone rang. Mum answered and told them to hang on, "I'll get him."

It was Mr. Norman for me.

"Rick, we have to make this quick. At this moment, two Interpol agents accompanied by two FBI agents are on the way to your house to arrest you for the murder of Haoran."

"What!"

"When the South Korean troops wearing blue UN helmets went to that resort, they were shown Haoran's body with your arrows in him. What were you thinking, leaving something like that at the scene of a black operation?"

"It was meant to be a message to the North Korean government."

"Which doesn't exist anymore."

"What should I do?"

"Get out of the United States as quickly as possible."

"Thanks, I will let you know where I end up."

Mum, who had been hovering in the background, understood part of the conversation. I brought her up to date.

"I thought I taught you better than that, leaving evidence!"

"But the US, China, and the UK all had parts in it."

"All deniable, now get going."

I threw some clothes in a carryall and went out the backdoor. As I was leaving, I heard a call to Mum from the front gate. The FBI was here with an arrest warrant.

I took a Jeep and drove over to the Forestry Service station. There I borrowed a phone from the front office. My jet crew wasn't immediately available. I planned for them to meet me in Vancouver.

I flew north in my Cessna. It was a beautiful day for flying but I paid no attention to that. I was trying to figure out what was going on.

Haoran's death must have been reported through UN channels, which in turn contacted Interpol. Interpol with a working arrangement with the FBI had tracked me down to California and was going to arrest me.

I could hold the thing up in court forever, from fighting extradition to challenging the argument that just because the arrows looked like mine, they were mine.

There was also the fact that a SEAL team had provided support on one of the missions. They wouldn't want that to come out.

I refueled and ate in Oakland and finished the twelve-hundred-mile trip in eight hours.

I had no problem with Canadian Immigration as I used my UK diplomatic passport.

Taking a taxi to a local hotel, I spent a restless night playing through scenarios in my head.

At ten o'clock the next morning, my 707 touched down. I was waiting in the private aviation terminal. While waiting, I hired a pilot to fly my Cessna back to LA. He was bonded to ferry private planes, so I didn't anticipate any problems.

I had decided to fly to Hong Kong. As the Duke of Hong Kong, I had the most power there of any place I could go.

Harold was on board the aircraft waiting with a handful of newspapers. They were all the prominent tabloids and all their headlines screamed about a murderer or assassin on the loose. Me.

They were all speculating where I would turn up. Hong Kong or China were high on their list.

Who said, "Any publicity is good publicity?"

The flight to Hong Kong seemed shorter than usual, but I suppose it was because of my starting point. The landing in Hong Kong was hairy as usual. They had flattened Checkerboard Hill so they could lengthen the runway, but it was still a challenge.

The press was waiting in droves. I went from my aircraft to a waiting helicopter and was flown to Jackson House. As the helicopter circled the field before landing, I could see cars and vans lined up behind the gates.

I was about to unass from the helicopter when Boris ran up to me.

"Boss, you got to get out of here. Interpol is in the house with warrants."

I hadn't even gotten out of the chopper, and we were airborne back to Kai Tek. I kicked myself all the way. Hong Kong is a British Crown colony, so Interpol could go there.

Back at the airport, the flight crew was still disembarking so they reboarded, and we took off to Beijing. They all thought it was a lark.

I wasn't laughing.

Chapter 2

Since my arrival in Beijing was unannounced, there was no fancy escort waiting for me. I hired a taxi; Harold would follow me later with my gear. I told him to wait until notified or he saw me running to the plane. I wasn't certain what my welcome would be.

I found out quickly as the guards at the gate warmly welcomed me home. It looked like I wouldn't be thrown in prison at once.

I had to wait in my room for a summons from the empress. It gave me a chance to clean up and refresh a little. I was still a bundle of nerves over this whole deal.

Within the hour, I was taken to the empress's private suite. That in itself was good news. That or she didn't want to be seen with me in public.

"Greetings, Richard. You have certainly set the cat amongst the pigeons. How are you doing?"

"Tired and confused."

"I'm not surprised. You will be glad to hear that we are working on fixing this problem."

"How?"

"First of all, South Korea overstepped itself when it looked into a crime committed on North Korean territory. Second, there never was a crime. Third, Interpol has no jurisdiction in former North Korea. Fourth, there was no murder committed."

I must have looked confused enough that she had mercy and explained.

"Haoran had been tried in absentia for High Crimes and Treason against the Imperial Throne and found guilty. A death sentence had been declared and a Chinese Citizen carried it out after former North Korea refused to extradite him."

As she talked, I felt the weight coming off my shoulders.

"One more thing, Rick."

"What's that?"

"Never leave evidence behind on a black op."

"I have figured that one out by myself."

"In the meantime, the US president wants to talk to you. He has been trying to reach you for the last twenty-four hours."

"Any idea what it is about?"

"He hasn't said; his people have just left messages. I would think he wants to make certain you don't reveal the SEAL's involvement."

"Also, Queen Elizabeth's people have called. They told me they were concerned that since the 22 SAS unit was in China at the time, they wouldn't be dragged into it."

"I've created a mess, haven't I?"

"Yes, but in doing so you eliminated a threat to China and my granddaughter. That outweighs everything else. Now, I suggest you make those phone calls, and we will then discuss what is next."

My first call was to Queen Elizabeth. She must have been anxious for me to call because I was put through in short order.

"Duke Richard, thank you for getting back to me quickly. I'm concerned that it might be implied that 22 SAS was involved with your trip into North Korea."

"I understand. I will make certain they aren't involved. I'm going to give an interview to a newspaper and describe how I did it by myself."

"We would be grateful if you did that. There is nothing worse for our special forces than getting publicity when it isn't planned for. In this case, it would make them look like hired assassins."

"I know. That has been bothering me. Those rogue MI6 agents wanted me to be an assassin for them, and I told them I wasn't an assassin. Now it appears that I am, not that I regret killing Haoran."

"I have been told that you wanted to play James Bond in a movie. Now you will be viewed as a real-life James Bond."

"Do I get a number?"

There was silence on the other end for a moment.

"Sometimes I forget how young you are. I would recommend asking the empress that question as you performed the deed for her."

I thought about that conversation for about two seconds.

"Maybe I don't need a number after all."

"Don't worry; the press will give you a number or a title. You have gone from All-American Boy to International Agent."

"Do you have any suggestions about which newspaper I should give the story to?"

"I think an American one would be best."

"You are right. It would help keep this matter away from the Crown."

"Thank you for being so understanding. We helped a little, but it was mostly a US-China event."

"I think I will work with the *LA Times*; I know them best, and they have always been fair with me."

After that, we hung up, and I made the second call of the day. This time to the White House. Again, my call was expected as I was put through right away.

"Rick, thank you for calling so soon. I need to talk to you about your being charged with murder and the fallout."

"Mr. President, I'm going to give the story to a US newspaper, probably the *LA Times*. I assure you that the SEALs will not be brought into it."

"That is what I wanted to talk to you about. After serious thought and consideration, we would like you to describe your first trip with the SEALs."

"Why?"

"They want the publicity to show them as a group that will go anywhere for our nation and perform under the most trying circumstances. At the same time, the lack of opportunity will demonstrate they aren't supermen. At my level, I want to show that we are a friend of the new China. I want to open up trade, and this will be the beginning of a partnership."

"I can do that Mr. President, but first I would have to make certain that Empress Ping will go along with that. It would be embarrassing if she denied us."

"I agree. I'm listing you with the State Department under seal as Ambassador Plenipotentiary to China."

"What does that entail?"

'You have the full authority to negotiate treaties between China and the United States. You will report only to me, and you will be given no public recognition at this time, maybe later if it all works out. You have a better relationship with the Imperial Dynasty than we could develop in years. Please help the United States."

"I will talk to the empress about all of this."

"That's all I ask. Please let me know as soon as you can what her decisions are."

"I will Mr. President."

"Thank you."

I had to sit and think for a while after that phone call. I decided the only way to handle it was to be open with the empress.

I went back to the office of her appointment secretary and asked for a meeting as soon as reasonably possible, and no it wasn't an emergency.

From there I returned to my suite to sip on a cup of coffee and to think about everything I was involved in. I was being pulled around like a puppet on a string. The string is being jerked by a three-year-old.

My many business interests and involvements with so many countries, the US, UK, China, Spain, and North and South Vietnam were going to cause problems eventually. I would drop a ball somewhere.

Of my business interests, there were what I considered to be my foundations and then the new ones involving computers and space exploration.

There was no way on earth I could handle all of these and keep my mind, much less have a life.

The appointment secretary called me and told me I was invited to dinner with the empress and May-ling.

Since it was a private dinner, I arrived informally dressed. The two ladies made me feel overdressed. They wore sweatpants and pullover shirts. I asked why the formal dress code, and I was informed it was the girls' night off.

What do you say to that, besides, "Okay."

We conversed casually at dinner. I learned that Ann was out at her deceased husband's estate arranging matters. She wanted to keep it but had to make certain her orders were in place.

I asked May-ling what her plans were now that she was not under immediate death threats. She told me she was planning to return to Hong Kong and finish her degree in Economics with a minor in Foreign Affairs. It would take her another year to finish up.

They wanted to know my plans, and I confessed that I was being pulled from pillar to post and didn't know which way to turn.

The empress suggested that I turn over all of my business to the operating heads and tell all the countries that they had to solve their own problems.

Easy for her to say since I had just solved her most immediate one. I glared a little at her and she had the grace to blush. Only a little, but it was a blush.

I went on to explain the British and American requests. She had no problems with any of them. She liked the idea of opening trade relations with the United States.

She did have one concern that US companies would want to take advantage of China's cheap labor. We talked about that for a while but came to no resolution. I told her I would give it some more thought.

She told me that she would have a working group look at the problem.

After that, I retired for the evening for a good night's sleep.

Chapter 3

Before falling asleep I thought about May-ling; I like her a lot and would like to get to know her better, but she always pushed me away. That is unless I save her, then I'm her hero.

Tonight, she was distant, all wrapped up in her plans to go back to school. The only conclusion I could reach was that she needed to mature and figure out what she wanted in life. At this point, it was not me.

As I drifted off, I wondered what I wanted in life.

The next morning, I called the *LA Times* in the US and asked for an editor. After what seemed like a hundred questions and reasons why I couldn't speak to anyone at that high level, I hung up.

I called Dad and asked for his help. He did understand why I couldn't present my side of the story with one of his papers. He took my number and told me not to go away.

Within fifteen minutes my phone rang. It was a senior editor from the *Times*. He apologized for me not being able to get through. I told him no big deal. I realized his editors were important people and had to be protected from such time-wasting people as the Duke of Hong Kong. Yeah, I was upset.

He took it in stride, basically ignoring my comment, and asked me what I wanted to talk about. I told him I was willing to be interviewed on the entire Haoran story.

He wanted to know when I could come to his office to be interviewed. I told him that I couldn't. I was in Beijing and staying there until things settled down.

They didn't have a reporter stationed in Beijing at this time, so we were at an impasse. There wasn't even direct regular air service. I told him that if he wanted the interview to fly to Hong Kong. A visa to enter China would be available.

He hemmed and hawed about budgets.

"Fine, I will call the *New York Times* or the *Washington Post*."

"It will take two days to get someone there. Would you please decide at your end? We will let you know what flight our reporter will be arriving on."

I had tried the carrot; the stick seemed to work better.

I spent the next several days wandering about the Forbidden City practicing my Mandarin. It was getting better, but there were still many laughs by the staff at my sometimes mangling of the language.

Once I asked a cook if I could have one of the sweet buns sitting on a plate. She slapped me. I wonder what I really said. No one would explain. They were all laughing too hard.

When the reporter arrived, he didn't meet the image I had expected. I was thinking of Mike Hammer and got Dagwood Bumstead. Since he was worn out from the trip, I allowed him a day to recover.

Once he had his wits about him, he started asking questions about everything he saw. No American reporter had ever been in the Forbidden City, so this was a chance of a lifetime.

I finally asked the chief of staff if he could assign someone to answer the reporter's questions about the palace and China in general, while I spoke with him specifically on my story.

He agreed that would be best. He also told me that an oubliette was available if needed. I had sudden visions of Mr. Dithers coming to hunt for Dagwood and told him I didn't think it would be necessary.

When we finally got settled in my office in my suite, I related the story as I knew it. I started with the murders of the Crown Prince and his son, and the agony the empress had gone through in concluding that one of her sons had killed his brother and nephew to gain the throne.

While she was coming to terms with that, there were the attempts on May-ling's life. Then there were our multiple flights to safety.

Finally, the empress had enough and had Haoran tried in absentia and condemned to death. Thus his flight to North Korea.

He was bouncing around as he took notes about the SEAL team's involvement. He had me go into great detail about the HALO jump into North Korea and how we had used the C-47 with corpses as a decoy.

The disappointment about finding a large North Korean unit camped right in our target area. Then there was how we scouted the place out and then hiked back to China.

He made a big deal about that hike and going on short rations. All I remembered was running out of coffee.

I then related my getting a call that another attempt had been made on May-ling and that I was given fast transportation from England to China. He tried to find out what I meant by fast transportation, but I didn't address that question. I didn't think the SR-71 was public knowledge yet.

I told him that when I arrived in China, the SAS unit 22 was there going through the Chinese parachute school to earn their Dragon Wings but that was only a coincidence. They had nothing to do with my mission.

I had to show him my Dragon Wings. He was suitably impressed that they had real rubies in the dragon's eyes. I explained they were a special set as being the first ones issued.

At this point, he had to start another stenographer's pad for his notes. We took a coffee break. Even there he asked questions. These were about my state of mind as events occurred, not the events themselves.

I surprised myself as I related them. I didn't realize how cool and calm I came across to onlookers while I was a bowl of Jello inside.

When I expressed that to him, he replied that he had come across this many times when interviewing people who had been in high-stress situations.

When we got back to the interview, he took me through my lying-in-wait for Haoran several times. He wanted to know where I had learned these skills. This led to a sidebar about archery and hunting.

I only said that my instructor was Rod Bell at the Warner Brothers studio. I told him nothing about who Rod was working for now. I gave full credit for hunting to the gillies and to the SEAL team for survival.

Besides the SR 71, I left out many high-altitude pictures taken in preparation for the first mission and of course nothing about Kim, the Bugatti, or four tons of gold. A guy's gotta have some secrets.

When I concluded with crossing back into China, I thought we were done. Instead, he wanted the names of people who could corroborate my story.

I told him that would be President John F. Kennedy, Queen Elizabeth, and Empress Ping to start with. It was fun to watch his reaction. I then broke down and told him his question had been anticipated and for the SEALs, he was to call Little River and ask for the public information officer. For England, Mr. Norman would be his contact. In China, the empress's chief of staff would answer his questions.

I called the chief of staff's office and made an appointment for him. Later I learned that while he was interviewing the chief of staff, the empress came into the room and told him that all my actions were legal.

My actions were with the full support of the Imperial Throne, and China greatly appreciated me removing the threat to the legitimate line of succession. Furthermore, these actions were only authorized after North Korea refused the extradition of Haoran.

This in turn also resulted in the loss of Chinese support for North Korea.

When Dagwood, the reporter (I had a mental block against his real name), published his story, the SEALs came across as America's answer to Superman. 22 SAS were innocent bystanders, and I was a complex mysterious person.

According to him, I was a mixture of Opie Taylor, Sean Connery as 007, Thomas Edison, and Armand Hammer. Figure that one out.

The murder charges were dropped, the SAS secrecy kept, and the SEAL's public image improved. A sweeping success. Of course, the tabloids couldn't stand for that and did many exposes of the real Richard Jackson.

Mum and Dad took great delight in telling me of my exploits according to the scandal sheets. I don't see how they can make this stuff up. My real life was very boring when compared to their version.

After the reporter left, I sat alone with my thoughts. One thing I realized was that I had to simplify my life if I was going to have one.

The first thing I did was to let the board of directors of Jackson Enterprises know that I was going on a hiatus from the company. I loved that movie term. They were only to contact me in emergencies.

Mum and Dad, my parents, as opposed to Mum and Dad, company directors, would know of my whereabouts. I let Boris know that my parents would be taking care of the gold in the hidden basement.

I instructed Mum and Dad that it was to be made available to General Booth and the space program at need. That took care of business. Next was to let the various countries I dealt with know that I wouldn't be available.

Chapter 4

How do you tell a country that you are taking time off, so don't call me for six months? I made a few phone calls and sent telegrams to others.

I called Mr. Norman in England. I told him that I was burned out and was taking time for myself. He asked where I was going.

"Someplace where I'm not famous and no one knows me."

"Oh, the jungles of Africa or South America?"

"Make that where few people know me, and those that do know me don't care."

"If I, were you, I would give some serious thought to Australia. You haven't done anything spectacular there yet."

"Why did you have to add the yet?"

"I know you, Rick. Trouble follows you."

"I can't argue with that. Anyway, I will be keeping my parents informed of my whereabouts. Other than that, I will not be calling in."

"Seriously, I think you have earned it. Go and enjoy yourself."

I had dinner with the empress. May-ling had left for school in Hong Kong. We had a long leisurely meal. In the end, I informed her of my intentions. She was supportive.

She also told me that it was good that May-ling and I were having time apart. This puzzled me, I didn't know there was anything between us.

I had learned to be direct when in doubt, rather than to let it eat at me. I asked her what she meant.

"Rick, anyone who sees you two together can tell there is a mutual attraction. You are both on the cusp of adulthood, you more than her. You need time apart to grow."

"You think we should be together one day?"

"I would like that, but only time will tell if you are right for each other."

I couldn't disagree with that.

I sent a telegram to the White House baldly stating that I was going on vacation and would be unavailable for the next six months. If they needed to contact me, do so through my parents.

I didn't call or send anything to either of the Vietnams. As far as I was concerned, they were now on their own.

I owed no one a call in Hong Kong, but I called the governor anyway. He told me to enjoy myself and come back refreshed and with a lot of money.

I wondered what that was about but didn't ask.

Now the only thing left to do was to decide where to go. I gave some serious thought to Australia. Mr. Norman had recommended it, but I had been wanting to buy a large ranch, or station as they called it, for some time.

I had no contacts there other than those I made when visiting the container operations. I didn't want to get mixed up with the government. It always seemed to cause me more problems than it solved.

The next day I asked the 707 crew to prepare for a trip to Australia. The heathens that they were, were all for a trip to Bondi beach.

I included my valet Harold in my planning so he knew it would be for an extended period. He asked if that were the case, could he take a long vacation of his own? I saw no reason he couldn't.

He informed me that he would accompany me to Australia and set me up with the proper local wardrobe, and then return to England.

I asked him if a girl was waiting for him. He grinned and told me there were several. I let it go. Some things you don't need to know.

The next day, with little fanfare, we left for Sydney.

Upon landing, the first order of business was finding a hotel. This was the first time in a long time that I came into a city with nothing arranged in advance. That was a mistake.

First of all, several conventions were going on, so there were no rooms available. Second, after viewing several of them, I wouldn't want to stay in any of them anyway.

That is the nice thing about having a plane with its bed. The crew spent the night in town at some pub place, The Lord Nelson Pub, but I didn't want any part of their party. I couldn't keep up with them.

I broke down and called the Governor General's office. I explained my difficulty. They agreed that housing was difficult at this time and would be for some time in the immediate future.

I asked what real estate firm they used for their higher postings. They gave me a name, Shorts and Sons, and an address.

I took a cab to their office. I felt like I was slumming it, a cab! No limo! I needed to get my head straight.

When I entered Shorts and Sons, I was greeted politely. I informed them I was going to be spending time in Australia, mostly in station territory, but wanted a nice home in Sydney when I came to town.

That was said to the receptionist. She never blinked. Instead, she made a phone call and a pretty, well-dressed young lady in her mid-twenties came up front. She introduced herself as Susan Short. I noticed she was wearing an engagement ring. Besides, she was too old for me.

I knew that with my age and casual clothing, she had to be wondering if this was a joke. I handed her my card. You could see her eyes widen.

"It is an honor, Your Grace."

I could see the receptionist's face when she heard that.

I commented it should be Short and Sons and Daughters. She laughed and said her grandfather wanted to do that, but she convinced him not to. It was a matter of branding. Pretty and into marketing, my kind of girl.

We went to her office where she offered me a seat on a comfortable sofa, and she sat in a wing-backed chair. We were no sooner seated than the receptionist was asking if we would like tea or coffee. We both asked for coffee, black for me, cream and sugar for Susan.

When the receptionist turned and left, Susan gave me a saucy grin.

"Doris has been with us forever, and she is very nosey. She is dying to know who you are."

"Are you going to tell her?"

"She will know soon enough, but I intend to drag it out as long as I can."

"You're mean."

"Please don't tell my fiancé that. He will find out soon enough."

I let that one go and explained in detail what I was looking for. She told me that they had several that fit the description, but they were pricey.

"What is the top price on them?"

"Five hundred thousand pounds."

"Then there are no price problems. I can always sell it later."

I didn't tell her that I had never sold a property once I owned it.

She had a picture book with all the listings. She showed me those that she thought would meet my needs. When she showed me the third one, I stopped her and told her I would buy that one.

"But you haven't even seen it or been in it."

"Still, I love that architecture and that is the house I want."

What were the odds, a third Talmadge house? That guy got around.

We drove out to Wolseley Road, in Point Piper, to take a look. There was no doubt this house had been built by Jason Talmadge. He must have bought one set of floor plans and used them over and over. I made a mental note to have all the major cities in the world checked out to see if there were other properties built by him.

The layout was identical inside. This house was in much better condition than the ones in the US and Hong Kong. It had been lived in and well maintained.

I asked if the owners were still in residence but was told no, that a recent death had left it vacant. The heirs felt like it was more house than they would ever need, and the upkeep would be too much.

I told Miss Short part of the story. This house was identical to our family home in the US. I had to have it.

On the way back, she asked what bank I would be using.

"I have to ask my London bank who they correspond with so I can open an account."

"I meant, who you will be financing it with?"

"This will be a cash sale."

"I have read a bit about you and know you have money, but that is still a lot."

"That is not a concern. Please offer the full asking price; forgo any inspections and close on this property as soon as possible."

"You do move fast, don't you?"

"I need a place to stay when in Sydney and it looks like I will be spending a lot of time here in the future, so I might as well have someplace nice."

"The furnishings are not included."

"Could we make an offer?"

"We can always make an offer."

"How much do you think I should offer?"

"I didn't see anything of great value there. I would ask them to come up with a price."

"Please do that."

What I didn't mention is that I couldn't wait to see if there was a subbasement and a wine cellar.

Chapter 5

It was a cash sale with a single heir who had never seen the place and didn't want to. She had lived in London all her life and saw no reason to journey so far from the center of civilization.

The title search did reveal that like the other properties, at one point it had been bank-owned. In other words, there was no family connection to Talmadge.

It took five days for the sale to go through. I slept on the airplane each night, as it was as good as any hotel in Sydney.

I didn't waste my time during those five days. I had my chief pilot arrange for the DC3 to be moved from South Vietnam to Sydney. I also went shopping. The type I like, buying another two-engine aircraft good for the Australian Outback.

A broker had just listed a 1960 Cessna 310D for 45,000 pounds. I grabbed it. I know I overpaid, but it was worth not having to get qualified in it.

It was hangared right here in Sydney, so it was easy to check out and take possession. It flew like a dream. The airframe and engines weren't due for checkups and rebuilds for some time yet; that is, if I didn't go crazy flying everywhere.

It is surprising how quickly hours mount up on maintenance items. At the same time, qualification hours are as slow as molasses.

Harold had done some shopping of his own. That is, he had identified the shops where I needed to buy clothes and accoutrements.

Contrary to what he told the flight crew, he didn't have to drag me screaming and kicking down the road. I only whined a bit.

When it was done, I had multiple outfits for everything from roughing it in the Outback to attending a formal ball in Australia. The clothes for the Outback made sense, but the formal ones weren't that different from those I already owned.

I think Harold just likes to buy clothes with other people's money. On the other hand, I was always dressed perfectly for the occasion, so I cut him some slack. I also think he is a spy for Mum.

One good thing was the press hadn't taken notice of me being in Australia. The international newspapers all carried the *LA Times* story. According to their editorial pages, I was either a menace to mankind or the long-heralded savior.

I voted for Dennis the Menace's older brother.

At long last, we closed on Jackson House Australia. A catchy name, that. I couldn't wait to get inside and check it out.

We closed in the Short's office. I had the cab that delivered me to the office wait to go directly to the property.

You would never have guessed the first thing I did was go to the master bedroom and check for the secret door. It was there. I had thought of bringing a flashlight, but the electricity was on.

It was like going downstairs on Christmas morning when I was four or five.

What I found wasn't much of a Christmas present. In the center of the subbasement, which was devoid of all furniture other than a large safe, were several pallets.

The pallets were loaded with bricks of heroin. The reason I knew that is because they were labeled. Now I know how Talmadge had so much money. Whether it really was heroin, I had no way of knowing. I wasn't about to touch it in any way.

This was going to be a headache! If I reported it to the authorities, the secrets of all the Jackson Houses would be blown. This stuff had been here for over thirty years, so it probably wasn't any good anyway.

I had to think of a way of getting rid of this stuff without getting caught. There must be a metric ton of the stuff.

Jason Talmadge was consistent in one thing. He used the same combination on all of his safes. It had stacks of Australian currency and Chinese round gold coins with a square hole in the middle. The gold coins were on a string, in this instance metal wire, with one hundred coins called a *diao*.

I counted the Australian currency; it was half a million pounds. I had no idea what the Chinese gold coins were worth, but since they were the same size as a US double eagle, I figured there was another half-million there.

There was also a stack of Swiss bearer bonds. A quick count was five million US, so I had made a profit on the purchase.

On the top shelf inside the safe were several account ledgers. They had names and dates of transactions. Talmage was a detailed keeper of records. You could follow his thirty-some-year-old trail of drug dealing.

I sat down cross-legged on the floor and leafed through the ledger. The entries were enlightening. He had numerous dealings in China before World War II, so they probably would lead nowhere.

There were several firms in Hong Kong whose names rang a bell. Also, Australian names, including one which was so prominent that I recognized it.

If it was the same person, they would have been thirty years old then; now they would be around sixty. Australian politics might be in for a big shakeup.

I wanted no part of this. I would let the police put it together.

Several American names jumped out. One was the father of a very famous American. This information was pure poison, and the sooner it was out of my hands, the better.

I now wish I had worn gloves. I don't know if they could get fingerprints. I would have to let the police know that I had leafed through the book but hadn't read it in any depth.

I put the book down and looked around the basement one more time. I tested the elevator system, and it worked like the others. You could go up from the subbasement but not down to it. It was a neat trick.

Next, I looked for the escape tunnel. I found the door and had to use my flashlight. The tunnel ran for about two hundred yards and came out in the garage of a house across the way.

I listened at the outer tunnel door and couldn't hear anything, so I took a chance and opened it after lifting the heavy bar. As in the other two houses, the door opened into a janitor's closet in the garage.

I listened again. Once more there was no sound. I tried the interior door from the garage to the house. It wasn't locked, and a quick peek showed the place to be empty.

I looked out a front window to orient myself. I would have to drive by to get the address so I could check into the status of the house. I would purchase it if it was available.

That brought to mind that I had been using taxis. I needed a car of my own.

I went back through the escape tunnel, making certain I hadn't left any footprints leading to the tunnel. Once back in the tunnel, I barred the door behind me and returned to the subbasement.

I then walked all around the perimeter of the subbasement to make certain I hadn't missed anything. I hadn't. There was no evidence of Mr. Talmadge's strange taste in sex.

Another place I hadn't looked in my haste to buy the place was the outbuildings. In the old garage behind the house were five vehicles covered with canvas.

You could tell that someone had looked at the first three and carelessly put the covers back on. I could see why. They were pedestrian-looking and well-worn.

I removed the fourth cover and found the same. The fifth was a treasure. It was a 1955 MG MGA. A white sports car. I didn't know the MG line, but I knew this was a good car.

It would need a complete checkover, oil replaced, new tires, gas tank emptied, carburetor cleaned, and a lot of other work but it was a beautiful machine. I now had my Sydney car.

The garage had a loft and I checked it out, even going so far as to move several ancient bales of hay. There was nothing of note stored there. I couldn't figure out why there was even hay there in the first place.

I then decided I would check out the view from the tower. I'm glad I did. It looked out over one of the best neighborhoods in Sydney. This included several houses with swimming pools.

I bet some pretty girls used those pools. Not that I was a voyeur. I just enjoyed looking at pretty girls, especially if they were topless. What teenage boy wouldn't?

Chapter 6

The question remained; what was I going to do with the ancient heroin? Since I now owned the place, the police would expect me to report it immediately.

The longer I waited, the worse my situation would be. I thought about burning it in the huge coal-fired furnace, but I didn't know what odors or ash would come out of the flue.

Remembering what we did with Talmadge's skeleton, I briefly considered airdropping it in the ocean. It would only take the DC3 and two or three other people.

I could visualize packing the stuff in weighted wooden crates. Smuggling it aboard the aircraft. Flying it out to sea and dropping it, where the crates would burst when hitting the water.

Passing fishing boats would report the strange white powder floating in the water, causing a huge fish kill. When the heroin was identified, all aircraft that had been flown in the area would be checked.

Mine would be the only one that could have done the job. When they searched the plane, they would find traces from when one box had broken open when I loaded it.

My next thought was of me being hauled off in handcuffs with the press taking pictures.

Scratch that idea.

While I mulled over what could be done, I went back to the secret panel behind the mirror upstairs. This led down to the wine cellar which I hadn't visited.

There were vintage cases of wine. Case after case. The cases were built so the wine was racked properly. I assumed they were of a good vintage, or why store them? Other than the wine and other spirits, it was empty. At least there was no artwork to dispose of.

I ended up doing what I always did when in doubt. I called my parents. I explained the situation to them as circumspectly as I could.

Dad asked a key question, "As far as you know, the realty company has been the only one in the house in years."

"That's right; the bank has had them trying to flog it for ten or more years, so the Shorts and anyone they gave a tour to would have been inside."

"Try to find out how many people have been through it, especially the first known basement. If not very many, you could discover the stuff there."

"I'll check with Susan Short and let you know."

After getting caught up on the family news, and hearing that all were fine, I called Susan.

"Hey, Susan, I have a question for you."

"What's that, Rick?"

"Since your family has been showing my place, have many people been down to the basement?"

"Only me and Dad, and we never went all through it. It is full of junk, and most potential clients didn't get past the first floor before saying no."

"That's all I need to know. You'll hear why later."

I went down to the first basement, which I had only looked at from the top of the stairs. It was full of junk. Nothing looked worth salvaging.

It looked like someone had intended to clean the place out at one time because there were several hand trucks and low trollies in a corner.

Thank goodness the freight elevator worked. I now had a plan.

I drove the car I had rented down to a work center where guys looking for day jobs were hanging out. I hired three of them and took them back to the house.

I picked them carefully. They were all loners, not a group. I could see hiring a group of three and being robbed. On the way back I stopped and bought some push brooms.

I had them clean out the junk with hand trucks and trollies for the rest of the day. They hauled the stuff up the elevator and dumped it behind the house.

I spent the afternoon sweeping.

After paying each of them enough that they would remember me but not enough to be stupid, I returned them to the work center. I'm sure they enjoyed their drinks or drugs that night.

I had learned enough about them that I wouldn't trust any of them as far as I could throw them.

I then went back to the house and did the real work. Using a pallet jack stored in the subbasement, I used the trick elevator to move the two large pallets upstairs.

I took the two ledgers that I'd stored in the safe and put them on top of one of the pallets. You never would know what would come up in a cold case.

I made certain the area was clean and had no evidence of pallet jack tracks. The area now looked like it was in the middle of a cleanout when I came across the pallets.

After examining the contents, I went to a corner phone and called the police as any good citizen should.

One patrol car showed up as I waited at the front door of the house.

"Sir, we have a report that you have found drugs in this house which you purchased recently."

"Yes, let me show you."

I don't know what they expected to see, maybe a bag of marijuana. Their eyes were bugging out as they saw what was there.

One of the policemen went upstairs to call it in on the car radio. The other stayed with me and started taking notes.

Who was I? When did I buy this place? Who did I buy it from?

I had decided to play it straight as all the truths would come out anyway.

I handed him my British diplomatic passport. It wouldn't give me immunity for something like this, but it did show that I had to be handled carefully.

This policeman was the calmest one I had ever met. He just wrote down all my answers. He never reacted to the Duke of Hong Kong bit.

We had been at it for about half an hour when half the Sydney police force descended upon us.

I was glad to see so many people wandering about as they ruined the crime scene as far as my cleaning and moving stuff went.

I was taken aside by two detectives who asked all the same questions over again. At least they didn't accuse me of being involved with the drugs. They could tell it was old stuff.

They got all the details of my purchase of the place two days before and descriptions of the guys I hired to help clean it out.

While they said nothing, I'm certain they would question the Shorts and try to find the guys who had helped clean the place.

There was a commotion over by the drugs. I figured they had found the ledgers. They had.

Since I hadn't worn gloves when handling the ledgers, I told the two detectives I thought the noise was about the ledgers, which I had opened.

I thought they would ask why I had opened them, but they didn't. I told them the books seemed to contain the details of the drug deals.

What I read told when, where, and from whom the drugs were bought. It even listed the cost and methods of transportation. Bribes paid and to whom. Mr. Talmadge was a very conscientious businessman.

I had moved to Lord Nelson Hotel from my jet after getting tired of planes taking off and landing all hours of the day and night. The next morning, the police picked me up at the Lord Nelson and drove me to the work center, where I identified the three men I had hired. They didn't see me as I stayed low in the backseat of the police car.

I then was taken down to the police headquarters building. I was introduced to the Sydney police commissioner.

I was treated like an honored guest.

"Your Grace, we would like to thank you for bringing this to our attention. Though after the reports I have received about you from the Crown, I would expect no less."

"Thank you."

My internal thoughts were, play this close and admit nothing.

"We have a favor to ask."

"What is that?"

"Say nothing to anyone about any of this. We have managed to keep it away from the papers and are investigating."

"As long as you get those drugs out of there."

"They are already gone. They will be dumped in a vat of molten steel at a forge."

Good to know.

"I have no reason to speak to anyone of this."

"Those ledgers have given us leads on companies and organizations that are still active."

"What were the Shorts told?"

"Only that you found a set of ledgers in the basement and turned them over to us. That is all the official record will show. Unless we could find and arrest Jason Talmadge who would be in his nineties by now, the case would never come to court."

I wished him luck with that one.

We shook hands as I departed. I thought I handled that quite well.

I called my parents that evening and relayed the events. I used a random call box. I had to trust that Jackson House California wasn't bugged.

Mum and Dad were pretty religious about having the phone lines checked out. I would have to start the same regime at all my places.

Chapter 7

I hadn't been up to the attic yet, so I decided to take a look at it. The police had been all through the house and hadn't found any more drugs but hadn't commented on what they did find.

After going up to the attic, I could see why. There was nothing but a bunch of old furniture up there. It was in good shape, not broken or anything, but none of it was in a style that I liked.

It seemed so formal. I looked for maker's marks and found a table and set of chairs that had a fancy crest on the bottom and the name Hepplewhite.

There were a couple of pieces by Sheraton and Adams. The best-looking furniture was a complete bedroom set by Chippendale.

I thought I recognized that name, so I had better have someone check the stuff out.

There was some artwork by people I didn't recognize and others that I did. I recognized the names Gainsborough, Vermeer, and Sargent. I thought I had heard of Klimt.

If the furniture was worth anything like the paintings, I had another small fortune on my hands.

It is a wonder the police hadn't seized them as part of the drug bust.

I went to a corner call box and dialed the governor-general's office. I wanted to keep a low profile, but it didn't seem to be working.

When connected, I explained to the receptionist at Government House that I needed to find appraisal experts in furniture and paintings. She transferred me to an office.

The gentleman I was transferred to recognized all of the names. He suggested that I contact the University of Sydney.

He gave me the name and number of a professor in the art department who should be able to help me.

I was lucky that the professor I was calling was in and available. He was very interested when I described my find. He asked if he could come by tomorrow and bring several other people with him.

I told him that I thought this was a very good idea and that 10 o'clock would be fine. From there I continued my exploration of the house. One room that I had not visited was the library. I had glanced in, and there were many books on the shelves.

If nothing else, this room needed a good dusting. I doubt if anyone had been in here since Tallmadge.

I randomly opened a few books to their title pages. The third book I picked up was a first edition, the first printing of *Oliver Twist*. The author on the title page was Boz. It was signed by Charles Dickens.

I had volume two of three in hand. The other two were next to it on the shelf. That meant this library had some value. I will ask the professor and his team to take a quick look tomorrow.

They showed up on time. I had been expecting the professor and maybe two graduate students. Instead, it looked like he had brought the whole department. They arrived on a bus. There must have been fifty of them.

I was waiting on the front porch for them, and the professor headed straight for me.

"Are you Duke Richard?"

"Yes, I am.

"I hope you will forgive me, but this is a rare chance for the students to do some real fieldwork."

"I've no problem with that as long as they have proper supervision. There appears to be a lot of value in the attic. Also, I would like someone to take a look in the library, as I think there are some first editions there."

I had a sudden thought.

"How long do you think this might take?"

"I would think all of today and maybe some of tomorrow. I will be able to tell you better after we take our first look."

"Have you made arrangements to feed this lot?"

He got the deer in the headlights look.

"Err, no."

"I will take care of that in part payment for your labors."

"Part payment?"

"I don't expect your department to do this for free, so I had planned to make a direct donation to your department's budget."

"Good show! Let's get started."

"Follow me."

The professor told the students to wait until he and his grad students reconnoitered the find.

Before we went upstairs, I asked the students in general if any of them knew of restaurants in the area that could cater lunch for fifty people.

Two raised their hands so I beckoned them forward. They both had the same restaurant in mind. The restaurant was close by, so I asked them to see if the manager could join us.

The two took off down the street before I could say anything else. Pointing to another student, I asked her to have the restaurant manager join us in the attic when he appeared.

He was to use the elevator in the entryway. To be certain, I showed the young lady the elevator. The controls were self-evident.

The professor and his aides rode with me to the attic. When we exited the elevator, Professor Johnson looked around and then looked around again.

"My word, from what I can see standing right here, there are over a million pounds in true antique furniture."

"That is what I thought from my art appreciation classes."

"Oh, where did you go to school?"

"Oxford."

"What did you graduate in?"

"I didn't. I was sent down."

"What! Sending a duke down; you must have done something terrible."

"I wasn't a duke at the time, and I did something terrible. I dyed the Chancellor a brilliant blue."

"That would do it."

The professor got a devilish look.

"Would you be interested in an Australian Chancellor?"

"I think I had better pass."

"Pity."

We then took a stroll around the attic. I had seen less than half of it. Most of the furniture was under Holland covers so the professor had the plain weave linen sheets removed so we could see what was underneath.

The surprises continued. None of the furniture was to my taste but then I didn't grow up in the 1700s.

He finally stopped and told me.

"These are all museum-quality pieces. It will take weeks if not months to document the condition and worth of each piece."

"Could we start a preliminary catalog of what is here?"

"That would be ideal. I'm going to break the students up into teams of five. We will write descriptions of everything and take photographs, and then recover them for protection."

"Professor, would you take a look at the paintings?"

"Certainly, I was about to ask about them. I'm almost afraid to look after seeing all of this."

He looked at them and had to take a seat. Even being as flustered as he was, he took great care sitting on the Chippendale chair.

"My word, these paintings are probably worth more than the furniture."

"I thought they might be."

"Again, we will photograph and catalog each one."

"This sounds like a plan."

I heard the elevator come to our floor and it was a gentleman I didn't know. I confirmed it was the restaurant manager. After introductions, I asked him if he could feed us and all the students downstairs lunch.

He would be delighted to; it was now eleven o'clock. If we could send them down to his restaurant in two groups a half-hour apart, it would work well. I had plenty of cash so paid for lunch for fifty-five out of pocket.

While all of this had been going on, I was having some grave reservations about what was going on. What was my legal position in all of this?

It wouldn't be hard to make a case that all these items were purchased with drug money and were subject to some sort of seizure.

While the group started work, I excused myself and made two telephone calls from the corner call box.

The first was for the phone company to have phones installed at Jackson House, at least one in the lobby, and more later.

The second was to the police commissioner.

He took my call immediately; he must have been wondering if I had found more drugs in the house.

I explained what was going on with books, paintings, and furniture that were included with my purchase. He assured me there were no laws on the books that would require the police to take them.

There also was the fact that they didn't want the drug bust to become public knowledge, as it would take them weeks or months to unravel the information in the ledgers.

"Though when it all comes out, Your Grace, I can see where you could be criticized for keeping or selling what might be stolen merchandise. May I suggest?"

"Please do. I don't need any more negative publicity."

"I understand. I have a dossier on you that is extremely thick. Most of it is good but some very dicey things also. Could you see your way to donating it all? From what I can understand, you have enough money as it is."

"That is a wonderful idea, especially if it is done anonymously."

Chapter 8

The only way it could be done semi-anonymously was through a shell company. Even then many people like the students would know that I was involved. That is why I say semi.

It was still worth a try to keep my name out of the papers. I ended up having a company created in Australia listing it as the owner of Jackson House.

The paintings were going to the Art Gallery of New South Wales, the books to the University of Sydney Library, and the furniture to the same school. I had to donate enough funds for a building to house the furniture. It would be a public admissions museum and also a source of study for students.

The different groups I talked to all wanted to create committees to study the issues and come up with recommendations. I listened for a while and then told them they had two days; then everything was going on the auction block. A little motivation works wonders.

The newspapers covered each, but the story ended with the company. They treated the company as a good corporate citizen in surrendering questionable goods, which may have been stolen.

Some cynics on the paper's staff wrote editorials that the company was trying to avoid legal complications from the purchase. If they only knew.

I had wanted to be in Sydney for two or three days. It turned into weeks. The time wasn't completely wasted. I was able to send the contents of the safe to America in the 707 for Mum and Dad to dispose of.

I also found from Government House recommendations a land agent who specialized in larger properties like those I was interested in. I had originally wanted a station of a million acres.

When I found that the only property that large was in the true Outback, which was effectively worthless at this point, I changed my mind.

I found that in Queensland, it was possible to find properties up to a quarter-million acres. Now all I had to do was find four adjourning ones.

After many hours spent in the agent's office looking at maps of available properties, I found that it wasn't going to be that neat.

The best I could do was buy five separate stations that were near each other and then try to convince the owners of the adjoining properties to sell so I could join them all together.

We spent hours discussing the best strategy. Buy the large properties upfront, then try to buy the properties that would connect them or offer for the connecting properties first and then the larger ones.

We decided, well I decided, to go for the connecting properties first so I wouldn't end up with four distinct stations to run. My life was complicated enough.

I requested dossiers made up for each of the properties. I wanted to know about the owners of the connectors, as it would tell me how to approach them. The large ones would have their own management. I wanted to know which ones were well run.

Six connector properties would have to be purchased. Three of them should be easy as the dossiers showed them going broke through poor management. Two of them would be for sale for the right price, which meant a high price.

I didn't see any way the sixth one would be for sale at any price. It was run by a McLeod family and had been a going concern for over a hundred years. Currently, two daughters were managing it. They were doing very well.

More study of the maps provided what I thought could be a solution. I only needed a corner of their ranch, which was only a thousand acres. It wasn't even the best land on their station. On the opposite side of their station was a failing ranch of five thousand acres.

The failing ranch was good land but owned by absentee landlords. If I could buy that land, maybe they would swap. It would be a very good deal for them.

My land agent contacted the absentee people in London, and they were more than willing to sell it. They only wanted twice what it was worth. The land agents fought well and got them down to only ten percent over the estimated value. That was close enough for me.

All the land in question was south of Mount Isa, about halfway to Bedourie. It was a few miles east of Dajarra. The land agent arranged a meeting with the McLeod sisters for Wednesday week.

The day before, I flew us in my new Cessna which had just finished a complete airworthiness check at my expense. I had learned to be careful with anything to do with aircraft.

We flew to Mount Isa and picked up a rented Range Rover. Leaving Mount Isa, we saw the huge copper mine. It was one of the largest open-pit mines in the world, if not the largest.

The Range Rover was exceptionally clean. A young man by the name of Greg Norman was wiping it down. I complimented him on his job. He stared at me for a minute.

"You're that amateur golfer who won the Grand Slam of golf!"

That is when I found out that young Greg was a huge golf fan and player. He recognized me from the magazines. I waited while he ran into the rental shed and brought out his magazine for me to autograph, wishing him luck in his golfing career.

So many young men wanted to be a professional and so few made it, I hoped he would do okay.

It took most of the afternoon, but it was still daylight when we reached Dajarra. The agent had reserved us rooms at the Dajarra Roadhouse. I was surprised when we got there. It was the only place to stay in town. It was a combination motel, service station, and general store. It was old but well cared for.

The next morning after a fine breakfast, we met with the McLeod sisters. They were very attractive. I had been told that men outnumbered women five to one in this area so they must have the guys knocking down their doors. They were too old for me, or I would have been right there with them.

After the introductions, I let the land agent take the lead. He didn't explain why we wanted those thousand acres, just the bare bones of the deal.

Their immediate reaction was positive, but as they talked, they wanted to know why that particular acreage. It went back and forth for a while with neither party wanting to back down.

I finally broke the impasse by speaking up.

"I will tell you the complete story if you sign an NDA."

The older sister looked blank, but the younger one who had spent time in the city knew what it was.

She asked, "What are the conditions?"

In anticipation of this, I had one prepared. They both read it and didn't see any problem with agreeing not to disclose what I was about to tell them. They signed it and the manager of the Roadhouse witnessed.

The manager loitered in the area as though he wanted to hear what was going on. I bluntly told him.

"This is none of your business. Would you please leave us?"

He left but didn't seem embarrassed by his nosiness. After he was gone, I told the ladies of my plans for a large ranch and how their thousand acres played a key part in this.

This was a bit of a gamble on my part as they now knew that the land was worth more than the direct sale value would indicate.

They huddled together in a corner and discussed the deal. From the way the arms waved, it was an energetic discussion.

They came back and asked if I was open to a counterproposal. It was noticeable that they now realized I was the person behind this deal and the land agent a representative. For his part, he seemed willing and ready to let me deal with this. To him, it was now a spectator sport.

"What are you requesting?"

"The land trade itself is a good deal. We aren't going to be greedy and ask for more money. What we would like is a verbal agreement of friendship."

I must have looked lost.

"What we would like is an agreement that we will be good neighbors with each other. If there is a fire, we will help put it out. If the cattle get mixed, we round them up together and split them up fairly. Good neighbors."

It wouldn't have occurred to me to be anything else. I did realize when I had the whole station put together, I had to make sure my people in charge understood that.

A handshake with them sealed the deal. The legal paperwork would be taken care of in Mount Isa. The first and most critical step was complete.

Chapter 9

While at the Roadhouse, I saw a sign for the spring fair in two weeks. It reminded me I was upside down from my normal seasons.

With the critical land deal in place now, it was imperative to move quickly on two others. The McLeod deal connected two of the large stations.

I couldn't assume anything done at the Roadhouse would remain quiet for long. This was a big event for a very small town.

My land agent had written proposals in place to present to the owners of the two stations. He had separate staff members present them to the listing agents that evening. Part of the offer was that it only would be good for twelve hours. Both of them were for the asking price, so they were accepted by the next morning.

We had managed to stay ahead of the bush telegraph. I was halfway to my goal of a million-acre station. When done, it would be around 1592 square miles or a box 40 miles on each side. What I was putting together would look more like a long squiggle.

The next move was to purchase the two connectors that would only go for a high price. This had to be done quickly because as far as pricing went, they were in the driver's seat.

That same morning the land agent had two of his staff make full-price offers to both of the connectors that were doing okay. Both of the asking prices were well over the market, but if they heard about what was going on, they might double overnight.

Our buying agents were to let slip that a rich American was buying a station and wanted one that was making money so as not to be embarrassed by a failure. This was true to a point.

By dinner time the deals were done.

The next day we made listing price offers on the other two large stations. They were accepted at once. We had signed deals in hand, well not actually in our hands, but in the staff's hands of our agent by dinner time.

That same afternoon offers were made on the last three connecting parcels. These were all failing stations. I felt slightly guilty as their asking prices all reflected this reality, so I insisted that we offer twenty-five percent over asking for each.

I just about had a row with my land agent over this. It offended his business sensibilities.

Everyone else we had dealt with had come out ahead. These people were trying to break even. When the entire deal became public, as it would, I didn't want to be seen as taking advantage of the down and outers.

There would be some who would complain no matter what, but the majority would think I had been more than fair.

When I explained my logic to the land agent, he accepted it with a grumble. I pretended not to hear, "Yanks with dollars and no sense."

So, in less than a week I had bought eleven properties for under fifteen million pounds and assembled a cattle station of a little over a million acres.

Every cowboy's dream.

We returned to Mount Isa by Range Rover, then flew back to Sydney for the weekend. I can't say I was sorry to leave the Roadhouse. It served its purpose but wasn't what I was used to.

Back in Sydney, the furniture and paintings had been removed from Jackson House. The books in the library were cataloged by students before being taken to the university library.

Several cute girls were working on the project and from the way they eyed me, I think I could have gotten a date. The only problem was that they looked so young!

None of them looked like they had faced real life yet. So innocent looking. What did that say about me?

The master bedroom had been cleaned out by a hired cleaning service and a new bed and furnishings installed. They were all off the shelf and would be replaced later, but they would do for now. At least I wouldn't be staying in a pub/hotel.

Things could get a bit noisy and even rowdy at Lord Nelson. It was a tourist-type place and not for those who wanted a quiet stay.

I didn't do much over the weekend. I looked at some stockman's hats and realized that my American cowboy hats would do fine.

I retrieved them from the 707, which was still parked at the airport. Harold refused to stay at any of the places I had been staying, so he spent the time on the aircraft in his cubbyhole in the hold.

Each to his own.

After he learned my schedule, he arranged for the entire wardrobe on the aircraft to be sent to Jackson House and put up properly. The plane would be deadheading back to London, and he would replace the wardrobe there.

He had a catalog of each item. Those that came from the States had already been ordered. I didn't even argue with him. I now had a full wardrobe at Grandmum's house, the Plaza on the Strand in London, the Waldorf in New York, Jackson House California, Jackson House Hong Kong, and now Sydney.

I didn't bring up Bellefontaine to him, or Spain. I had over a hundred thousand dollars in clothes scattered around the world.

I think he may have been in a bragging rights contest with his father. I had given up and went with the flow. I had several pairs of jeans, outdoor shirts, boots, and belts with large buckles. Those along with socks and underwear were all I needed right now.

I don't think showing up at my new stations dressed in Coldstream Guards mess dress would impress anyone.

I could carry a pistol and rifle on my ranch while in the Outback, but it wouldn't be wise to carry them into any town. This wasn't Texas.

I had a large-scale map of Queensland and another of my area. I outlined my new station/ranch to the best of my ability. I laid out a new ranch house area. It would be a self-contained small town.

The buildings on each of the properties that I had purchased had to be evaluated to keep as is, repaired, or torn down.

There would be a need for housing for the many ranch hands and their families. I laughed at myself as my thinking kept switching back and forth from American ranches to Australian stations.

There were also cowboys and stockmen. Then there were jackaroos and jillaroos. I'm not even sure what they did.

I spoke American and British English, and now I had to learn Australian. I was going to stick with my British accent. At one time my normal accent was American, now it was British. Would it change to Australian?

Don't even ask about my Spanish anymore. I didn't even know what you would call my accent when I spoke in Mandarin. From the way many Chinese looked at me, I suspect it was pretty bad or at least different.

Accent aside, I spent time considering what I would want on my new property. I realized that flying into Sydney and then flying to Mount Isa to then drive wouldn't cut it. I would have to have a long runway built on the station that would handle the big jet.

That wasn't as crazy as it sounds. To run the station, I would need light aircraft and helicopters. I'm certain the Australian Royal Air Force would appreciate a runway for emergencies to be a good thing. I could even let good neighbors fly in, like the McLeods.

There would have to be full maintenance buildings stocked with the correct equipment and spare parts, similar to what we were doing in Spain.

There would be paint shops, woodworking shops, and electronics. That made me think of a full radio station with AM, FM, and Short-wave capability.

Next was a health center for the hundreds of people who would live at the station.

I got so wrapped up in these items I almost forgot what the purpose of the station was, a cattle ranch.

I would have to have the economics of butchering on station and shipping frozen beef versus sending live cattle to market.

This was beginning to sound like work.

I went back to the basics of cattle ranching. You needed water, feed, and cattle. Everything else is supported.

Each of the stations had a water supply, but I thought a new survey of the entire area with test drillings would be in order.

We could grow the grain to feed our cattle. The soil was fertile, but we would have to do crop rotation to ensure we didn't erode the fertility of the fields.

The fifteen million I had spent on the land was nothing compared to what I would have to invest to do this properly. That didn't faze me as I was in this for the long haul.

I couldn't wait to have the Duke down to show him what a real ranch looked like. That made me think of our movie-making days. From there I jumped to the thought that I needed to have a documentary team filming the building of a million-acre ranch.

It wouldn't do well in theaters but might make a TV special. If nothing else, my kids and grandkids would enjoy it.

Kids and grandkids, where did that come from?

Chapter 10

I decided now was the time to start visiting the properties I had purchased. I had a rental ute that looked ragged but ran well as I drove to the first large station.

When I drove through the gate of the first station, I was unimpressed. The fences were down and didn't look like they had been tended for years.

I drove up to the main house to check in with the station manager. A middle-aged man came out of the house as I drove up. He was what you would call wiry. I outweighed him by at least seventy-five pounds and had six or eight inches on him.

That didn't stop him from charging right up to me.

"I get tired of you jackaroos coming around for a job."

That was when he realized how big I was compared to him.

"Well, maybe I do have some work for someone your size. You ever do any fence repair?"

"Yes, sir."

"You're hired. I'm the boss and you are labor. We pay cash at minimum wage. You will have to rebate ten percent to me every payday. Also, bunkhouse rent will be taken out of your pay."

As he turned to walk away, he said, "Got it?"

"Yep, you're fired."

He turned as quick as a snake.

"What did you say, boy?"

"I said you're fired. I'm the new owner of this station."

"We'll see about that. The only ground you will own here is a six-foot deep hole."

Two other guys who had been lounging on the porch joined him. Whatever happened would be three on one. They were big guys but looked soft from too many beers.

They didn't seem to want to play fair, so I wouldn't either. Australian law let me carry a weapon on my property, especially this far out. I was glad I had the foresight to wear my Colt Peacemaker that John Wayne had given me.

I drew it and told them they had one hour to gather their things and get off the property. Their eyes got big when I cocked the hammer back and aimed between the leader's eyes. Actually, I was aiming slightly above his head, but he couldn't tell that. All he could see was the round hole pointing at him.

They all backed up and raised their hands above their heads. I didn't even have to tell them. They robbed me of my chance to say, "Reach for the sky."

A group of guys was watching us from about twenty yards away. I signaled over the oldest one there, a guy who looked forty or fifty—with the weathered skin you couldn't tell.

When he came over, I told him, "I'm the new owner of this spread, and this thief and his two toadies are fired. Would you and some others follow them around as they gather their gear and make sure it is only their stuff they take?"

"Be delighted, Boss; been waiting for this day for a long time."

In less than an hour, they were gone, each in a ute in worse shape than mine, if possible. At least mine didn't emit smoke out the tailpipe.

While this was going on, I went into the main house. It looked like a pigsty. The office was a mess, and I couldn't find any ledger books. There were handwritten notes all over the place.

It would take a team of accountants to straighten this mess out. When I bought the place, I was shown a set of books that indicated they were at least breaking even. Now I knew why the place was being sold.

The older guy came back to the house. He introduced himself as Frank, no last name, just Frank.

"Frank, can you tell me anything about the real state of this operation?"

"The guy and his friends who you just ran off were looting this place. When old man Winters died with no heirs, the court ordered the place to be put up for sale."

"Todd Spencer, the station manager who worked for Mr. Winters disappeared, and the next thing we know, these guys showed up with paperwork saying they were to run the place."

"Hmm, maybe I ran them off too soon. Let's go in the house and see if we can find the paper that said he could run the station."

It didn't take us long to find a coffee-stained letter issued by a law firm directing Ned Kelly to run the station until it was sold.

I took it to my vehicle and put it in my briefcase as evidence. I wanted to know where the law firm got the authority to issue that letter.

As I was closing the car door, I noticed a cloud of dust being raised by several vehicles approaching at high speed. I had been dealing with rocket scientists in my space program, but it didn't need that much thought to figure out where this was going.

I was wearing a six-shooter, but I had my Henry lever action rifle in the car. It is chambered for forty-four magnums. I levered the action and waited with the rifle down by my side. I had the ute between me and them as I waited.

It was Kelly and his clowns, as I thought. They came to a screeching halt and jumped out of their utes. They all had rifles. I suspected they had gone down the road apiece, stopped and unpacked their weapons, and were coming back to show me my place.

The rifles looked like single-shot bolt action guns. Typical of a varmint rifle.

The first hint I had that I was right was when one of them fired a shot at me. He missed by a mile. When someone is shooting at you, if they are aiming right, the flame you see coming out of the barrel looks like a round dot.

This shot had flame shooting out in a line for about six inches. That was enough for me to declare open season on Ned Kelly and his gang.

Since the guy who had shot at me had to work the rifle bolt to reload, I ignored him for a moment.

Instead, I shot Mr. Kelly first. At thirty yards it didn't take great marksmanship to hit him center mass. As soon as I pulled the trigger, I stooped down. It was a good thing as I did as two shots went through my ute's windows, breaking them.

I stood back up and dropped the first guy who shot at me. The third guy put a bullet hole in my Resistol hat, sending it flying. To this day I swear I didn't kill him because he ruined my hat.

It didn't matter why I killed him; dead is dead.

So much for keeping a low profile in Australia.

I told Frank to call the cops. He asked if he could have one of the other guys do it. I gave him a long look and told him to pick someone to make the call.

I also asked him to write down the names of the eleven other witnesses to this gunfight. I thought we should rename this station the OK Corral, but I knew that was just adrenaline talking.

I laid the rifle on the hood of the car and walked over to the porch.

Frank came back and told me the police were coming from Mount Isa and it would take them three hours to get here.

I used the time to call the police commissioner in Sydney in hopes that he could help with the Queensland Police Service. He said he would let them know that I had been an assistant to them in a drug bust. He would also tell them I appeared to be a good guy for half a Yank and half a Pommy.

Thanks a lot.

I called the governor general's office to let them know what was going on and to ask for the recommendation of a solicitor's firm. One that could defend me if needed and start an investigation into who had hired Ned Kelly.

Lucky for me the station's copy machine still worked, so I made a copy of the letter giving Kelly authority over the ranch. I left the copy with Frank and told him to hang onto it.

This all was a superabundance of caution on my part, but I didn't know the players around here. For all I knew, the police were in on it.

After a long three-hour wait, the police showed up.

From their actions, I immediately knew they weren't in on it. They were professional when they questioned me. They didn't challenge me as to the veracity of my statements, they just took them down.

This was after they had secured the crime scene. They were in the middle of taking statements from everyone present except Frank. He seemed to have disappeared.

While this was going on, the coroner arrived and pronounced Kelly and his men dead. Kelly had fallen face down so the police hadn't got a look at him.

"That's Ned Kelly! He's wanted for murder and bank robbery in three states!"

That took care of my worries.

Chapter 11

I went from a possible murder suspect to a hero in no seconds at all. I found out I was eligible for over a hundred thousand pounds in rewards.

The press would be all over this story. Again, so much for a low profile. The police had many more questions, but they were asked in a friendly tone.

They were extremely interested in the lawyer's letter giving Kelly authority over the ranch. It only took them a few phone calls to establish that no such law firm existed, and the address given in Sydney was an empty lot.

When they searched the cars, they found several bags of cash. The police would have to sort out where it had come from.

I imagined most from their looting of the ranch, but some may have been left over from their robberies. I didn't count on ever seeing any of it again.

It took a few more hours and after having the bodies removed and all the evidence bagged and tagged, they were gone.

I turned to go back to the office and Frank was there.

"Hey Frank, I was going to look for you. Could you take care of this place for a few days? Make certain everyone keeps getting fed, and the necessary work done, and make a list of what everyone should have made less Kelly's share and the bunkhouse rent. I intend to pay them back for all of that."

"I can do that."

"Frank, I'm not going to ask why you avoid the police, but if it is for a serious crime, I would advise you to move on."

"I'll be staying for a while."

"Good to know."

That was the last conversation Frank and I ever had on the subject.

I got in my old ute with the windows shot out and moved on to the next property. It was one of the connectors.

The family that lived there was trying to maintain the property. The husband kept the stock fed where needed and kept the water supply running. Other than that, it was too big a spread for one man to handle.

We sat on the front porch and discussed what all needed doing. It was a lot. While we were talking, a girl about six years old came up and asked if they would be eating dinner tonight or if it was their night to fast.

That got my attention. Was this religion or something else? It was something else. Upon questioning, the father admitted they weren't paid enough to afford food.

His wife was on him to move on, but they had no idea where to go.

I handed him two hundred pounds and told him to go into town for dinner and buy groceries. I did think to ask him if he had enough fuel in his ute to make it to town. He did.

They did have a working phone, so I called Frank and asked him to send two jackaroos over to help this small station. Also, have them bring bedding as I suspected there wouldn't be any extra here.

I let the guy know that help was on its way and that I would be reviewing everyone's pay within a week and making sure that they got their due and any shortages made up.

His wife who had been listening from inside the house came out and thanked me. The little girl came with her and from the smile on her face, I thought she could be a good playmate for Mary.

I moved on to the next large station. This one was more like a station. The fences were all up. Gates closed. The road was well maintained. It looked like a grader had been run down it recently.

When I pulled up to the main house, it had a neat front yard outlined in white stone. No one was idly sitting around. I could hear the sound of machinery running in the distance.

It was spring, so I figured they were getting the fields ready for planting. This was more like it.

I knocked on the front door of the house and a lady answered the door. I introduced myself and handed her a card.

She replied that they were expecting someone, as they had been informed the station had been sold but nothing about the new owners. She looked at my name on the card, but you could tell all the titles didn't sink in.

"My husband who is the station manager is due in for lunch anytime now. May I invite you in to eat with us?"

"That would be my pleasure."

She poured me a cup of coffee while we waited. Her name was Jean and her husband was Walt. Their children were grown and had stayed in Sydney when their university days were finished.

Walt showed up a little later, and we introduced ourselves. He paid attention to my card.

"You're a bloody duke, the one who goes around killing people!"

Ouch.

"Only those that need it."

"I heard about that Ned Kelly gang this morning; if anyone needed killing, it was them. That Chinese prince sounded like a bad one also."

"He was the worst of the lot. He killed his brother and nephew and was going after his niece. His mother would have been next."

Jean put her hand to her mouth in shock. Walt shook his head. I thought it meant that he agreed that Haoran needed to be stopped.

After a nice lunch of cold meatloaf sandwiches, Walt took me on a tour of the close-in station. It was all neat and orderly. It also had a shopworn look like no money had been put back into the place.

I asked Walt directly about that thought. He told me that I was correct in my thinking; the absentee landlord kept them on a tight string. They were only left with enough money to keep the place going, nothing for improvements.

I asked Walt how he would run the place if he could. From his answers, I gathered he would bring everything up to snuff and not try to improve things any further.

He sounded like a good person to maintain the status quo but not the sort of person I imagine being in charge of all my stations. I had to find a general manager, as I didn't intend to take on the job.

I guess that would make me one of those absentee landlords, but not one trying to milk everything out that I could. I think what I was doing in Spain would demonstrate that.

That gave me an idea. I would send whoever I selected for general manager to Spain to see what was being done there. It would show them how I wanted things done and was willing to provide support for.

It was getting late in the afternoon, so I asked Walt if I could stay in the bunkhouse with the stockmen overnight.

He gave me a sharp look and told me that would be fine. He saw through me. I wanted to stay with the stockmen to see what they thought of things.

I had finally figured out that the stockmen were cowboys, pure cowboys in their function. The jackaroos and jillaroos were more general help around the station. They were always younger and doing the job to get experience so they could become better-paid stockmen.

Until they gained the experience, they were looked down on by the stockmen. The class system was alive and well on Australian stations. I knew better than to ever express that opinion.

I privately thought of the roos as apprentice cowboys.

My evening with the stockmen was interesting. They had nothing bad to say about Walt's management. They had a lot to say about the lack of funds to do things right.

It appeared that Walt was open in his sharing of the station's books, everything but salaries. The men knew the truth about the station's situation.

I was grilled on my intentions. Aside from Walt and Jean at lunch, these were the first people to hear about what I was putting together.

Interestingly enough, they never questioned me about my background or finances. It appeared the bush telegraph had been working overtime.

Several of the older hands had a quiet conversation to the side, then came to me.

"If you want to see a well-run station, look at the place run by Ron Ferguson. It should be next on your list. He does wonders with that place. He learned to work with the old owners and showed them that by leaving him some money to work with, they could make more."

I thanked them for their insights and moved on early the next morning. If nothing else, Jean fixed a nice breakfast. I needed it after my morning run.

I then drove on to the next connector. It was one of those that were well-run and profitable. It looked like it when I drove up. Everything was in tip-top condition.

By this time everyone knew that I was coming and all about me, so it was no surprise that several people were waiting for me when I showed up.

We all introduced ourselves. We settled in on the front veranda on this fine spring day with coffee.

I had my spiel down pat. I told them what I was trying to accomplish and in general how I would go about it.

What struck me the most when they were talking about progress on the station, they kept mentioning Ron Ferguson as the father of the innovations.

I couldn't wait to get over to Ferguson's Station.

Chapter 12

Ferguson Station was a dream. If Disney had built an Australian ranch, it would look like this. Everything was organized and in its place. There was no worn-out equipment sitting around.

Everything was painted and clean. The main roads were asphalted. If the rest of the place lived up to this, it would be perfect.

I had seen the balance sheets of all the properties. This one was the best of the lot, by far. When I pulled into the main station house, there was a banner posted, "Welcome, Duke Richard."

I felt positively shabby in my Outback jeans and hat. My ute seemed like a junk heap next to the others sitting there.

A teenage girl about my age ran out to meet me as I got out of my pickup truck.

"You can't park here, all jackaroos around back. We have a new owner coming today and want to put our best foot forward."

She wasn't being mean about it, just a little frantic as they didn't want to disappoint the new owner, So I tipped my hat, got back in my ute, and drove around the main house to another parking lot where the vehicles were more like mine.

Several younger cowboys or jackaroos were loitering there waiting for a chance to see the new guy. At least that is what they told me when I walked up.

I was asked, "Are you looking for a job?"

"Could be. What's this place like to work at?"

"If they take you on, it will be the best job you have ever had."

"Why wouldn't they take me on?"

"Rob Roy Ferguson is careful about who he hires. He will even run a police officer check on you."

So, no Franks working here.

"Why do you call him Rob Roy? I thought his name was Ron."

"He's a Scotsman who is tough as nails, but he is also fair."

An older man came up to me.

"Are you looking for work?"

"I might be."

"Do you have any experience working with cattle?"

"No, but I've played an American cowboy in several movies."

That confused him for a moment, then it sunk in.

"Oh shit, you're the duke."

"John Wayne is The Duke, I'm just an ordinary duke."

"Are you going to fire us for this?"

"Why would I do that?"

"For not bowing and scraping."

"Do I look like someone who needs that?"

"No, you don't."

"Does Mr. Ferguson have a sense of humor? No, don't answer that. Introduce me as the latest hire. If he asks about a police check, tell him the only thing they have is I killed three guys the other day."

"The Ned Kelly gang?"

"Yeah, but don't tell him that right away."

"Well, you're the owner, but it is your fault if things go wrong."

"No problem."

The guy introduced himself as John Sloan as we walked over to the house. He took me in through the kitchen door. What seemed like a whole family was waiting there.

"Hey boss, I would like to introduce you to our latest hire."

"You did tell him it is dependent on him passing a police check, didn't you?"

"There is no way that he would pass one of those; he killed three guys yesterday."

Talk about the cat amongst the pigeons!

The guy who I figured must be Mr. Ferguson came out of his chair ready to fight. An older woman who must have been his wife let out an eek!

A young man in his middle teens was ready to join his father. The young lady who sent me around back got it at once.

"Dad, he's the one that did Ned Kelly in!"

That took everything into slow motion. Dad caught on quickly, "Are you Richard Jackson?"

"Yes, sir."

"Why are you sneaking through the back door?"

"I was told to go around to the back. I ran into Mr. Sloan here, and he brought me in. The new hire idea was mine."

"Who was dumb enough to send you around back?"

I looked at the young lady, "It was some old coot, must have been over sixty, dressed like a farmer."

Mr. Ferguson asked Mr. Sloan, "Who could that have been? We don't have anyone who meets that description."

"Daddy, it was me. His Grace is being kind to me."

I nodded my head to acknowledge her statement.

To change the subject, I asked him, "Is it possible to get a cold soft drink around here?"

Like magic, I was handed a Coke. After taking a refreshing drink, I started with, "This is a mighty fine-looking station. Is it like this with the cattle?"

They could paint everything they wanted; this was a cattle ranch no matter what name they gave it. If the cattle weren't taken care of, they were wasting a lot of paint.

Mr. Ferguson, who had been getting up on his high horse, came down to earth.

"Let's go take a look."

"Okay."

I thought I was going to be driven around a ranch. Instead, we walked across a field to a flight hangar. There was a neat little two-seater helicopter there. It said Fairey Ultralight on the nameplate on the control panel. I hadn't even heard of these, but it seemed to fly nicely.

Mr. Ferguson took me on an hour's ride around the station. The cattle below us seemed to be in fine condition. At least no skeletons were lying about. There were windmills all over the place, and the water tanks were full.

We were able to talk through headphones. He gave a running commentary on things as he went.

I was convinced this station was as good as it looked.

After we landed, I had some more questions for him. That seemed fair, as he had many for me.

Three hours and one fine dinner later, we had talked ourselves out.

I knew he was itching for a bigger challenge, as he had this property as good as it was going to get. He knew I had such a challenge.

I asked him his opinion of each of the station's designs. His opinion matched what my land agent had presented to me.

We spent the evening hours discussing what could be done with the new spread. When I told him there would be a landing strip that would take my 707, he just shook his head.

"You don't think small, do you?"

From there it went on to schooling, medical care, housing, and veterinarian staffing. I just thought I knew what went into a dream station. He had been thinking of it for years.

I told him what I had done with the *estancia* in Spain. He liked what he heard. Though he did tell me that he would have thrown the Church off his property if he were me.

That's where we got into a serious discussion about respecting local cultures. I was more liberal about it than he was.

He wanted to know how I felt about the Aborigines crossing the land. Or as he called them the Abos.

In turn, I asked him, "Why would I have a problem with that?"

"They steal everything to feed themselves when they go walkabout. If they are hungry, taking a cow means nothing to them."

"Well, we will have to come to an accommodation with them. Something like a setup out in the rough where we leave food and shelter for when they are passing through.

He told me that would just encourage them. I could see that we weren't about to see eye to eye on that tonight, so let it go.

It seemed to me that we would come out ahead if we treated them like humans and respected their culture.

They put me up in a guest room. It was the most decent room since I had arrived in Queensland.

I ran into the daughter of the house, Linda, at breakfast. She was shy after her goof-up yesterday.

She seemed like a nice enough kid for an eighteen-year-old. One year younger than me and I felt old enough to be her father. Life was making me old before my years.

She seemed starstruck. She couldn't wait to tell her friends she had met me. This was innocent high school stuff. She was starting uni in the summer session in Sydney.

Her brother was there, and he was a bundle of teenage resentment. He didn't talk at breakfast, and I let him alone. He would sort things out or not. I think he resented me at my age being his dad's boss.

Mr. Ferguson joined us, and I let him know I still had two of the connector ranches to visit and the last big one.

In the meantime, why didn't he start writing up a plan to develop the station as we talked about last night? That included the large new house, airstrips, road improvements, and a butchering operation. Also, estimate the costs where possible and have an idea of when it could all be profitable.

In those cost estimates, he is to double his salary.

He smiled at that, and his son sat up straight. I think the young man had just come to terms with the situation.

Chapter 13

I took off after breakfast to continue my tour of the stations I had bought. I still had three connectors to go and a large station. It was interesting that the next connector was one of those doing well.

Those doing well were connecting the number one and two performing stations so far. The three failing stations were connected to the first large one and the large station I had yet to visit.

That didn't bode well for my last large station.

As could have been predicted, the next connector off Ferguson Station was doing well. It was in the black according to the books and the way it looked.

It was surprising how first appearances usually told the truth. I found that if the appearance was poor, then the maintenance of equipment would follow suit.

If the equipment wasn't maintained, then the cattle weren't supported with feed and water, or fences maintained. This in turn led to a non-profitable station.

To use a navy term, the station could also be gun decked; that is, made to look good on the surface but rotten underneath. A little experience could see through a gun-decked operation. Painting rotten fencing white still left rotten fences.

The first connector from the Ferguson place to the next big ranch wasn't gun-decked at all. It was neat and trim but didn't look like the Disney crew had done the set decoration.

The station manager and his wife were pleasant, and we had an open discussion about the state of the station while going over the books.

They thought that the only thing that was left to do on the station was to asphalt the major roads, both of them. I agreed with them. If we were to process our beef here, rather than sending it to market, we needed good roads.

The people who had sold me the small station didn't have access to enough funds or a compelling reason to pave the roads.

That brought up another issue. There was a rail spur to Dajarra, but it stopped there. Could we run it to the new station?

The manager Jack Thompson didn't think that the railroad would run tracks or trains out to us. I responded they probably wouldn't, so we would have to pay for the tracks and buy a locomotive or two and cars.

This left them stunned for a moment.

"Can you afford that? Will the banks loan you the money?"

"People don't understand how rich I am. I will pay for this out of pocket. It will be a capital asset to the station and increase its value. After we are hooked into the mainlines, we may even extend it to other areas. It would be good to connect Mount Isa and Bedourie.

"We could even put on some flatcars to haul semi-trailers and utes."

I asked the Mrs., "How would you like to be able to catch a morning passenger run out of here to Mount Isa and go shopping and still be home in time to make dinner?"

She liked that idea. They must have thought I was some crazy kid having wild dreams, but I put this wild dream on my to-do list. Railroad freight costs were way less than over the road. The new station would be shipping millions of pounds of beef.

After lunch, I wished the nice couple well after assuring them their positions on the new combined station were safe.

As far as their hired hands went, we would evaluate each one individually. Since I anticipated having to hire more to accomplish all my plans, only the bad ones would fall by the wayside.

My next stop was the fourth large station. It wasn't a disaster, and it wasn't that good either. After a long talk and look around with the manager, I thought the problems were seventy-five percent with the old owners and twenty-five percent with the current manager.

He was a nice enough bloke but didn't seem to have much drive to him. He was the sort that you would put in a boring repetitive position. No energy or imagination required. Since every company has positions like that, I saw no reason to fire him but had no desire to keep him in a top management position.

I would leave that up to Ron Ferguson. I had made up my mind that he was the man to run the new superstation, as I had begun to think of it.

This left the last two connectors; they attached this station to the first one I had visited.

Neither of them had people starving like the first station. Even though that little girl had been acting, they were truly short on food.

These were just bone-lazy people who only tried to get by and cared nothing about the station or the livestock. The men working the ranch were the dregs of the industry. These would all have to go.

Even most of the buildings would have to be torn down. Several of the buildings were managing that on their own.

I had to drive after dark, but I returned to Ferguson's. There was no way that I would spend the night at any of the last three places I had visited.

The next morning, I sat down with Mr. Ferguson and went over the plans he had been working on. His son kept looking in on us, so I asked if he could sit in. That was the right thing for me to do, from both the looks of father and son.

I was very pleased when the first item on his list was to bring in a team of auditors from Sydney to go over the books of each station and then consolidate them.

The audit was to include a full physical inventory of each station.

He also had a proposed organization chart that looked more like a city organization chart. When I thought about it, it seemed appropriate.

What we were putting together was a lot like the Firestone Rubber Plantation in Liberia. I told Ron that I could introduce him to the plantation's managing director who was running a city in the jungle that faced the same problems that he would.

He liked that thought. I gave him the name and number which I had written in my little black book. That is what I thought of it as, though it wasn't little and had a red cover. Instead of my back jeans pocket, I had it in my briefcase.

The first time I had mounted a horse carrying a briefcase in hand, they made so much fun of the "briefcase cowboy," that I had a set of saddlebags made for that sort of stuff.

I had even thought of asking the Beach Boys to write a song with that title, though it had more of a country-western flavor.

Ron didn't want to get too far ahead of himself. He wouldn't try to develop an education plan for the ranch until he had the superintendent of schools on board. That person would have to identify the student base, teachers, and infrastructure required and then obtain state certification from the school system.

The same went for our health care system.

What I envisioned would be a station that would employ five hundred people. A small town.

Those five hundred people would be a magnet for supporting services like bakeries, barbers, and beauty shops, and probably a setup like the Dajarra Roadhouse.

I would lease the land to build those facilities on the side of the station's main road. Then those people would need housing. Maybe the station should have a construction company as a subsidiary.

Then there would have to be a bank, and the state would want to place at least a post office there, then a police substation. In the end, Ron and I figured that we were building a small city of twenty thousand people.

Then there were the politicians to think of.

That is where I was able to contribute. Not that I had dealt with them directly, but I knew how power structures worked.

Because of that, we planned a trip to Sydney. His whole family would be going. I made several phone calls and found that Jackson House had been made habitable enough that we could all stay there.

I had the DC3 flown to Mount Isa as my little Cessna wouldn't hold all of us. There had been some work performed on the DC3 so that seats could be put in and taken out.

These were first-class seats. Slots in the floor made it easy to put them in and remove them.

In Sydney, the house had been put in good order. At least the bedrooms had. The sitting rooms were still bare. A phone had been installed in the lobby so we wouldn't have to keep running to the corner box.

While Ron, his son, and I were going to a lawyer's office to create a contract between us, mother and daughter wanted to visit the University of Sydney.

They would have to take a cab. I gave Mum enough cash to ride back to Dajarra if needed. I also called my professor's contact and asked him to arrange a tour for them.

Chapter 14

The contract Ron Ferguson and I came up with was pretty straightforward. We saw eye to eye on what we expected from each other, so it was easy to tell the lawyer what we wanted.

Being a good lawyer, he came up with a dozen or more situations we hadn't considered. We finally left it with him to draft, and we would review it.

Ron's son accompanied us for the day. You could tell he was seeing a world he didn't even imagine existed. Before the day started, he had looked at his dad with the resentment most teenage boys had.

Now there was hero worship in his eyes. He did ask how we learned about all this stuff. I let his dad reply, "Education son, education."

I did add not all education comes through schooling. Some you have to learn on your own, and some of it the hard way. I shared with him my experience in high school where I learned that studying ahead paid off big time.

He wanted to know where I went to uni. I told him Oxford and let it go at that. I didn't want to ruin the good path we had him going on.

Next, we went to a civil engineer's office. I had made an appointment with a firm recommended by the governor-general's office.

Whilst we were waiting for our appointment, we toured their extensive lobby. They had models of their most prestigious project. Ron and I made eye contact at the same time.

He said it first, "We need one of these."

"Agreed."

It would be a good visual representation of our plan. We had to sell the idea to several government bodies, so the more attractive we could make it, the better.

I hated the thought of all the contributions that would have to be made to various political campaigns and entities. That was the reality that we lived in and not a battle to be fought.

I expressed that thought to Ron.

"Unfortunately, true; I'm glad you see the reality."

His son was listening with wide eyes.

"But that is the same as bribery!"

Ron answered, "Welcome to the world of grownups, son."

I spoke up, "Evan, think of it as a football team paying a bonus to players to join our side."

"But politicians can't be bought and paid for!"

His dad couldn't help himself as he laughed and shook his head at the same time.

Evan shut up at this point as he realized he was new at this game.

We were soon escorted by an attractive young lady to the managing director's office.

Once there, introductions were made, coffee or tea offered and accepted, and then, seated comfortably at a conference table, we got down to business.

That is, we got down to business after me having to tell the story of my gunfight with Ned Kelly. So far, I had managed to dodge the reporters but would have to give in soon.

"Your Grace, I was told by the governor-general that you have a large project in mind and that he recommended us."

I thought it was a good sign that it was the governor-general who made a direct call and not his office.

I proceeded to give him an overview of the project.

"May I ask if you have filed the proper paperwork in the Torrens title system?"

"Yes, we have. It's through a company I have had my lawyers create here in Australia. It will be headquartered in Queensland."

"What about Foreign Investment Board approval?"

"Application has been made, and I anticipate a quick approval."

"May I ask who is backing your application?"

"The Throne."

"I expect we will have rapid approval."

"I hope so. My lawyers have been instructed to identify all the key players and make certain they are on board with us."

He gave a little smirk at that; he knew bribes when he heard of them.

He suggested that he assemble a team of engineers to start work on the project. I didn't wait for him to ask for an advance to cover the costs. I pulled out my checkbook.

"How much to start work?"

"A quarter million will do."

I wrote out the check. While I did that, I heard Evan take a deep breath. I turned and winked at him.

"I will get with my bank and set up a drawing account to keep you paid to date on the project.

"Our next stop is at an accounting office to audit the current state of affairs at each of the stations and then continue to monitor the ongoing costs of the project."

That was my way of telling him to keep his hands out of the till.

"Of course, Your Grace."

I just hoped the finder's fee he would pay the prime minister would keep him on my side. Maybe I should throw a reception at Jackson House for the prime minister when we unveil the project.

After leaving the engineering firm's office, I mentioned that to Ron.

He countered with, "We should invite all the political players and the press. Show how good this is for the nation."

"Excellent idea, and it would also publicly lock them into supporting the project."

Evan spoke up, "All this just to raise some cows for market!"

His dad corrected him. "Son, this will also make Rick a power player in Australian politics. He won't be in office, but he will be a power to reckon with."

At the accountant's office, it was like deja vu all over again, talk of Ned Kelly and then down to business.

They also had been recommended by the governor-general, but I thought his finder's fee, in this case, might be handled more delicately. Maybe through his wife?

They were eager to take on the project. It was money and prestige. I was even asked if I gave appointments, such as Accountants to His Grace the Duke of Hong Kong. This was the first time I had been asked that.

"I will have to consult with the Palace to see what etiquette allows and requires."

That was a non-answer but the best I could give at the moment.

After that meeting and another large check written, Ron, Evan, and I went to lunch. It had been an interesting morning.

While seated at the restaurant, an enterprising young reporter came up to us. He asked politely if he could interview me on the Ned Kelly incident.

I requested to see his press credentials. He was a freelancer for the University of Sydney newspaper. I'm not certain if you could get any lower on the reporting food chain and be credentialed.

He looked so hopeful I had to give in. I had decided not that long ago that I would have to give an interview, so why not now?

Once he sat down and had pen and notebook ready, I gave him the first run-through of the whole incident. Then I started answering the questions. They were all the ones that I expected.

"Was I scared?"

Of course, I was. Only a fool wouldn't be frightened when the shooting was about to start.

"Did I know who it was?"

"Never heard of him before this."

"If you had known who it was, would you have backed down?"

"I shot two bank robbers when I was fourteen."

Me and my big mouth. That gave him an opening to ask about my entire career.

I shut him down, just so I could eat lunch.

"All that will have to wait for another time. I have told you about the Ned Kelly incident. You will have to do your homework on my background. In the meantime, I have lunch to eat."

That last comment cost me some in my public approval rating. The reporter wrote that I was cold-hearted, worrying more about my lunch than killing three men.

Since I wasn't running for office, it didn't matter.

From lunch, we returned to Jackson House. There we met the ladies who had just returned from their tour of the university.

They were both excited about the school and their treatment. It seemed I was in good order with the administration.

While the family caught each other up on their day so far, I made a phone call to England. I wanted to know about this By Appointment to His Grace the Duke of Hong Kong stuff.

Being the middle of the night there I had to leave a message, but I knew Mr. Norman would get back to me.

By this time, the guys and I had to leave for an appointment with the governor-general. So far it had been phone calls through his office with no face-to-face contact.

We were ushered in immediately.

After describing once more my gunfight with the Kelly gang, we got down to business. He asked what he could do to help my project.

"I have to get a lot of lower-level players on board. I think at this time if you are questioned, you reply that you are aware of the project and wish me success. Don't imply that you are sponsoring. While your direct support would help in some areas, in others it would be a hindrance."

"Very astute, Your Grace."

And it would let him stay on the fence.

Chapter 15

The next steps in establishing the station as a functioning entity would have to wait until the civil engineering firm completed the model we had commissioned.

Ron would be working with them from this point forward. Once the model was complete, then we would bring in officials from the various governing bodies to sell the idea and gain their support.

The civil engineering firm wasn't new to this game. Our model of the station would be set up in a large separate room. The room would have conference tables, refreshment areas, and even a sitting room arrangement. Everything that is needed for a good sales meeting.

They would even provide catering staff. We planned several events, one as an evening social with formal dress. This would be the full Dom Pérignon and canapés route.

We also planned a daytime event for the press with beer and shrimp on a barbie.

This would take weeks to set in place. In the meantime, Ron's family would be staying in town at Jackson House. I set up an account for the ladies to purchase furniture and whatever else they thought the place would need to be livable.

I could always throw it away and start over if it was too horrible.

I found out that the only place where I could obtain land directly by freehold was Western Australia. This land at the time was considered worthless and could be purchased from the Crown for one shilling an acre.

In Queensland I had to first lease the land, then convert it to a freehold. I intended to do that, but I was intrigued by being able to buy land directly.

The only thing that held me back was a freehold didn't confer mineral rights on the land. I would have to think this through. I didn't want to buy a huge parcel and then have a fortune in copper found, then lose it to the finder who could file a claim.

I would need to survey the land before purchase. The most important question would be, is there any water?

Since I had a lot on my plate with the station deal, I decided to let the idea of a huge station, like three million acres in the Outback, simmer for a while.

Instead, since I had some time on my hands, I decided to head back to Hong Kong to take care of business there. I also arranged for Ron and Evan, and the ladies if they desired, to go to Spain and see the *estancia*. This would let them know how I wanted things done.

It took several days to get the 707 back to Sydney. It had been at Oxford getting scheduled maintenance performed.

It costs a bundle to keep it flying. That said, I didn't see how I could function without it. Less than five years ago I was hitchhiking around. Now I needed something faster and able to cross oceans.

It was like an old home week when the 707 and its crew showed up. They had been one of the few constants in my life over the last few years.

Several of the stewardesses had gotten married and left the flight. The next time I saw Harry Beal, I would have a few words with him for stealing one of the better ones. I did send them a nice wedding present. At least my office informed me that I had done so.

The flight to Hong Kong was uneventful. Harold had to show me that the wardrobe on the aircraft had been completely replenished so I wouldn't have to go dressed in a rain barrel.

The fact that there was another one waiting in Hong Kong didn't matter. Who knew if we would have a forced landing in some jungle and I would be invited to a formal gathering?

We arrived in Hong Kong late in the evening, so I took a helicopter to Jackson House. Boris was aware of my coming, so my rooms were ready.

The next morning, he gave me an update on the state of the house. The most important item was the gold had been moved to China and put in the space program. From what he heard, that was going well.

The house had been completely redone, including all furnishings. It looked good. I would have to see about having a formal reception here one day.

I had a lunch appointment with the royal governor, so I took the helicopter back to the airport.

I missed driving, but security concerns kept me out of the public's eye as much as possible. Even in Australia, I hadn't been out and about in town. All were business appointments, no public appearances.

The reality was that a lot of people had reason to wish me ill.

The governor and I discussed the state of affairs in Hong Kong over lunch. Since we had started the quality program here, things had done nothing but look better.

Hong Kong manufacturing and subsequent orders were at an all-time high. This in turn resulted in increased tax revenue. The local infrastructure was being upgraded as quickly as possible.

This included roads, the seaport, an airport, and electrical. Because of the increased revenue, they were also able to reduce port fees. This led to more business, more fees, etc. A virtuous cycle according to my economic textbooks.

While I had stopped going to school, I hadn't stopped my education. While visiting the University of Sydney, I obtained copies of their economics class schedules and bought all the class textbooks.

I was working my way through each one as I could. I had also done the same with political science. I suspect I will continue my education for the rest of my life. Although I had no intention of attending any classrooms or worrying about getting a degree.

I did stop at my bank in Hong Kong and go over my accounts. My checking account was flush with cash as a quarterly dividend had come in from Jackson Enterprises.

Spending a ton of money on the stations and committing to another ten tons hadn't made a dent in my cash flow. It was getting to the point where I couldn't even fathom how I could ever spend what I had, much less what would be coming in.

The space program was helping me pump money back into the worldwide economy. I had to keep the money moving or it would create an imbalance in worldwide cash flow.

I made a point of calling home that evening to let my parents know where I was at. I had forgotten to tell them I was leaving Australia for a while.

They took it in stride as they were used to my gadding about, as Dad would say.

I was told about Mary and her Girl Scout Cookie selling experience. I thought it was as funny as all get out. I could see Mary in her limo going door to door on Rodeo Drive. Especially with Jim and Sally letting their weapons show.

Her idea of testing if showing a weapon helped or hurt sales was great. I suggested they make it more in-depth, maybe a bazooka or even ride in an armored car, with quad fifties. Dad thought that a bit much. Mum seemed intrigued.

That bit of silliness left me smiling. It was good to be able to talk to them. It did get lonely on the road. I wish I had someone to accompany me. May-ling came to mind.

After the home call, I placed a call to North Vietnam. The president seemed pleased to hear from me. He had nothing in particular that I could help them with. The port in Haiphong harbor was now open for business.

When he started talking about the latest models of American cars, I knew it was time to hang up. I had bought the officials new ones last year; darned if I would do it again.

South Vietnam was better. They were able to support their army without my funding. With Australian guidance, their officer corps was coming along. It would still take a few years. It seemed good sergeants were the hardest to bring up through the ranks. Generals could be had for a dime a dozen.

They were managing to interdict the border with Laos, so, they weren't a drug gateway anymore. I think you would have to take flamethrowers to the entire Golden Triangle and then salt the earth to stop that trade.

I thought interdiction and harsh laws were necessary but had to question why the citizens of a country would feel the need to turn to drugs. That to me indicated a failure in public policy and also that corruption was rampant in that government. The corruption didn't have to be out-and-out bribes. It could be the creation of a class dependent on the drug trade. Lawyers, healthcare professionals, and police came to mind.

None of those would encourage the drug trade. It just wouldn't be in their best interest to eliminate it, keep it down to a dull roar, yes. They would have no incentive to hurt their standard of living.

All good people, trapped in an unvirtuous cycle.

Chapter 16

After catching up on things in Hong Kong, I decided to visit the Space Center. The reports I received indicated tremendous progress.

Once there I found the reports to be understated. All launch pads were now in use. The rocket factory was now in full production.

There was a launch going on every five days right now, and it would soon increase to one every three days. Not all would carry passengers. Most would be capsules carrying construction materials for the first space station.

The capsules were launched into high earth orbit and were constructed in a modular form so that they could be joined together.

The station would be able to be staffed by fifteen crew members. We planned to have most of the crew involved in getting ready for a moon landing.

Five of the crew would be dedicated to running experiments for a fee for private industry and educational organizations. Who knows, NASA might even hire us when we announce our success.

The world of rocket science was abuzz about what we were doing. It was obvious we were building a space station; the question was its purpose.

That was being closely held. Our Space Ladies when questioned answered that they were being homemakers as all ladies should be doing.

NASA could smell a rat and tried to spy on our operation. Since the only workers were the ladies or Chinese, they weren't having much luck.

From the number of launches, they knew we were doing something big, but it was never publicly speculated that we were in a race with them to the moon.

I guess they couldn't comprehend those women would be the high workers on such a project.

The first habitats had been joined, and we now had ten ladies up there for a month at a time. Any longer and their muscles atrophied too much.

Since we now had thirty astronaut-rated women, we could rotate them up every three months. Qualifications were in process for another ten women.

When the first women were brought on board, it was because they were the only ones available. Now it was a matter of pride. The ten women in the new group were all Chinese.

I wondered how I was ever going to talk the women into letting me go up at least once.

Soon after arriving at the Jiuquan Satellite Launch Center, I was given a presentation. A space station in high earth orbit was good, but a space station at LaGrange Point L1 was even better.

It is an unstable point requiring course adjustments about every twenty-three days. L3, 4, and 5 are stable but much further out.

We could build a much bigger station there for the same energy costs as the high earth orbit. Once out of Earth's gravity field, the spacecraft would coast to its destination and then use the same amount of fuel to "stop" as it would in high earth orbit.

This would be a monster at half a mile in diameter. That worked out to over nine billion cubic feet. They planned to have a double hull with the space in between filled with water as protection from solar flares.

This would be a city in space, more than a city, almost a country in its own right.

I asked them where they would be getting all the metal and water from as it was impractical to launch it from the earth. Silly me, the asteroid belt is full of asteroids with metal and ice.

They realized this was a very long-term plan but wanted to start the whole process. The first step would be getting the capability to get to the asteroid belt, and then bring an asteroid back with them.

I permitted them to proceed but put it as a low priority.

A more interesting proposal that had a quicker payback was to make a spaceplane. It would have the payload of a rocket but would be able to come back to Earth and be reused.

I was all for that as the next logical step would be to have a plane that could fly to orbit and return without being launched with a rocket. Of course, I had no idea how this could be done, but I was ready to blast off.

Other projects in the works were vehicles to drive on the moon. Batteries would be the easiest to use and they could be recharged with a solar panel. I had never heard of those things before. The only problem was that the panels weren't very efficient.

As an alternative to the machines, they were talking about using mirrors to focus sunlight and direct it to melt tunnels. That sounded like science fiction to me.

That shouldn't be a problem on the moon, as we could have enormous "arrays" of them. Another problem with batteries was the size of the charge they could take; it would limit the distance they could go.

Gasoline-powered engines were a possibility. We would have to provide a source of oxygen. Compressed air tanks would fill the bill. We would need these because batteries couldn't run the huge tunneling machines, and we would need to dig underground living quarters on the moon.

They also were talking of hydroponic gardens to help with food. Until we got to the moon and checked out what the soil was like, we didn't know if we could grow any crops using traditional methods.

They were even considering fish farms for protein. That would be so cool, going fishing on the moon!

All was not peaches and cream with the program. I was sitting in a presentation when the most godawful racket started.

One of the Proton rockets exploded on the launch pad. We all ran out of the room to see an enormous cloud of smoke where the rocket had blown up. Thank goodness it was an unmanned launch.

The failure wouldn't stop the launch program. This was the seventy-second launch. The prediction from NASA for their program was a failure rate of one in twenty-five.

This was our first. There would be an investigation as to the cause, but it wouldn't stop the launches. I even asked Jerri Cobb about it, and she told me they knew the odds and still would play the game.

We talked for a little while. It came up in our conversation that the ladies had a TV recording camera up there. They couldn't broadcast back to Earth yet, but that was only weeks away.

One of the things they had done was a PSA for Mary's "Feed the Puppies" campaign. They had a puppy up there! The punch line of the PSA was when one of the women told Jerri it was her turn to take the dog out for a walk.

It was cute and would certainly get NASA up in arms. I didn't have that much against them other than not letting the better women fly. I'm sure they would be downplaying it as a fake commercial. Women couldn't be up in a space station! Nobody had that capability.

On a more serious note, I approved a project to put communication satellites in a ring around the Earth. We called it a constellation. We planned on an equidistant grouping so there would be complete coverage of the world but also extra ones orbiting above the US and Europe as they would be the biggest users at first.

In the US, Jackson Enterprises had been approached by the CIA wanting to launch satellites that would take high-altitude pictures. After much thought, I drafted a reply that we would do so but would announce to the whole world what they were intended for.

Also, JE would under no circumstances put weapons into orbit. After hearing those conditions, we were told they would get back to us.

Rather than wait for them, I commissioned our satellites to take pictures from high earth orbit and we would sell them to anyone who wanted to buy them. They wouldn't be cheap. All of a sudden JE was the only provider of high-earth imagery. We would even take special orders, for a special fee of course.

It became like the old saying—why buy the cow when the milk was free? In this case cheap pictures vs expensive launches and satellites.

The first few times we had the film from the satellites be ejected and fall to earth. Finding the film was a problem, so we came up with a manned small rocket-powered vehicle that we could fly up to the satellite and unload.

This also enabled us to refuel or repair satellites at need.

We also came up with a program for sending low earth orbit rockets up with small science projects or to take site-specific photos.

These were called sounding rockets. They were much smaller than the big boys. They would be anywhere from three feet in diameter to six feet and anywhere from ten to thirty feet long.

These launches were complicated because we had to bring the science package down safely and then retrieve it.

Our new desktop computers were able to handle the orbital mechanics. It would have taken weeks to calculate them by hand, but the computers did it in minutes.

All and all, I thought we were making great progress. Within a year or so we would have a woman on the moon.

Chapter 17

Several issues were being worked on in the space program. From Earth, they could launch a rocket and capsule that would reach the moon.

Once the capsule/rocket combination reached the moon, it would have to go into orbit around the moon. Then a moon lander would have to go down to the surface, and then return to the capsule in orbit.

Then the orbiting capsule would have to return to Earth and land. Without our new computers, I didn't see how the orbital mechanics could be worked out.

Then there were the slight physical details such as the various launches. There would be the launch to the moon, the launch down to the moon, the launch back up, and then the return launch to Earth. That was a lot of launching!

I was assured that we had the technology well in hand to do all of it, but it still left me concerned. If any of the launches failed, I could envision a crew stranded in space until the air ran out.

I asked for a meeting with the team leaders on the space program. When I expressed my concerns, they agreed with me but then tried to tell me that to keep it cost-effective and the schedule on track risk would have to be taken.

That got me hot under the collar.

"Are any of you taking the risks?"

One guy, I think in charge of the moon lander, told me yes, it was their reputations on the line.

"I mean, are any of you putting your lives on the line?"

Dead silence.

"Have you been told that there are any budget constraints?"

Dead silence.

"This schedule that has been put in place, is it arbitrary or is there a reason, such as saving the planet, to keep to it?"

Dead silence.

"Here is what we are going to do. One, it won't be a launch from Earth. It will be a launch from our space station or another orbital site.

"Two, the objective will be to build an extended stay station which orbits the moon. There will also be in place a system of launches to resupply it and a method of returning from the moon station.

"Third, moon landings and returns will be with multiple vehicles, each of which is capable of carrying the whole crew.

"This is not a space race which must be won at all costs. It is the building of infrastructure like a superhighway. You must be able to travel it safely multiple times. We are building for the future, not trying to run a soapbox derby!

"As far as cost goes, I'm right now considered the richest person on earth. My income keeps growing, so why should we try to do this on the cheap? I know you are used to working for the government and politicians. This isn't true anymore! I want this done right and for the long term, not dusted and done!"

I may have got a little excited, but I had to make the point.

It was also a wake-up call for me. I couldn't remain hands-off until they understood what this was all about. It wasn't a space race between Russia and the United States. It was Rick Jackson extending mankind's reach.

While things were being put in place on my Australian station project, I would spend time here on the moon station project. I would have to change the culture from the moon landing to the moon station. It would be another mindset.

I also realized that there were several more people I had to bring on board in their thinking. The empress and the queen. Since I was providing the cash for this project while they provided in-kind, I'm sure they would go along. They just needed to understand what the objective was.

In turn, they would have to pass this on to their people. Thank goodness the politicians wouldn't be involved. It would double both costs and time.

One huge advantage we had as a private company, we didn't have to put anything out for a competitive bid unless we wanted to. This saved us time in not having to wait for bids and then evaluating them.

Then having to give the losers hearings as to why we were being unfair. Then having to wait for court cases to be settled after they sued when they lost the hearing. All this and the politicians they supported trying to pressure us in the background.

The cost savings in not having to have an organizational structure in place to accomplish all of the above was enormous.

This also meant I didn't have to announce what we needed to the world by placing public bids. I don't see how poor NASA could ever get anything done.

I could see a competitive bid put out for a launch vehicle and then one of the parties having theirs fail on launch. If this would happen, they wouldn't be selected to build the launch vehicle. I mean, who in their right mind would select a company that failed in what you were trying to accomplish?

Under the rules, they could appeal the bid selection as unfair. It could set the project dates back a year or more. This would give the failed company time to build a successful rocket. They would try again, and if they failed, the judges would conclude they weren't able to build a rocket that would work.

Then the failing company would appeal that ruling. They could set the program back years and never achieve anything.

This could go on forever or until the failing company went broke. If I were a competing country, I would make certain they never went broke.

Hurray for private enterprise.

I suspect it costs more to fight this system than to build and launch the payload.

I made appointments with both the queen and empress in two weeks. I set them out that far, as I wanted to sit in on the meetings my tirade had set off. I wanted to make certain everyone got the message, and no empire builders would stall the program.

I was glad I did when the very first meeting with the overall mission planning group had a problem child. One individual insisted that it had to be a one-and-done launch as proposed originally.

When asked why it had to be done that way, we were told that was because the original plan called for it. The original plan was developed by NASA.

"Don't you understand we aren't NASA and don't have the same mission?"

"Well, we should. They are the premier space group in the world."

"I thought we were."

"Bah, just a bunch of amateurs thinking they know best."

This couldn't have worked out better than if I had planned it. I needed to show everyone how serious I was about the whole program.

"You're fired. Someone get him on a flight back to England."

'Make that to the US; I have to get back to my real job."

"What's that?"

"I consult with NASA on their lunar landing program."

"On second thought, let him find his way back. He is in breach of his contract."

I found out later it took him over a month to get back to the US. It seems he had trouble finding transportation from Mongolia to Beijing, and then couldn't afford the flight back to the US.

He was staying at the US Embassy. They finally got him a ride on a US military flight out of Japan just to get rid of him.

I thought about sending him a thank you card, as the incident motivated others. I think my having our Jiuquan Satellite Launch Center daily newspaper track his trials and tribulations helped.

There was one set of meetings that proved to be helpful to the overall program. It seems there was a company in the US that had designed inflatable space habitats. So far, they had had no luck in finding a buyer who would work with them.

The objections to them were the amount of oxygen that would be needed to fill one, replacing losses due to leakage, and the opening or closing of the hatches.

Then there were micrometeorite punctures to consider. There would be no radiation protection. The side exposed to the sun would heat the place, and the side not exposed to the sun would bleed off the heat. Going too far in either direction would either broil the workers or freeze them.

The plus was that workers could perform in shirt sleeves if you could even out the temperature.

Before I could open my mouth, a young engineer spoke up saying that we could do a balloon inside of a balloon, filling the space in between with water. It would seal off most of the air loss and provide radiation and micrometeorite protection.

The water would act as a giant heat sink averaging out the temperatures. Fans to keep the air circulating would make the inside liveable.

My contribution changed to, "Let's buy this company."

I was originally going to bring up everything that brilliant engineer said. That's my story, and I'm sticking to it.

Chapter 18

I issued orders that we look into purchasing the space habitat company. It seemed to be the answer to some of our problems. I didn't doubt for a minute that there would be issues to resolve, but it looked too good to pass up.

I scheduled a trip to Beijing and then on to London to explain my vision to the empress and the queen. I just hoped they agreed with my long-range plan and weren't hung up on the short-range space race.

The Soviet Union and the US had started the race. Then the Soviet Union collapsed. So, since there was no race anymore, it was now political theater to show that the US was number one.

I thought the US was number one. That is number one in being short-sighted. Here they had a chance to truly be the first in the solar system; instead, they were going to land men on the moon and call it a day.

My space vehicles would display the flag along with the British and Chinese flags. Maybe it would be better this way.

I caught one of the regular shuttle flights from the space center to Beijing. It was only a few hours, but I decided that coach seats were torture. I don't see how airlines could ever make seats any smaller.

Since I had an appointment with Empress Ping, I didn't have to wait long. An hour after landing I was in her office.

I had given a written memo of why I wanted this meeting. I just think I had time problems. I was trying to be respectful.

"Richard, I don't understand why you are here. I thought this was what we had agreed upon. Taking the long view has always been the Middle Kingdom's approach."

"I needed to make certain that this is understood from the top down. At the launch center, I found plans and attitudes in place that were favoring the short term. Granted, they were being championed by a NASA employee."

"How did he end up in a position of power?"

"Security is still tracking that down. His background checks didn't show this. It has the fingerprints of the CIA all over it. NASA isn't in the spy business."

"No matter what, I will back you in this program. The bigger it is, the better it is for the Chinese and even the whole world's economy. Now give me a quick update on the program."

I told her of all the successes and challenges we were facing. When I got to the inflatable habitats, she got a thoughtful look.

"Rick, all the most powerful emperors of China built landmark palaces. Maybe my legacy will be a Chinese Space Palace."

The look of horror on my face said it all. Before I could open my mouth, she burst out laughing.

"Your mum is right; you are easy!"

At that, I made an unflattering face at the most powerful woman on earth. It is a wonder I didn't hear, "Off with his head."

Instead, I just heard gales of laughter.

She managed to say, "I can't wait to tell the girls about this."

I didn't dare ask who the girls were.

I had dinner with her, and we talked into the evening about how China was doing. Siberia was proving to be a challenge, now that we were on the verge of winter.

The Siberian railway was almost completed as projected. The side spurs still had a way to go, but they now could truly send railcars across all of Asia. If Russia would allow them to connect, it would open travel to Europe.

Russia was still having internal upheavals but seemed to be settling down. They hadn't found anyone to be tsar. Maybe people remembered what happened to the last one.

She had heard about my gunfight in Australia. I think everyone in the world has heard about it. She wanted all the gory details. I think she would have been a range rider if given half a chance. That or hanged for being a horse thief.

She thought my idea of a huge station in Australia would work. It would be a good investment for the future.

I was to think about a large farm in Mongolia to grow grain. She wanted this so I would bring modern practices to the country.

I told her that I would provide contact information for large grain farmers in the US. Maybe they would like to expand.

We said good night, and I headed to my room.

When there, I had a phone call placed to Jackson House California. I hadn't talked to my parents in several weeks.

We exchanged family news. I had nothing exciting to tell them. That got me nowhere as Mum and Dad filled me in on all the things I had done since I had called last. I asked how they knew all of this. It seems they read the daily newspapers.

I did ask Dad if he knew any large grain farmers in the US. He didn't directly, but he knew people who knew people so he would ask around.

Mum had one more question before we hung up.

"Rick, do you think we could build a Jackson House in space?"

She then had to start laughing as she told me how easy I was. At least I now knew who one of the girls was.

The next morning, I boarded the 707 for the flight to London.

I spent most of the flight with economic and political science textbooks. I made a list of questions about the concepts that I didn't understand. I would have to find someone to answer them.

I took a short nap and then had dinner before landing. The head stewardess took the opportunity to see if she could ask a question. I told her to go ahead.

"Rick, do you think we could have your flight headquarters based in space? Maybe in an inflatable habitat?"

Grr!

From the aircraft, I went to my hotel suite for the evening.

The next morning, I went for my run on Rotten Row where I usually ran when in London. I saw an old friend. She came riding by on her horse and gave me the finger as she passed by. I would love to know who she was. I was also glad she didn't stop and ask if she could have a stable in orbit.

I was on time for my appointment with the queen. She had Mr. Norman sit in with us. I explained how my trip to the launch center had raised concerns in my mind about people understanding the mission as I saw it.

She was honest enough to tell me she hadn't personally given it a lot of thought but agreed that my plan was a better use of resources than the US government's.

She blamed that on the "everything right now" attitude in America. Rise in the stock market, the space race, everything had to be at once. If it didn't have instant payback, they weren't interested.

I kept my mouth shut when she stated that America would have been better off staying a Crown Colony.

The look on my face must have shown how I felt as she started laughing.

"You are easy! Can we move Buckingham Palace to orbit?"

I think I'm returning to Australia and living in the Outback.

I did have to give her updates on my activities. She wasn't as into the gory details of the Ned Kelly shootout, but she listened to my description.

She also let me know that the Sydney police were making great strides in their investigation based on the Jason Talmadge account ledgers I had provided. She doubted that I would ever have to worry about speeding or parking tickets in that country.

When I explained the scope of the station that I was putting together, she was suitably impressed. I was to call Mr. Norman if there were too many obstacles. They might be able to help.

She loved the Space Lady program and wanted some English women included. I didn't see why not, as we would need hundreds of people before it was over.

Mr. Norman was to inform the RAF that they were to provide suitable candidates. That was interesting from two angles. It gave me a better insight as to Mr. Norman's role in the scheme of things. It was much more powerful than I thought.

Secondly, from what I knew of the RAF, they would have problems as they made NASA look like a bastion of women's liberation. I had read that term recently. I could see where they were coming from, but from my experiences recently, it looked like men needed some liberation of their own, at least from the ladies' propensity to tweak us guys.

From the palace, I went up to Grandmum's and spent several days with her. She and I chatted all day long. It was fun hearing the antics of her and the Queen Mum. It is a wonder the two of them didn't ask for a ride into space.

"Oh no, my dear boy. We are going to wait until you move the palace there."

Chapter 19

I thought about knocking up my friends from school and seeing if they wanted to hoist a few at the pub. I decided not to after remembering our last get-together, where they thought I was too dangerous to be near.

This time I did remember to visit the Roman ruins to see how the dig was going. It was going, slowly. There was hardly any activity at all.

The guards we had hired were still in place, preventing people from just motoring up and starting to dig for treasure.

I had to show ID to get in, which was fine by me. On the site itself, which previously had fifty or more students working, there were now five or six roaming around with little purpose.

I stopped one and asked if David Randel-MacIver was around.

"He's been banned from the site."

This was news to me!

"Do you have any idea about why he was banned, and who banned him?"

"Some bigwig don at Oxford claimed he wasn't directing the dig correctly and filed a complaint with some government commission, so they banned him."

"The government?"

"Yeah, some department I never heard of. Word is that it was a setup job, as the don was on the oversight board of that group."

"Do you have any idea where I can find David now?"

"I think he went to a dig in Egypt."

"Thank you. I guess I will be going to Egypt."

It took long enough, but the guy I was talking to finally twigged as to who I was.

"It happened when you were in Siberia, Your Grace."

"That explains that."

I was now on a new mission, find David and get this project back on track. Also, destroy the don who had done this and his pet government commission.

My first stop was to change clothes. I was going to Oxford and wanted to look serious. After consulting at Grandmum's house with Harold, I chose a business suit. I had never worn it before, but it was a perfect fit and screamed "money".

When I mentioned it to Harold, he had to chuckle. "This is the most expensive suit you have ever worn. It cost over fifteen hundred quid."

Yikes!

For a trip this serious, I borrowed Grandmum's Rolls-Royce and driver, the esteemed Hamilton. I wanted to make an impression.

He drove me to the bursar's office. I kept reminding myself on the way that I had to be cool and calm. This wasn't the Ned Kelly gang. They were easier to face.

I was asked if I had an appointment.

"No. Please inform the bursar that Colonel the Duke of Hong Kong Richard Jackson is here to see him. I handed her my card which had my titles plus my honors, GC, KG, OBE, KCVO, LoH, GBM, OEoD, and HC. If you got 'em, use them.

It lit a fire under her. She almost ran into the next office. Within a minute, the bursar came bustling out. It wasn't the same one that I had met before.

He bowed and scrapped me into his office. It was satisfying and disgusting at the same time. Strange.

"I have just been informed that my dig out at The Meadows has been halted. I would like to inquire as to why?"

"That was before my time. I had been told that an incompetent person was tearing up the dig and that it had been halted. I know that it is now in various committees in the antiquity department to decide who will run the dig."

"Are you aware that I'm paying for the dig on my family property?"

"No, I'm not aware; as I said, this was all before my tenure."

"Do you have a way of finding out how much money I have contributed to the university, directly and indirectly?"

His face lit up; he could do this! He called the young lady from the reception desk back in and asked her to retrieve the Richard Jackson file. It only took her a few minutes.

I was offered coffee or tea in the interim but turned it down. No way was I taking a chance with this suit.

The bursar took his time with the file, making notes as he went.

"I must say you went out in a burst of glory!"

"It had its moments."

"There have been several chancellors I would have loved to dye blue. Unfortunately, one has to eat, you know."

"One of the true pleasures of being rich."

He had been adding up numbers as we talked.

"It seems you have been one of our major donors! I hope you are here to continue that tradition."

"I'm here to get my incompetent dig director back on the project, get the project out of whatever stupid committees that are holding it, destroy the career of the don that started this, and have the government committee that allowed this to be disbanded."

"I think we need to see the chancellor on this. I don't want to make you think that I'm a coward on this issue, but it is really beyond my scope."

"I do understand that, and I also realize it happened before you started here. I consider you an innocent bystander."

"Do you intend to shoot the chancellor?"

"What!?"

"I read about that gang in Australia and how you took them down. I wondered if you were going to resort to violence here?"

"Only if needed."

At that, he had his young lady make a call to let the chancellor know we were on our way. I couldn't believe it. He thought I would go around England and shoot people! What sort of reputation did I have?

The chancellor didn't seem pleased to see me. I wonder why.

The bursar and I were invited in and had the usual amenities offered. I declined, wanting to get the heart of the matter. I told him how I had been out of the country for a while and had come back to find the Roman dig shut down.

He dryly told me that he had heard of my adventures around the world. Everything from Siberia to North Korea to Australia. I had left a trail of bodies in my wake.

When he said it that way, I understood the bursar's concerns.

"Who is the don that complained to the government, and what committee was it that stopped the work?"

When he named the don, I realized it was the guy who had stolen David's work in the first place.

"I thought that after it came to light how much of his student's work he was taking credit for, he would have been let go."

"That's not how things are done in academia. He is tenured, so we can't let him go. He successfully made the argument that all professors take credit for their student's work, that maybe he had overstepped the bounds a little, but not by much. Based on that he has continued to be the dean of his department."

"What is the name of the government department?"

"The Department of Antiquities is a group for ancient finds in England. A subgroup under them is called the Project Approval Board. They decide if groups applying to work on sites are competent. They have professionals in the field review the proposals and decide if the people are competent."

"Let me guess. The professional the board chose was the dean?"

"Correct."

"And no one saw a conflict of interest?"

"Not our problem; this is outside of the University."

"I see."

The chancellor continued in his plummy voice. "As you can see, everything has been done within the rules, so our hands are tied. I suggest you let this go."

I turned to the bursar, "The Richard Jackson Foundation has been donating a million pounds a year to the university. I let it continue even though I was sent down. Consider it stopped."

The Chancellor told me, "You can't do that."

"I can, and it's within the rules, so I suggest you let it go."

I stood at that point.

"Good day, gentlemen. I have a government department to put in order."

I left them sitting there in semi-shock. The university certainly wouldn't be hurt by the loss of the funds, but it would inconvenience them as they had to revise budgets.

I called Mr. Norman from The Meadows and asked for an appointment in the morning. He set it for ten o'clock. I was there on time wearing my new suit with a clean shirt and a different tie. I liked this power look.

It only took a few minutes to explain my situation. He made a phone call and set us up for a meeting with the Department of Antiquities after lunch.

At lunch, I wore a bib to protect my new suit. I may have looked strange, but I wasn't taking any chances.

It was a good thing because mustard dripped off my hotdog.

Chapter 20

That meeting went well. They denied all responsibility and blamed the independent board for its actions. You have to love large organizations.

"Then there is nothing you can do to help us with this situation?"

"I'm afraid not. It is within the rules, I suggest that you let it go."

Right.

"Where can I obtain a copy of the charter that this organization is working under?"

He made a call to the young lady at the front desk and asked her to bring a copy in.

When it arrived, Mr. Norman would read a page and then hand it to me. He stopped on the third page.

"This is what we are looking for, 'all decisions as to the competence of dig supervisors will be made by an impartial party.'"

"Again, our department doesn't decide who is an impartial party. It is the board's prerogative."

I spoke up, getting a little hot under the collar.

"And it is my prerogative to give this story to my father, who owns one of the largest newspaper and television chains in the world. I assure you that your name and the department's name will play a prominent role."

All of a sudden, it seemed his department had an oversight role on this independent board. Maybe they should look into how things were handled.

I told him I thought that was a wonderful idea and that I was certain the result would be the removal of a certain Oxford professor from the board and whoever appointed him.

He thought that might be a reasonable solution.

Mr. Norman had said nothing, but I noticed he had worn his metal lapel badge with a crown on it. He was tapping it.

I love the subtle approach.

My next item on my new list was to fly to Cairo, then charter a plane to Thebes where David was doing scut work in the Valley of the Kings.

It didn't take as long as the other flights I had been taking. Only across the Mediterranean rather than the Pacific. Don't ever let anyone tell you differently. The Pacific is one big ocean.

I was able to charter a light plane to Thebes and then a taxi to the Valley of the Kings. Once there, it was easy to hire one of the many tour guides working in the area to take me to the dig that David was working on.

I arrived at lunchtime and caught David in camp. If nothing else, he looked healthy. Working outside and the tan made him look good. He was sitting and eating with four other kids, at least they looked that to me. There were two boys and two girls.

He was surprised to see me. He thought that I would have written off the project after my adventures.

I told him where things stood, and I wanted him to come back. He agreed immediately. His onsite boss had other ideas.

"I need you here; you can't walk out on me."

David replied, "I have no contract, and you don't pay worth a damn. I'm out of here."

The guy flexed his fists, "I can make all of you stay."

"May I introduce you to the Duke of Hong Kong? If you remember, we were talking about his gun battle with the Ned Kelly gang last night."

The wind went out of the guy's sails.

I spoke up, "David will need additional help on-site. If any of you want to come along, you have a job."

All four of them got up and ran to their tents to collect their belongings. I thought the guy in charge would have a fit, but he just stood there glaring at me.

We needed two taxis to get back to the airport, and I had to charter a larger plane, but we made it back to Cairo by dinner time. We checked in at the new Shepheard Hotel. It would have been great to stay at the old one, but it was destroyed in a 1952 fire.

The new one didn't have the historic feel that the old one would have had, but since we were only there for one night, it didn't matter.

The only reason we were staying the night was the aircrew needed the downtime.

We left early the next morning. I had forgotten how the 707 appeared to people who had never been on it before.

I talked one of the stewardesses into giving a complete tour while I read business reports that had been sent on board before we left England. I had been reading them for two days now and wouldn't finish before we touched down in Oxford.

One item of interest in the report was the theme park that had been built next to the Roman site. It wasn't completely done, but enough that it was open and making a ton of money. I had never even thought to look in its direction when I visited the site. I must have been upset.

When we landed, I made a couple of calls from the private passenger terminal. My first was to Mr. Norman to see if the government investigation was started on the competency board.

"Done and dusted, my boy. They all have been fired and the agency shut down. It took about ten minutes to find out the organization was corrupt.

"Now the whole Department of Antiquities is under review. I think there will be some changes there."

My next call was to the bursar's office at Oxford. My call was taken quickly. I asked the bursar if any steps had been taken at the university to rectify the situation.

"It seems the don in question has been involved in a scheme of corruption with a government agency. Moral turpitude is one reason a tenured professor can lose his position. He is losing his position as we speak."

"Good."

"Does this mean we can count on your annual donation being renewed?"

"That ship has sailed. I no longer have any relations with Oxford University. Burn me once, and all that."

We had Grandmum's limo waiting for us, so we went straight to the dig. While David was starting the process to get it up and running again, I had a meeting with the onsite security supervisor. I explained to him that Oxford University no longer was associated with the project and none of their personnel, unless approved by David or me, were allowed on site.

He had me give that to him in writing. I appreciated his doing that.

Back at The Meadows, I had a phone message waiting for me, the chancellor at Oxford wanted me to call.

I knew he would be trying to get my funding back, but it wasn't going to happen. I called him back out of common courtesy.

"Your Grace, thank you for returning my call. I know you have hard feelings about being sent down, but I wish you could get past them."

"My actions got me sent down. I have no hard feelings about me being stupid. What I have hard feelings about is how your school allowed the corruption in your antiquity department to continue and do nothing about it."

"But we have, we have fired the professor who was involved."

"Only after I forced the whole issue out into the open."

"Is there a way we can get you to change your mind?"

"Not at this time."

"I'm sorry you feel that way."

"I'm sorry that the school is so hidebound that it can't police itself. Now good day."

I had a place to invest the money that I wouldn't be donating to Oxford. My FreightEx company was doing well and ready to expand out of California to all the states west of the Mississippi.

I wanted that company to do well, as my board of directors at JE had shot down the idea.

With that on my mind, I made a call to check up with my manager. His reports were glowing. They were making money hand over fist and hadn't even put on a major advertising campaign yet.

I told him that I would be depositing a million pounds in the company's capital account. That made his day.

It was time for me to head back to Australia. The engineering design firm should have the first plans in place for the large station. I didn't call ahead. I wanted to see what state they were really in rather than hear an optimistic phone call.

I had to wait for another day for the 707 and crew to be ready to fly. While waiting, I wandered the streets of London looking for odd little stores that might have something unique in them.

I did find a few small items. One was purported to be a bead from Zulu Chief Dinizulu. These are the beads that Baden-Powell used in Scouting to reward the completion of an advanced scouting course. I would donate it to the BSA, as they had significance in Scouting but were little known elsewhere.

One of the other items was a wooden doll that was supposedly Anne Bolyn. She was beheaded at the order of King Henry VIII. The doll was old, and the head was removable. I thought Mary would love it.

When she played princess, it was always, "Off with their heads."

Chapter 21

We took off to Australia late in the afternoon on a rainy English day. As they would say, a normal day. Once above the clouds and in the sunshine, it was beautiful as usual.

I spent many hours at the controls picking up flight time as the pilot in command. I had even done the takeoff under the eagle eye of the chief pilot. The only things I hadn't done were those that would be required in my check flight, like putting the aircraft in a stall. For some reason, the 707 crew was reluctant to let me do that.

I slept and ate well, showered, and changed clothes three times on the trip. I had time to read the books on economics and political science. I still had trouble with the thought of elastic and inelastic demand. Either people wanted it, or they didn't!

I even managed to lose fifty-three dollars to the stewardesses playing gin rummy. I'm a slow learner. Don't swim with the sharks.

Like most flights, it had a good ending. I landed us without bouncing down the runway, so I counted it as a win.

Upon landing, I immediately drove to Jackson House in the MG MGA that I had found in the garage there. I had left it at the airport in long-term parking.

I had a pleasant surprise when I arrived. Margaret and Linda Ferguson had done a wonderful job in furnishing and decorating Jackson House.

They cheated a little. They had pictures of Jackson House California and kept the design in the same spirit. While they couldn't duplicate everything, it was certainly in the same style. Don't even ask me the name of the style. That is one area I don't pretend to know anything about.

When I asked how I should describe it, Margaret told me that it was formal art deco with overtones of California modern adapted for current Australian taste.

I kept repeating the sentence to myself. I would regurgitate it when requested and hope like heck that no one would ask me what that meant.

Margaret and Linda gave me a complete tour of the house. You could tell that they were nervous about what I would say. As each room exceeded expectations and I let them know that, they relaxed a little.

As we started to enter the large dining room which would seat fifty people or more, Margaret brought up an issue that had been bothering her.

"Your Grace, this has cost a lot of money. I hope that we haven't exceeded what you had in mind."

"First of all, cut the 'Your Grace'. I'm Rick. Second of all, you have exceeded my expectations. The costs are immaterial. I demand that you and Linda go on a shopping trip, charging at least five thousand pounds to my account."

That was a lot of money, almost a year's salary for the average family. They had earned it. If I had paid a decorator for this, it would have been at least three times the amount plus the design fees.

The only thing missing were library books. The ones that were in the house had been shipped to the University of Sydney. I wondered aloud what to do about that.

Margaret informed me that she had talked to Mum and that a copy of the Jackson House California library was being shipped. In the meantime, she had contacted Angus & Robertson to provide all of the significant Australian literature from since its founding.

The large dining room was impressive. The table was set with fancy table settings to rival Buckingham Palace. I did have a twinge about the cost at that point. I'm still stuck somewhere between Bellefontaine paperboy and stupidly rich.

When I saw the ballroom, a coin dropped. I needed to show this off, a grand reception. After giving it some serious thought, I realized it would have to be a series of receptions.

I would have one for all the government officials, bureaucrats, project engineers, and their spouses.

Another for prominent British expats to gather support among the biggest investors in the country. I wasn't looking for investments but trying to avoid opposition.

Then the American expats so they wouldn't feel slighted and oppose my project or feel left out.

Last, I would hold an event on the station itself for all the people who worked there and the locals, just to get them on my side. Maybe a rodeo.

I passed these thoughts by Ron, and he thought it was a great idea. He did ask who my hostess would be. I told him I had to think about that.

I suspect he had Linda in mind, as she was about my age. I hated to tell him she seemed like a little kid in my mind. I would have to tread carefully here.

As we started to plan the events, I got saved, at least for the first one. My parents notified me they were coming for a visit. They wanted to see the new Jackson House and the station. I would ask Mum to be the hostess. That saved me from having Linda thrown at me.

She's a nice kid but would never make it in the pressure cooker that is my life.

I was scheduling the events for four consecutive weekends, to get it over with. The first group then had a countess as hostess. Who could I have as hostess for the British expats? They might grumble that the first group had a countess, and they didn't rate.

I had a thought. I would swing for the bleachers. I made a call to Mr. Norman, and he helped me broker a deal for Princess Margaret to attend. Since it was to be a quick trip, her husband Anthony Armstrong-Jones wouldn't be accompanying her. My 707 would pick her up and return her to England.

I decided once more to swing for the bleachers. I called the White House and asked the president and his wife Jackie if they could make a trip to Australia. My timing was good as he was going to be in Singapore anyway.

I didn't even have to send my jet; he would come on Air Force One. I would have to pay for the fuel, but that was peanuts.

I did let the royal governor know who was coming and as an afterthought the prime minister plus the NSW governor. It was a good thing I did; they would be present, and it would have been a tremendous faux pas not to let them know.

Once things got going both the princess and the president arranged other meetings while in Australia.

One thing for certain, this would cement my place in Australian society.

The royal governor's office helped me develop the first guest list, the British ambassador the second, and the American ambassador the third.

The last event on the list, the one at the station, I asked Mrs. Ferguson and her daughter Linda to be my co-hostesses.

A lot of high-powered people were involved to avoid telling Ron Ferguson that while he had a nice daughter, she was not for me.

My parents arrived two days before the first event on a Saturday evening. That gave them a day to recover from their trip, then a day to look things over.

They brought Mary with them. It seems lately they have been afraid to leave her alone, even with a lot of adult supervision. It seemed she had upped her quota of mischief recently. This quota was already high. When I got a chance, I would have to ask them what she had been up to.

If I asked Mary, it would be all sweetness and light. You know all nine-year-old girls were innocent.

While my parents were taking a nap on day one, I gave Mary the run of the house. She knew all the secrets of the first Jackson House, so she would know her way around this one.

I figured she would get tired of everything when she realized all the good stuff had been hauled away. No treasure was left behind for her to find.

That turned out to be a big mistake because about an hour later she returned, declaring finders, keepers. She was carrying a Thompson submachine gun; it was as big as her.

The round drum was attached and the way she was carrying it, it was full. I looked and the safety was off.

I about had a heart attack. I was supposed to be watching her. Mum would kill me, probably with the Thompson.

I asked as I relieved her of her superior firepower, "Where did you find that?"

"There is a little room off of the escape tunnel. You have to be small to fit in the entryway. It has all sorts of stuff.

"You had better make sure that gun is safe. I tried to work the bolt but I'm not strong enough."

I not only removed the drum but cleared the breach and set the safety, then locked it in my office.

Chapter 22

"Good find Mary. Would you please show me the little room?"

"It will cost you."

"How much?"

"Two quarts of tutti-frutti ice cream."

"Ouch, one, and it's a deal."

With Mary, you always have to negotiate.

"Include whipped cream and a cherry."

"One squirt of light whipped cream and one maraschino cherry."

Also, be clear on the details.

If she wanted more, I would have demanded it in writing. If she was serious, she would ask for a lawyer to review it. Not really, but we were getting close to that level. By the time she is in the fifth grade, I suspect I will have to sign contracts with her in blood.

"Deal."

We shook hands, and that settled it. Neither of us cared to face our parents if we reneged after a handshake.

She took me down to the escape tunnel and showed me the room. I could have found it if I knew it was there, but not by accident. The opening was only about three feet tall and not very wide.

Mary found it because she is so much shorter than I am.

There were all sorts of weapons inside. Some I had never seen before, but I recognized them. Why did Talmadge have a grenade launcher? There was also a canvas carryall. It must have been his go-bag.

He could go a long way on the two million dollars in bearer bonds inside. There were also ten thousand Australian pounds and several gold watches.

I delighted in telling Mary, "Finders, keepers."

"Then I get to keep the machine gun."

"Okay with me, if it's okay with Mum and Dad."

My little sister was growing up. She only stomped her foot. She didn't stick her tongue out at me."

"Tell you what, I will share."

I handed her about half the Australian pounds. She tried to put them in her little purse, but they wouldn't fit. She just carried the stack in her hand.

We went back upstairs just in time to run into Ron Ferguson. He looked at Mary, then at me.

I told him, "She wants to go buy some ice cream."

He started to say something and changed his mind. He walked away muttering, "They really are different."

When Mum and Dad got up from their rest, Mary and I showed them what she had found. She was told in no uncertain terms, no machine guns until she was at least twenty-one.

Being Mary, she got it down to eighteen. From the look Dad gave me, I knew that gun would be long gone before she was ten.

From there I gave my parents a tour of the house. The drugs, furniture, paintings, and safe contents were long gone, so there wasn't much to see. He did tell me the wine cellar had some interesting vintages and that I should have them served at the receptions.

He agreed to bring up the bottles and separate them by events. As he stated, the best stuff would be for the Brits, the Americans would get the second rate and never know the difference.

I argued him into good stuff for the president and first lady. He agreed as they were Democrats. If it had been Ike, he would serve him dishwater in a bottle.

Dad did look at the weapons in the tunnel and told me there were none of any real value and that I should consider the grenade launcher too dangerous to use because of its age, not the rifle but the grenades.

I decided to leave everything as is; you never know. Well, everything but the bearer bonds. Even then I had second thoughts and left them there. You never know when you'll have to run for the hills.

Mum approved of the decorating that had been done. I asked her if there was anything called formal art deco with overtones of California modern adapted for current Australian taste.

She replied as though I was the village idiot, "That is what this is."

Okay, on decorating I'm the village idiot. It's official.

When Margaret Ferguson joined us, Mum complimented her and Linda on their fine work. She couldn't have done it any better. The adaption to current Australian taste was the perfect touch.

No comment.

The hardest part of all the dinners was coming up with the dinnerware. After some frantic shopping by the Ferguson ladies, they asked for my help. They must have been beyond desperate.

Knowing absolutely nothing on the subject, I called Mum. When she was done laughing at me, she told me to call someone, either at the White House or the palace.

That was an easy decision for me. I called Mr. Norman who in turn had me talk to the Master of the Household. The Master, whose name I didn't get, recommended place settings by Royal Doulton, and the glassware by Waterford in the Marquis pattern.

In a surprise move, he recommended Lunt Silversmiths, a US company, in their Eloquence pattern. I asked him how he had this all off the top of his head.

"We receive calls of this nature every week, Your Grace."

His use of "We" was the royal "We." I guess one of the perks of the position. He also suggested I ask the Royal Doulton people if they had any patterns that were not released yet but were ready. That way I would be a trendsetter.

He gave me contact information for each of the companies, again off the top of his head. He sure kept a lot of stuff up there.

He then went on to counsel me that this was just a quick order starter ware. I needed to visit each vendor later and pick out a pattern that would be special to Jackson House.

When I asked if we should use the same pattern at each of the Jackson Houses, I think even he was impressed. I was to select a common pattern for all Jackson Houses and pay for that pattern to be sold to us only. Why in a mere two or three hundred years, it would be worth a fortune.

I made a point of calling Mr. Norman back and letting him know how helpful the Master of the Household had been.

"Who might that have been?"

"I only got his title. I didn't catch his name, even if he gave it."

"I was hoping that you got his name. No one who works in the palace knows it. We all call him Master."

"Wouldn't the payroll people know?"

"They are tighter than MI6. I think it is a joke dreamed up by him and the queen. We have been trying for years and have made no headway."

"Sorry I can't help, and thanks for yours, please pass on my comments to the Master."

After calling Royal Doulton and the others, I had arrangements made for a 707 flight to pick everything up. I ordered seventy-five place settings. It was more than needed, but things broke.

Then there was the menu for each of the events. My initial thought for the British was fish and chips wrapped in newspaper. The Americas would get hotdogs and hamburgers.

I mentioned it to the ladies, and they rounded on me. It seems those dishes don't go well with formal place settings or ball gowns.

After that, I didn't mess around and placed calls to the palace and the White House.

For the British dinner it would be:

Steamed fillet of halibut with watercress mousse, asparagus spears, and chervil sauce.

Saddle of new-season Windsor lamb with herb stuffing, spring vegetables, and port sauce.

Strawberry sable with lemon verbena cream.

Then a selection of assorted fresh fruits.

Finally coffee and petit fours.

The Americans would get:

Crisped Halibut with Potato Crust, to be served on a bed of braised baby kale.

Salad of a variety of spring garden lettuces with a shallot dressing.

The main course, Beef Wellington, prepared with Australian cattle in a British style.

For dessert, a lemon sponge pudding in the American style served with Newtown Pippin Apples.

The menus would have the rationale behind each dish written on the back. Again, some of the ingredients, such as the unique Newtown Pippin Apples, would have to be shipped in by air.

While working on these hurdles, we also worked on the guest list. I would never have guessed formal events could be so much work and so time-consuming. We hired the calligraphy work out.

If there were many of these, I would hire someone on staff to manage these events.

Maybe I could have a master of Jackson House and have him move at need between the properties. I could already see this person and Harold trying to one-up the other.

It also brought home the fact I had been running Jackson House Hong Kong and Australia as a bachelor pad. That worked to a point.

Mum had a staff at Jackson House California. I needed the same. A call to my ever-reliable Mr. Norman made me understand I needed to hire a butler. One would do for both my houses, and he would hire a housekeeper for each of the residences.

Between them they would hire the necessary staff, he the men and she the women. The only place it could get sticky was if I insisted on a male chef. I was smarter than that.

As I worked myself through all of this, one afternoon I went up to the top of the tower, taking two beers with me.

I thought long and hard about things. I had been used to being on my own. Things had grown on me. I had a basic decision to make. Go back to Rick Jackson sometimes hitchhiker, or be Colonel the Duke of Hong Kong Richard Jackson.

It's the simple things that help make decisions in life. I had been up there for two hours and wanted another beer. I would have to fetch it myself. It was a shame there wasn't a maid or footman available.

Now, how to start the process? Once again, a call to Mr. Norman. He is turning out to have the patience of a saint. He thought I should hire an experienced butler rather than a recent graduate of a butler school.

Another thing learned! They have schools for butlers.

"Where do you find experienced butlers? Do you put an ad in the *Times*?"

"Heavens no, this is all done through the upper servant gossip system. I shall mention to the palace butler your need and the conditions, and the word will be passed through their network."

Within two weeks, a Mr. Jeeves Wodehouse was my butler. I was to call him Jeeves. Our relationship started formally and remained that way.

Since I was only in attendance at each house on a limited basis, they could be managed by ten on staff. I asked if that was the total and was told that was at each.

I suspect I won't be leaving my underwear on the floor in the future.

Chapter 23

After all that, the dinners themselves were anticlimactic.

The first event the next evening went well. The governor-general was delighted to meet Mum and squired her around all evening as though she was his trophy. He had better watch it. Dad knows where the Tommy gun is.

All the government officials, engineers, and bureaucrats seemed pleased with the event. One older man, an engineer, had the nerve to say that the governor-general got a countess. When he showed up for the British expats, it would probably be a housemaid.

I couldn't wait to tell Princess Margaret that. I couldn't decide if I would point the old guy out to her or not. She had a wicked tongue on her.

Many people made a point of telling me that the New Station, as they started calling it, was a fine idea. It would help the Australian economy in many ways.

They weren't telling me anything that I didn't already know, except that if I wanted to name my station, time was running out.

I hadn't given it any great thought, maybe something like the Rocking R. That was my American West speaking. Maybe I should go with what the Australians were thinking of. It's their country and traditions after all. They tended to go with the name of the nearest town. Or the town went with the station, I'm not sure which.

Using that logic, New Station worked because it was the joining of a group of stations. That is, unless I wanted to keep the name of one of the original stations.

That didn't work because the largest and the best was Ferguson Station, and he wasn't the owner anymore.

So, I hunted up the head engineer who I found hiding by the bar and asked that he have the model labeled New Station. He asked me why I would do that; all the legal papers would have to be changed. They had been filed as Jackson Station.

I can overthink things at times.

Always moving around the room, I made a point of talking a little to everyone I could. Dad called it working the room. I thought of it as being a good host.

When it looked like I was going to be pinned down by someone trying to sell their pet idea, whether it was a bureaucrat wanting to expand their empire or an engineer with a hundred reasons to modify the project with only a delay of a year or so and a few more pounds, I would do my best to escape.

I had prearranged with one of my security guards to pull me away when I gave a signal. It was a touching of my ear lobe. The guards thought this was great fun.

That was another thing that was now different in my life. I had to have security around me whenever I was at a public event. I thought a dinner reception at my own house was taking it a bit far but try to argue with Mum.

When it was time for dinner, I escorted Mary. Dad was with Mum. Mary was allowed to stay up late tonight to keep me safe from all those Sheilas, as she called them. I wondered how she picked up the slang so quickly.

I asked her and she informed me that she had a dress line especially for the well-dressed Australian girl. Its seasons ran counter to the US, so they had special ads.

I gave a short speech about Jackson Station; the speech was like a politician's stump speech. These had small variations in a standard talk to fit the local audience.

Here I emphasized that Australia was benefiting from the farsightedness of the government and its staff, elected, appointed, and civil. The design itself is due to the professional engineers of Australia.

As a friend of Mary's, Patty would say, "Gag me with a spoon."

At dinner, I sat with Mary on one side and Mum on the other, so I was well protected. After dinner, it was once again open game on me. We had a small orchestra playing soft swing music.

I had to dance. Invitations had been for the engineers, etc. plus one, so I wasn't inundated with eligible daughters. Instead, it was the divorcees who were after me. Who knew that many bureaucrats and engineers were divorced women?

They had brought a partner but were willing to throw them over to dance with me. It wasn't so much dancing as being embraced by an anaconda.

I'm a male so I had the expected reactions, but I knew better than to try to play around in this crowd. It would lead to nothing but trouble. I must say though that several of them might have been worth the trouble.

Then there was the one married woman who acted as the others in front of her husband. Seeing the ring on her finger, I kept pushing her away in a slow dance and she kept moving in. In desperation, I about yanked my ear off signaling my guard to rescue me.

And so went another social event that the tabloids pictured as Duke Ricky having a good time as usual.

Princess Margaret flying in for the British expat's dinner made Australian national news. And I thought I was going to remain in the background.

I did make it a point to introduce Margaret to the guy who complained about a countess being present for the bureaucrats and engineers while the expats would get nothing. He looked like he swallowed a lemon when I winked at him.

I hadn't informed the princess about what he had said. Let sleeping dogs, or in this case, princesses lie.

Dinner was good, better than the political rubber chicken circuit. The entertainment was okay. I saw the magician palm a card during his act during an intermission in the dancing.

When he did it a second time, I think everyone in the room noticed. Next, the rabbit peeked out of his hat early. The endless scarves had lady's knickers tied in. By that time, I was laughing so hard I thought I would cry.

Who would have thought of a comedy magic act? I was so impressed that I followed him out of the room and asked him how he had dreamed it up.

"I didn't start that way, but I was so bad at sleight of hand I was going to have to quit. One day at a child's birthday party, I realized all present were smiling and laughing at my mistakes."

"I went from twenty pounds a show to the thousand pounds you are paying me tonight."

I had to ask.

"It was worth every penny. If anyone asks, I will give you a good recommendation."

"Thank you, Your Grace."

"Better yet, I know a guy in the US, Ed Sullivan. Would you like to be on his show?"

"Most certainly."

"Consider it done."

Mr. Sullivan owed me. I had negotiated peace between him and the Beatles on a delicate subject. Do you think "Lucy in the Sky with Diamonds" is about Lucy and Diamonds?

Since this was an event for the British, I wore my military uniform. I didn't get to wear it very often with all the gewgaws. I was glad I did. All the sharp medals and badges I wore kept the anacondas at a distance.

I swore a couple of them would have bruises and indentations from trying.

Chapter 24

The American expat reception went off well. The menu was well received. Since it was an American event, I would have thought a barbeque would have been more fun, but no, it seems that Americans like formal events as much as the rest of the world.

Almost all the people were from the East or West Coast. I couldn't find any mid-westerners there. Maybe that is why they liked the formal stuff. I wondered if we had two different countries. I'm a mid-westerner but can hum the coastal tune. Can't sing it but can hum it.

Harold wouldn't let me wear boots and jeans to the event. He insisted on a white dinner jacket. A red bow tie and cummerbund made it look sporty, according to him. I thought the red carnation in my lapel was over the top, but he nagged and nagged. I wasn't going to a prom!

That is what I thought until I received my guests. It was exactly how they were dressed. You would think I would get used to this high society stuff by now. I had been to enough events exactly like this, but every time I was astonished that people enjoyed this.

I was cornered as expected by men who had the deal of a lifetime for me. I learned a long time ago that asking them to submit their deal in writing to my headquarters sent most packing. Those who did submit had an honest review. We rarely accepted any of them.

The women were different from the British. Instead of anacondas, I thought of them as boa constrictors. The result would be the same, my life squeezed out of me.

The highlight of the evening was when President Kennedy and Jackie made an entrance. This cemented me as a power player. They were gracious as only they could be. It was an eye-opener to watch them work a crowd. Dad could learn a few things. I learned a lot.

After dinner, while others danced, the president and I had a private conference. He made certain I understood that he wasn't at my beck and call and that he had intended to make a state visit to Australia about this time, so it was easy to work me into his schedule.

I asked him if it would ease his pain if I donated to his re-election campaign. He smiled at that. Speaking of pain, since I knew he was coming, I had a rocking chair waiting for him.

We made some small talk, about how miserable the flight could get, even if you had your bed. Especially since Jackie snored so loud!

I bit on that for a moment and then he gave his trademark grin. I just shook my head.

After that, he got more serious. He wanted to talk about the further opening of trade with China. In turn, I asked him if that was a good idea. Why not let China grow itself internally?

I had to explain that the US would lose until the Chinese standard of living came up. Where did he think multi-national industries would move to? One dollar an hour American wages or Chinese ten cents a day? That was the American minimum wage. How would high-paying auto workers earning almost three dollars an hour react?

"I don't see good American car manufacturers moving overseas!"

"Listen to yourself, Mr. President. You depend on the goodwill and loyalty of capitalists who have to satisfy Wall Street. They will move in a heartbeat if the quality remains the same. If quality improves, the factories may be lost anyway."

"What about the shipping cost?"

"Sorry to say, but I have ensured that ship has sailed, literally. My containerized shipping has had an enormous impact on shipping cost."

"So, we can't open up China at all."

"I didn't say that. Just consider the consequences of each trade sector and keep trade balances equal. The worst-case would be shifting the average Chinese wages up by lowering the wage structures of Americans.

"It could be made to look equal through some smoke and mirrors but overall, the people will know they are working for less. Frankly, they won't care about the Chinese workers getting more. Let the Chinese raise their economy by internal measures. The sheer population numbers will ensure that America will lose on the deal."

"That gives me a lot to think about. The more financially conservative members of both parties are pushing for more trade with China to help the US."

"I would think long and hard about this. Ask your economic team to do some projections on each trade sector and see what the short and long-term effects would be. If they would be bad, let the American people know. Get enough shop stewards bending Congress's ear, and they will not be so eager to give the workers' jobs away."

I knew studying all those economic and political science textbooks would pay off. Imagine me lecturing the president of the United States.

"Rick, I now respect you more than ever. My economic team has given me the same advice. Since you talk to the empress, I now know she probably sees things the same as we do. It will make negotiations easier for both sides. Be sure and tell her of our conversation."

Dumb me, his team probably wrote the textbooks I had been studying.

"Let's change the subject. What are you up to with your space program? NASA feels like you are trying to embarrass them."

"I think they are doing a good job of that all by themselves."

"What do you mean?"

"You know they colluded with LBJ and Glenn to keep women out of space, at least until the heroes went first. Well, they had all the astronauts. I needed some, and only the women were available. It's not my fault the women are more qualified than the men."

"But the women aren't combat qualified."

"Then I guess we are in trouble up there when the little green men show up. By the way, how many machine guns and cannons are being mounted in each capsule?"

He ignored that dig.

"Your program has launched many more rockets than ours, and I understand that some of the capsules have been joined to form a space station."

"That is correct. They are going to start the TV broadcasts next week. I understand they will be giving out homemaking tips, like how to bake cookies for when your astronauts come in from a hard day of spacewalking. Also, how to get stubborn stains out of their spacesuit."

"You are mocking us."

"Yes, sir. I'm allowing this. Not only because of how women have been treated but to show that it will be private enterprise that will open up space to mankind, not a bloated bureaucracy depending on congressional pork."

"How do you truly feel, Rick?"

"I guess I did get a little carried away. But I tend to get excited about this program. It is my way of giving back the good fortune that has come my way. Besides, they may let me take a ride someday."

"Do you want to go up?"

"I would love to. You can't count the number of people who have tried to get a ride up there. We may even open up a space tourist group. Why, even my sister Mary has been lobbying for a ride so she can pitch Girl Scout cookies to the astronauts and the whole world."

"At least I will be out of office before she is a teenager. That's assuming I don't run for reelection or die in office before my term is up."

"I have heard that Queen Elizabeth is considering accommodations for Mary in the Tower until Charles is King."

"What would your parents have to say about that?"

"They are considering it, and even talking about waiting until one of Charles's children is on the throne."

"It must be an interesting life at Jackson House, California."

"You can say that again."

A knock on the library door broke our conversation up. It was time for the president to give private interviews to important American expats, read donors.

I went out and valiantly allowed the American black snakes to wrap themselves around me.

I did dance with one young lady who came with her dad, a widower. She was very nice, and I managed to steer her out onto the terrace where it was cooler.

We had a wonderful half-hour talking about our experiences in Australia. It was good fun, and I enjoyed her company so much I asked if I could call her at home.

She gave me her number. She lived here in Sydney. She and her father wanted a change in scenery from Columbus, Ohio after her mother died. He had enough money that it was no issue. He had retired from running his own company in Worthington. They made specialty steels.

She was nineteen like me, and attractive. I don't mean a beauty queen; I mean a good-looking Ohio girl. Susan Knowlton seemed like a lot of fun.

She seemed to know a lot about me. I asked her how she knew all this.

"Your dating Judy King made the gossip pages of the *Columbus Dispatch*. We were all jealous of her, dating a movie star and singer."

Shows you how much newspapers know.

Singer?

Chapter 25

The reception was on Saturday night. I called Susan on Sunday. I asked her for a date next Friday night. She agreed. We spent another hour on the phone talking about our lives in Ohio.

She did ask a few questions about my life now. She told me that if she believed everything she read in the papers, I was bigger than life.

I assured her I wasn't. I resisted telling her about some of the seamy things I had been forced to do along the way. It might scare her off.

Not that I wanted her for anything but friendship at this point. After all those aggressive divorcees at the reception, I was ready to spend time with a real girl.

I can't even remember when I had a relationship where the girl wasn't trying to get something from me. Did it go back to Judy?

May-ling didn't count as I never considered her a girlfriend. She had always made it clear that she would marry a Chinese that fit her station. We had both felt an attraction, but she would never act upon it. I had certainly sent enough signals.

I spent the week before our date continuing to set up my household. This included a whole new security setup. Jackson House in California had gate-controlled access with armed guards. Here there was no gate. There was room for a secure entryway; it just had never been installed.

That was unlike Jason Talmadge, but I would never know the answer. I no sooner had that thought than I found out the answer.

There is a right of way that runs close to the house. It is for underground water and gas pipes. When the engineers filed the construction plans and tried for the permits, they found out these existed.

All they had to do to get an exemption was to have access points on either side of the new gatehouse. This required permission from not only the city planning board but also the mayor's office.

Talmadge probably didn't want to draw any attention to himself or didn't have the political pull. I now didn't care about the attention but did have the pull.

CCTV cameras were placed around the perimeter of the house, with steps being taken to ensure there were no blind spots. A twenty-four-hour watch would be kept on the screens.

Then there was the staffing interview. My new butler Jeeves flew in from England. I had hired him with Mr. Norman's recommendation. He was in his mid-forties and had been a butler for fifteen years. The house in England in which he worked had to be sold to settle death duties when the last of the line died. The estate was to be split up between five different people, none of whom wanted or could support the mansion.

This was happening all too frequently in England as the two world wars and the Depression all but destroyed the ranks of the noble class.

He was glad to get this job. Technically, he was moving up from a count to a ducal household, no matter if it was in the sticks. Who knew, maybe besides Hong Kong and Sydney, I would establish a hall in England?

I didn't think it was likely; two events and I was sick and tired of the social life of a nobleman. Doing that in England full-time sounded like a living hell to me.

When he arrived, I dumped the hiring of the rest of the staff on him. He would sink or swim based on the team he put together. There probably would be some turnover as we wouldn't be hiring from the local village where everyone's history was an open book for the last five generations.

Heck, go back six generations and you will find transported convicts. No matter how some Australians tried to romance it as stealing a loaf of bread, some of those convicts were bad news.

Susan and I went to an American movie, *Charade*. It starred Cary Grant and Audrey Hepburn. I had only met Mr. Grant once and never Miss Hepburn, so I didn't have any good stories about them. The movie was good and had us both guessing until the end.

After that, we went to a dance club with Johnny O'Keefe performing. He was okay, but he would never make it big in America. That took a lot of nerve for me even to think about it.

We had a fun time, talking about everything and nothing. She gave me a light kiss on the cheek when I walked her to her front door. We had a good time, but I don't think a spark was lit between us.

I called her the next day, Saturday, and told her I enjoyed the evening very much. She responded that she had a good time. I asked her if we could go out again, but she declined. Her boyfriend was coming back to town, and she was hoping that he would propose.

I wished her the best. I wonder if she knew that the photographers took snaps of us at the dance club. She better hope that the guy proposes before he sees the papers.

Then again it was a very innocent evening, so why should she worry? As for me, I had fun, but as usual, it would go nowhere. Maybe I could get the Beatles to do a song about that. "Alone Again (Naturally)" would be a good title.

I was glad to get back to Ferguson's station where we were having the reception for our employees and the locals. Except we didn't call it a reception; we called it a festival to celebrate the new station.

It was to be a combination of a US county fair, carnival, horse and ute racing, barbecue, square dance, and rodeo. The whole thing was being filmed as nothing like it had ever occurred in Australia. Bits and pieces, especially the fair and rodeo, but not all together.

Word of the event got out, and we had people drive over five hundred miles to attend. Some invitations had been sent out, but most people came because of the posters that were put up in every little petrol station and restaurant in this part of Queensland.

It was scheduled to be a week-long event. Some portions of it became permanent. When touring the newly built fairgrounds, I asked how we got a small carnival to come way out here and set up.

"You bought them."

The Ferris wheel attracted the natives. When it got about that anyone could ride for free, it became a walkabout destination. We ended up hiring a guy and his family to run it whenever someone showed up. It looked like it would be running for years.

That and the Tilt-A-Whirl. What was considerably strange was to see a train made for children ride past you containing the tribal elders.

That was all in the future. In the present, we had a lot of fun. I had to give a short opening speech, and we turned it loose.

I was pressured by the Fergusons to ride a bull in the rodeo. I didn't win the event but didn't disgrace myself by falling off. I lost on points, which worked for me. My point was that I lived. I wasn't young and stupid anymore. Or any less for that matter.

We had planned on five hundred people. Five thousand showed up. To feed everyone, we had flights coming in on a newly cleared airstrip. It was a dirt strip but long and wide. I hired a couple of pilots to keep the DC3 continuously flying supplies in from Sydney.

Not everyone stayed the whole event, but later we calculated we had fed an average of three thousand people a day for five days. That is a lot of food.

I had to be a judge for many of the fair exhibits. Some were fun like tasting all the pies and cakes that had been submitted.

I got tired of the pickles pretty quickly.

I spent the whole event in boots, jeans, and a cowboy hat. The festival was so large that I rode a horse from event to event.

Since so many more people had shown up than expected, we hastily arranged for the Queensland police to set up a temporary station. They sent police to stay in caravans. Several did along with their families.

As we saw what was developing, I told my people to go with the flow and not turn people away. Arrange for more tents, food, and whatever it takes to make this remembered as a fun time.

If you put that many Australians together with free beer, you will end up with a punch-up or two. At one point the drunk tank, a series of tents, had almost one hundred residents.

Several guys spent half the five days drinking and the other half sleeping it off in our tents.

My hands hurt after the first three days of shaking hands. Not painfully but enough to notice. I must have met all five thousand people. At least it seemed that way.

There were first aid stations, port-a-potties set up in male and female tents, and rest stations cooled by fans blowing over ice. Most of the infrastructure was set up on the fly.

The highlight of the event was that we had a baby born there. The Fergusons opened up their house to the young lady, and there were more doctors and midwives present than at a Sydney hospital on any given day.

One hour I would be riding in a ute race, never winning—those Aussies are crazy; the next judging pickles—those Aussies are crazy; square dancing—those Aussie girls are crazy; and finally, eating barbeque.

You can have your formal events. This week I had a ball!

Chapter 26

I had considered a reception for the Chinese but realized they were too few and had no prominent Australian citizens among them.

I contacted the people making a video for TV about the space project and arranged for them to do one on the building of the Jackson Station.

The idea was to gain popular support for the huge project in Australia, similar to how Ike gained support for the interstate system.

I would also send copies to some heads of state to demonstrate what a Jackson project could do for their country, not all countries, those that I had facilities in, and those that could be of interest in the future.

I was exhausted after the last several weeks. This being a big shot was tiring. I liked people but not having them thrown at me constantly.

I always carried business cards with me. Each day since the first reception I have had to increase the number I carried. I learned early on to write notes on the back of each card I received in return about the person and what they wanted. They all wanted something.

I bought several plastic boxes made to keep business cards in alphabetical order. The only problem with that system was if you couldn't remember the name of the person or company you were looking for, you were out of luck.

I soon started noting the date and event where I met them. Some were to be stored for future reference, some needed action taken, but most were stored because as soon as I threw it away, I would need it.

I had always saved business cards, but never on the scale of the last several weeks.

Then there was the sad fact if you handed someone your card in return, they now had your phone number. Jeeves had to hire an operator to answer the phone at Jackson House and have two private lines put in for us to use.

I spent the next couple of days at the beach. I took along a couple of new books to read. I didn't care for *Cat's Cradle*, too doom and gloom, and loved *The Spy Who Came in from the Cold*.

I could tell several different girls were eyeing me from time to time, but I was too tired to care. Now that is tired.

After two more days, I was feeling recharged and decided to do something I wanted to do for a long time and that was to go see Ayer's Rock.

Early one morning I flew from Sydney to Mount Isa, refueled, and took off toward Ayer's Rock. I wanted to see it from the air first. If I wanted to climb it, I would land at Connellan Airport.

I took off intending to fly the 281 miles in a direct line. When I was about fifty miles out of Alice Springs, flying southwest to Ayers Rock and Connellan Airport, I saw a sandstorm approaching. It appeared to be a strong one.

I had been flying at ten thousand feet so climbed to twenty thousand in hopes of going over it. My rate of climb was slow enough that I saw I couldn't get high enough quick enough and that it was probably over twenty thousand feet anyway.

If I turned back to Alice Springs, the storm would catch up with me before I was on the ground with the aircraft undercover. I elected to turn due west and avoid the storm; I would let it pass me by and then turn toward the rock.

I was able to carry out my plan. I was right on the edge of the storm and took some pretty good buffeting. I bet some of the paint was scoured off the airplane.

I was at about fifteen thousand feet, and I saw a brilliant flash of light from the ground, about five miles ahead. I was curious, so I kept on the heading and started losing height.

The sandstorm was swirling around a lot of sand on the ground, but I realized that I was looking at a highly reflective outcropping. It could be quartz.

As I reached its position, the sand swirling around kept masking and unmasking the outcrop. I was down to five hundred feet and things were getting as bouncy as I could take. Looking at it this closely, I realized it was a giant quartz outcrop. I couldn't tell the size of it, but it had to be miles long and wide.

Remembering that small outcrop of quartz I found in California and the amount of gold it contained. This was possibly the largest gold deposit ever found, or not.

The first thing I had to do was get a fix on the location. There would be no landing of fixed-wing aircraft in this part of the world. A helicopter could do the job.

The only problem with that was I would have to have someone fly me in. Is there anyone who I know as a pilot who I could trust? I couldn't think of anyone offhand.

Back to the immediate problem, finding this spot again.

I had changed direction and been buffeted around so much that I had a rough idea of where I was, but only a rough idea.

I thought I was about one hundred and fifty miles from Alice Springs. While circling the outcrop, which was coming and going due to the residual of the sandstorm on the ground, I climbed back up to twenty thousand feet.

Once at that height, I turned on what I thought was a reciprocal heading back to Alice Springs. I made certain I was writing down my speed, time, and headings. I had gone up to twenty thousand feet because the higher you were, the farther out you could intercept the line-of-sight VOR signals from the airport. In this case, within forty miles of the airport, I would catch the beam and could ride it in.

I wasn't going to land. I just wanted to get a good fix on the airport. That worked. I only had to fly a little over a hundred miles, which didn't take long at one hundred and fifty knots.

When I received the signal, I turned the aircraft toward the airport after noting the heading. I then timed how long it took to get to the airport.

I now had what I thought would be good headings to get back to my find. I immediately turned and flew back, using the headings, speeds, and times I had recorded.

When I was nearing the area, I descended back down. The sandstorm had pretty well passed through. It also had almost completely covered the quartz outcrop. There was still enough uncovered that I got the occasional flash from reflected sunlight, but nothing like the great flash I had originally seen.

I would be able to fly back to this area. Next, I decided to play it safe by then flying towards Connellan Airport using the same technique that I had used to get back to Alice Springs.

I once again documented everything as I went. The VOR at Connellan came in loud and clear on schedule. Once I flew over the airport, I turned and went back to the outcrop.

Aside from one little flash, you would never know that anything was there. Even as I circled it, it disappeared.

I then went back to my original goal of seeing Ayers Rock. It was beyond impressive. I landed at Connellan to climb it. I had a day pack with me and several bottles of water. I wore good climbing shoes and rough clothes.

My understanding is that it was only a difficult climb if you weren't dressed correctly or weren't prepared for the heat. I was ready.

I landed at Connellan and decided for the plane to be refueled. There was a taxi ready to run me over to the visitor center.

The driver, an Aboriginal, asked me about my plans. When I told him I was going to climb the rock, he asked me not to.

I inquired, "Why shouldn't I?"

"It is a sacred place to my people. How would you like it if we crawled around the altar of your church?"

"I'm not very religious, but I take your meaning. What do you recommend I do?"

"Do the base walk. It is about ten kilometers on flat ground. You will see all sides of Uluru while not upsetting the Dreamtime gods."

"I will do that. I never intended to intrude on a religious site. No one told me about this. It was only that I had to see and climb this enormous rock that they called Ayer's Rock, after the guy who first saw it."

"My people saw Uluru thousands of years before Ayers did."

"I stand corrected. Of course, they did."

It was coming up at lunchtime, so I ate at the visitor center, chips and a Coke. From there I went on the walk with a hired native guide to lecture me on the way.

He told me all about the geological history of the rocks, the plant and animal life that we saw on the way, and those in the area that we didn't see. The one takeaway I had was that there was a lot of unfriendly wildlife in Australia.

I asked about the native legends and stories about the rock. That is when I learned two things. They didn't talk to outsiders about them, and his taxi driver cousin had told him I would understand.

Even in the middle of nowhere, you had to watch what you said.

Chapter 27

My guide told me that my flying in had been a good idea. Lasseter Road from Alice Springs was a terrible road. He went on to tell me that the road was as crazy as old man Lasseter himself.

"How crazy is he?"

"He dead now, buried out in the desert while on one of his wild chases to find the quartz outcrop which he claimed held millions in gold."

"Would you tell me what you know?"

"The story comes up in the newspaper every couple of years. It always seems to change a little, so take everything with a grain of salt.

"Lasseter claims that as a seventeen-year-old he discovered this huge gold find somewhere west of Alice Springs. It could be anything from one to seven hundred miles west. This would have been either 1897 or 1911. That right there makes the whole story suspect.

"It was thought to be on the western edge of the McDonnell Ranges. He reported it to officials sometime after 1913, but no action was taken. Since he had been in a reform school when he was younger, they probably didn't believe him.

"In 1930 he retold the story to a member of the Australian Workers Union. In this telling, it was somewhere near the border of the Northern Territory and Western Australia.

"Sometime after 1897, he got in trouble in the desert and was rescued by a passing Afghan camel driver! He was taken to a surveyors' camp run by Joseph Harding.

"Harding and Lasseter returned to the reef to fix its location but couldn't do it. Later they claimed it was because their watches weren't accurate enough.

"Lasseter then spent the next three decades trying to raise interest in funding an expedition. As you can see, the timeline is a mess and the location keeps changing.

"Finally in 1930 when the Great Depression was at its height, he secured around 50,000 pounds in private funds towards an expedition. It included motorized vehicles and aircraft. This was unusual for the time. It should have been camels and mules.

"The expedition was accompanied by experienced bushmen, prospectors, engineers, explorers, and a pilot.

"Lasseter was sullen and uncooperative for some reason. The group had many logistical difficulties including the loss of an airplane. Finally, Lasseter declared they were one hundred and fifty miles too far north. The exasperated bushman leader stated that Lasseter was a charlatan and ended the expedition. They parted with Lasseter.

"Lasseter and a dingo-shooter along with a team of camels continued. Lasseter, whose behavior was increasingly erratic set off towards the Olgas.

"One afternoon he returned to camp with concealed rock samples, claiming he had found the gold reef. The dingo-shooter, who now doubted Lasseter's sanity, called him a liar. A fight ensued and Lasseter was left to his own devices.

"The dingo-hunter returned to 'civilization', and Lasseter trudged off with two camels. Later a search for Lasseter was conducted by a bushman who found Lasseter's emaciated body at Winter's Glen and his personal effects in a cave at Hull's Creek.

"From Lasseter's diary, it was found that after the dingo-hunter left, the two camels bolted. He encountered a group of Aboriginal people who rendered him assistance with food and shelter, but he was weakened and blinded and eventually died of exhaustion and malnutrition trying to walk to Uluru.

"Later, Lasseter's son spent years hunting for the gold reef. It was never found. It is the most famous lost gold mine in Australia, and many people have searched. The trail left by Lasseter and then the expedition zigzags all over the place. There is no way of knowing if anyone got close.

"Movies and songs have been made. None have any proven facts."

That was interesting, I had found a quartz reef that met the conditions of Lasseter's gold reef without being biased by knowledge of the story. Add to that the fact that I could get back there; it was worth following up.

The only practical way to get there on the ground was by helicopter. I couldn't fly one and didn't know any pilots who I could trust with the knowledge. The first thing I had to do was learn how to fly a helicopter.

Flying back to Sydney via Alice Springs, I gave it a lot of thought. Back at Jackson House, I started making a Gantt chart of what had to be accomplished and a timeline. I didn't try to refine it too much. Just the highlights with generous achievement dates.

Until I knew there was gold there, it wouldn't do to spend too much time on it. The first action item was to find a helicopter school and find out what I would need to do to get a license.

I found that I could get a Private Helicopter Pilot License (PPL(H)). This license enabled me to fly any Australian-registered helicopter, subject to endorsements and ratings, by myself or nonpaying passengers.

The requirements are:

A minimum of 50 hours of flight experience following the CASA-approved flight training syllabus.

A Class 2 Aviation Medical Certificate.

Demonstration of adequate aeronautical knowledge in a PPL helicopter theoretical examination.

And then successfully passing a practical flight examination.

This sounded like a piece of cake. They didn't even require me to strafe airfields! I had wanted to be able to fly helicopters, so this was the excuse that I needed. It would only take a month since I could dedicate a lot of time to it as the station was being put together.

I signed up at a school operating at the Sydney airport and went to work. During breaks from my ground classes, I asked what sort of small helicopter I should have for the Outback.

The basic response was that I shouldn't be flying any helicopter by myself beyond the black stump, said stump currently being at Alice Springs. That stump seemed to move around a lot, depending on who you talked to.

I finally decided on a Fairey Ultralight just like Ron Ferguson had. Then it dawned on me that I didn't have to buy another helicopter; I owned that one. I could use it for a couple of days and return it to the station.

I spent time at the ranch familiarizing myself with the little chopper. It was a good machine. Ron flew it down to Sydney for me to use as part of my training. I couldn't fly it as I wasn't trained yet. Ron had to do the flying. All I can say is it is one sweet handling machine.

After a month of continuous classes, I was able to pass my check ride. I used the Fairey as I was now very comfortable with it.

I put together my gold prospecting kit. This wouldn't be panning for gold. It would be crushing ore and testing it. Sydney had stores that carried everything a gold miner could need. They called them pawn shops.

I found a pickaxe, a shovel, and a rock crusher, which operated on the same principle as a fence post driver. From a chemical supply house, I was able to get a test kit for various ores, among them gold.

That and plenty of water. I only intended this first trip to be an afternoon outing. I waited until the weather was predicted to be as calm as it ever gets.

I had marked up my maps with the headings, times, speeds, and distances so I should be able to fly right to the spot.

I was using Alice Springs to start the investigation. If anyone asked, I was looking for more ground to buy. I wanted a larger station. I even got to tell my tale to the airport manager who wandered over to see what was going on. I guess with only a few flights a day that was easy for him to do.

He looked at me like I wasn't too smart but didn't say anything. I had stowed my kit out of sight in the little storage compartment.

Before I took off, I made calls to the surrounding airports to confirm weather conditions hadn't changed. It was only an hour of flying time, but why take a chance? I rechecked all fluids and had the fuel tank topped off.

You know me, Ricky never takes a risk Jackson. Well, calculated ones or unavoidable ones like jumping for my life.

This time my planning paid off. I was able to fly directly to the coordinates on my map. When I got there, it looked like nothing I had seen before. There was no quartz sparkling in the sun. The entire area was a series of sand-covered hills.

This was not unexpected as I had seen the wind covering the area in sand before. From the topography of the area, I thought I had a pretty good idea of which hill it had to be, and it was only a short walk there. Lugging my equipment with me, I began to dig.

It didn't take long before I hit hard rocks under the sand. Using a little whisk broom, I cleaned the sand off the rocks. They were quartz. I next broke the quartz into small chunks that would fit in the rock crusher.

After pounding the chunks into small pieces, I used the test kit to determine if gold was present.

It was.

Chapter 28

Before I got all excited, I collected nine more samples. I walked about a hundred yards in a straight line along the reef, then took another sample. I repeated this four more times.

I then went two hundred yards at a right angle from the last sample and took another one. I worked my way back parallel to the first sample line collecting another every hundred yards.

That sounds easy, but with the hot sun and having to trudge through the sand, it was tiring. I drank all of my water doing this.

The first thing I did when I was finished was to collect more water from the helicopter. It is a good thing I had brought two gallons; I also popped a couple of salt pills. This desert was murder.

After I rehydrated myself, I tested the samples I had just collected. They all contained gold. My simple test kit would only test positive for the gold. It wouldn't tell me what percentage or the purity.

Now all I had to do was have the samples assayed, and if they proved to be worth anything, purchase the land and obtain the mining rights, map a route in, put together an expedition to set up camps along the way, and a base camp. Then start to mine.

If we were doing serious mining, heavy equipment would have to be brought in. For this, a road and quarters for the mining crew would have to be built, and other amenities. Ore would have to be extracted and smelted, the environment kept clean, and arrangements made to ship the gold out safely.

There were probably a hundred other details I hadn't thought of, but that was a starter list.

The first and most important was to have these samples assayed. The gold content and purity would tell if any of the other steps would be worth taking.

I couldn't just walk into an assay office here in Australia and ask them to take a look at this stuff. People talked. I would be followed and hounded.

I put the samples in unlabeled burlap bags brought along for this occasion. No sense in using the bags normally used, which had stamped on them in red, "Assay Sample".

I wondered if anyone used them.

While refueling in Alice Springs, the friendly airport manager came out to visit. He appeared to have less to do than I thought.

"Did you have any luck out there?" he asked.

"A little. I saw a few places where if water was available, we could work with."

"Good luck on that. They have been hunting for an aquifer out here for over a hundred years."

"I'm thinking about bringing in some equipment and doing some test bores to see what's down there."

"Your waste of time and money, though if you could find water you would increase the value of this land tenfold if not more."

"I have to give it some thought."

"As I said, good luck."

All the time we had been talking, he had been maneuvering himself to get a look into the little helicopter. I'm glad the samples weren't that big and the whole bag would fit in the small storage compartment.

I even let him turn me while talking so he could get a good look to confirm I hadn't brought any samples back.

On the flight back to Sydney after returning the helicopter to the station, I thought my telling him that I might bring equipment to drill for water was brilliant. I could bring some machinery in and pass it off as drilling equipment. A large flatbed trailer with tarp-covered machines would help keep the secret longer.

Landing in Sydney, I carried the bag of samples in a metal toolbox. It looked like an oversized lunch pail.

Checking the time in Sydney against US time, I placed a call to Mum and Dad. Dad answered.

"Dad, I'm sending you a present. It is very much like that one I found in California on my hitchhiking trip, but even more so."

"How big of a present?"

"Oh, I'm not certain. These are just samples; they have to be checked out. I didn't want to do it here as it might get people talking.

I continued, "If I were you, I would do it through a cut-out, as privacy is a major concern here."

"Rick, you are making this sound like a big deal."

"It has the potential to be the biggest deal I have ever been involved in."

"How are you sending the samples?"

"I'm having the 707 make a special delivery. The crew will be bringing the Ferguson ladies to check out your Jackson House as a cover. They will have a 'present' for Mum in a box."

"I've never known you to be this serious."

"You will soon understand."

"Okay, we'll be waiting for your package."

We chatted for a few more minutes and hung up.

Just call me, "Jackson, Richard Jackson."

After hanging up, I called the Fergusons and asked for mother and daughter to go to the States and see the first Jackson House. My story to them was that I wanted them to redo Jackson House Hong Kong as formal art deco with overtones of California modern, adapted for the current Hong Kong colony taste.

They were impressed that I had such a fine grasp of fashion. I was impressed that I could remember that stuff.

"By the way, there will be a box waiting on board the aircraft with a present to my mum. Please give it to her."

After that, I called the 707-flight crew to schedule the flight back to the States. They weren't at their hotel; it seems they spent all their time on Bondi Beach. How do you get a job like that?

I spent the next couple of days finding and installing an aerial photography rig that could be adapted to the Cessna.

Taking pictures would wait until the assay results were in, but I wanted to be ready.

A few days later I was called to the phone at Jackson House by our new operator. I had a long-distance call from my father.

"Hi, Dad. What's up?"

"You certainly know how to throw the cat amongst the pigeons. That present you sent me is high grade both in content and purity."

"All the separate ones?"

"Yes, all of them."

"I hope you had someone else submit them for testing."

"I did. I told your mum, and she advised a double cutout. I'm glad we did. It has the whole business here in the US going mad over where the stuff came from. I didn't know it, but every find has other minerals mixed in, so a sample is like a fingerprint. These prints don't match any known ones."

"Will the cutouts keep their mouths shut?"

"Both are on vacation in other countries, none in your neck of the woods."

"Good to know. Keep them there for a few more months. It will all get out, but the longer we can keep it quiet, the easier this will all be."

"Rick, I have some bad news for you. Your grandmum's health is failing. She may not live out the year."

"Oh, no, I will have to get to England soon."

"Your mum is there now and will be staying for the next few months."

"That is bad news."

ED NELSON

"Things are even worse. I have to watch Mary in the interim."

That gave me a chuckle despite the bad news about Grandmum. Mary had Dad wrapped around her finger. What could go wrong?

After hanging up and shedding a tear about my grandmum's health, I had several things to do.

I had to buy the land that contained the quartz reef. I could have just made a mining claim on the majority of it, but it would be simpler if I owned it all outright. That way no one could deny or limit my access to the reef.

The only problem was how to explain the large purchase of a large piece of worthless land.

I had a bright idea; it was so outrageous that it might work.

I first approached the prime minister's office. I was able to obtain an appointment with him.

"Your Grace, how may I help you?"

"Mr. Prime Minister, I need help in winning a bet."

From the way he turned in his chair, you could see this made him uncomfortable.

"I have bet that before the end of the year, I would own the largest ranch or station in the world. The bet is with a Texan who currently has the largest."

"Isn't the Jackson Station large enough?"

"No, I miscalculated. It misses the mark by about ten thousand acres, and the station is surrounded by others which can't be bought."

"That is embarrassing. So what are you proposing?"

"I would like to buy three million acres in Western Australia. Nothing was said about the land having to be developed."

"That must have been a big bet."

"Five million dollars, US. I think the desert in the Outback can be bought for a shilling or so an acre so I wouldn't win as much but would still be three million ahead."

"I would advise buying five million acres. You aren't the only one who has thought of this. I found the man to be overbearing and would love to see him get his comeuppance."

I had no idea what the prime minister was talking about, but if it could get me the land I needed, I wasn't going to argue about it.

"Thank you, sir. If you would pass the word to the land people that my purchase sees favor, it would make it easier."

Much later I found out that I had just been played. No other person wanted to buy that much land. The prime minister just saw a chance to sell another two million acres of worthless land.

Maybe I'm not as brilliant as I thought, but I did end up with what I needed. I also made a large contribution to his opponent in the next election.

Chapter 29

I had to go to the main office for Western Australia. Needless to say, it was little compared to the large active states like Queensland. When all you have is desert, there isn't much going on. There were a few stations on the edge, but that was it.

In the state land office, they had a huge map. It didn't have any areas marked "Here be dragons," but they didn't have much in the way of detail.

I asked what the desert land with no proven water was going for. The cost for that sort of land was one shilling per acre. Or 250,000 pounds for five million acres.

That was equal to 7,812 square miles. Rather than do all the math, I bought a chunk of land one hundred miles by one hundred miles which was 10,000 square miles or 6,400,000 acres for 320,000 pounds.

It would be easier to say 100 miles a side at over six million acres. This would give me room to swing the cat, as they say. Shy of being a government, I now owned the single largest plot of land in the world. I hoped the desert snakes would be impressed.

It took several days before the lawyers were satisfied with all the details. My largest concern was that the reef would be totally on my land and that it would have access to the nearest road to Alice Springs.

The closest road out of Alice Springs came within twenty miles of my property, so I would only have about one hundred and thirty miles to develop. Much easier said than done.

Once the ownership was settled, I inquired about the mineral rights. As I thought, all gold found belonged to the Crown, or in this case, the Australian government.

I asked the manager of the surveying office what I would have to do to mine any minerals found on my property.

"You would have to have a license from the state to mine. The license would spell out what royalties you would owe the state based on what is mined."

"What would the agreement be for a copper mine?"

"For commercial mines like that, we would ask for ten percent of all minerals, plus taxes of course on profits made."

"What about gold and silver?"

"Ah, you've found Lasseter Reef I see."

I about choked on that one.

"That would be nice. I just wanted to know the rules before anything is found, to see if it is worth the effort to explore."

"I would think you would explore, as that is the only use that land will ever have. To answer your question, the government would want thirty percent."

"Why so much more?"

"Because there will be less tonnage mined."

"That makes sense. So can I negotiate an agreement before a find?"

"Yes, that is the way most of the agreements are made out there. Just in case a find is made."

"What do I need to do?"

"Fill out this form and pay a fifty-pound registration fee."

"That's it?"

"Yes. Your prospects are low on finding anything, so we don't make a big deal out of it."

That's how I got the mineral rights. It took days, lawyers, and thousands in fees to buy almost worthless land, while it took minutes and fifty pounds to buy mineral rights that could be worth billions. Go figure.

Now that I had the mineral rights, it was time to mark out a trail to the Reef. That is where the aerial photography equipment mounted in the Cessna proved its value.

I spent the next week flying back and forth over the land between Alice Springs and the Reef. I wanted to map out the best trail to place a road.

The film was developed in Sydney every night. I used the first basement in Jackson House to lay it out on the floor. At the end of the week, I had what seemed a viable route, not too many dunes or gullies to negotiate.

For a reality check, I flew the route at a low altitude in the station helicopter. It seemed level enough, straight it was anything but. What would be one hundred and thirty miles in a straight line was almost two hundred miles of winding back and forth.

Once it looked good in pictures and near the ground, I had to drive it. I wasn't stupid enough to even think about going it alone.

I bought five MK 5 5-ton cargo trucks from the Australian Army surplus depot. These trucks were a newer model and had to have seen some hard use to be sent off so early. I had every one of them gone over with a fine-tooth comb, or in this case, trained mechanics.

They rejected one for a severely bent frame; it seemed it had been rolled over. We picked up another one that we only had to replace its rear axles, both of them.

We had an excess of jackaroos and jillaroos on the Jackson Station at the time, so I didn't feel guilty about pinching them from Ron. He didn't complain too much. They were eating a lot and sitting around.

We had talked about laying some off, but they were good people, and we would need them later. It costs more to hire and train new people than to keep some around.

I also had a 1960 Land-Rover 109 series pickup truck for myself. The only drawback to it was it used gasoline while the trucks were diesel.

We had three five-hundred-gallon water buffaloes to tow behind the trucks. Fuel was carried in fifty-five-gallon drums spread between two trucks.

One of the older jackaroos explained to me that I didn't want to have a point source failure, or as my grandmum would have put it, not all my eggs in one basket.

I had been calling England every other day and talking to Mum. She told me that Grandmum didn't have much time left so I should come for the last visit.

While all the trucks were being readied and supplies, such as tents, gathered, I flew to England.

I was glad I did; Grandmum looked so frail. She still had her smile, but it was a tired smile. She was ninety-eight years old, so she was allowed to be tired.

I sat with her for two days talking about the trouble Mum was in while she was growing up. I just thought Mary was a holy terror. Now I knew where it came from.

She talked about the old days before the Great War. She didn't appear to remember there were two world wars. They were fine days, as she related them. The good ole days as we said in America.

There were a few bad times she remembered besides the Great War. There was the Spanish Flu where she lost two brothers and a sister. Then the Great Depression where they had a hard time keeping food on the table.

Some nights she and Ernie her husband went without but never the children. There were more good times than bad, at least in her memories. She told me how they would sit around a table with a mixing bowl with the radio headphones in it to act as a speaker, and while she knitted, they would tell of the day's gossip.

Such gossip they had. Prince Edward, the Teddy Boy, and his scandals; such a shame the old queen had to leave it all to him.

And the clothes they wore in the roaring twenties were enough to make a sailor blush. Though Granddad, who had been a sailor, was never known to blush when the flappers came into their green grocer's market.

Though failing, it didn't seem to be quite her time yet, so I decided to head back to Australia. I promised to be back by Christmas. She told me that I would be back sooner for her funeral. I cried at that.

She told me not to be silly. She'd had a good run of it and enjoyed it all; that was life. I hoped I could have her attitude at the end. Though at the rate I was going, my end would be sudden, as in gunfire sudden. They couldn't always miss.

The trip back to Australia gave me plenty of time to think. The flight crew left me alone as I seemed to be withdrawn. I didn't ask to fly the plane, open any textbooks, or show interest in the eternal game of gin rummy.

Grandmum would be the first grandparent dying whom I had gotten to know. It seemed hard and unfair.

I did think about my expedition to the Reef. The locals would be going crazy about my leading a group into the Outback. They would be speculating why.

I had an idea. It was based on my conversation with the Alice Springs airport manager. I would add several water drilling rigs to my group. That way they could talk about the crazy duke and his hunt for water, rather than the crazy duke and his hunt for gold.

If we did find water, it would probably be worth more in the long run than the gold. Not that we would find any, but it would be a good distraction.

I wasn't even going to dig any more samples while there, I just wanted to confirm a viable path.

Chapter 30

I decided that we would do some serious searching for water. I checked with the University of Sydney, and they had several hydrologists on staff who would love to be part of our expedition.

After I explained what I wanted, they had mixed reactions. There had been many searches for water in the desert and none had yielded results. Yes, there were the soaks, which were minor groundwater concentrations, but no drilling had ever found an aquifer.

When I explained what I was willing to pay, they came around. They would end up ahead of the game no matter what.

I gave them an overview of the equipment I had gathered so far. They went to great lengths to explain that if I was going to find an aquifer it would be deep, most likely over a thousand feet down.

I would need a lot more pipe casing than I had allowed for. One drill hole wouldn't be enough. I needed at least five drilling rigs to make enough boreholes for the seismograph equipment to detect differences in the geology.

They assumed I had seismograph equipment. When I confessed the lack, they looked at me like I was the village idiot, a rich one, but still an idiot.

Not being a complete idiot, I asked them to draw up a list of needed equipment. One of them had experience purchasing seismographic equipment, so I gave him that task.

I had the lead jackaroo order more trucks and drilling rigs, along with several miles of pipe casings.

Then there were the explosives to be used with the seismographs. The same place that sold the drilling rigs could provide all we needed.

This extra equipment required the hiring of fifty more jackaroos and jillaroos. That, in turn, meant more tents, food, water, etc. This meant more trucks and drivers.

Before it was over, we had twenty-seven MK 5 5-ton cargo trucks towing trailers and water buffaloes.

This expedition was approaching military standards.

My hydrologists told me that I should have done an aerial survey before thinking about starting the trip.

I took them to Jackson House to the first basement where I had all my aerial photos laid out. I had marked the best route.

I explained I had taken the pictures, picked a route, flown it low with a helicopter, and then driven it, marking the route with flags.

I was able to show them the route which I had marked on the photographs. I was no longer the village idiot, maybe just the dim one in the family.

They were glad to see that I had marked a route, but their real interest was in the topography of the area that we were going to. I explained that I wanted to establish the station headquarters there.

They never once asked me, why there? Now, who were the dim ones?

With that large of a caravan, it appeared we would be doing good to do thirty miles a day. This mileage was given to me by an experienced trekker whom I hired to advise us on the best way to do this.

He recommended that I send a small group of three trucks ahead to establish base camps along the way. They could establish fuel dumps, have extra food, and have tents set up for the main group's arrival.

I thought this was overkill but when I expressed that thought, he shared a few stories that changed my attitude.

We also added ten more Land Rovers for people to ride in. These weren't the pickup truck types but made for passengers. For some reason, not many people wanted to ride in the back of the MK 5s.

We even added a beefed-up school bus. I didn't even know they made any six-wheel-drive buses. If they were needed anywhere, it was here.

I had a last-minute thought and asked him if we should establish an airfield on arrival. He thought it was worth doing. This added one more truck with a bulldozer mounted on a trailer. Landing lights, radio equipment, VOR setup, and windsocks were carried in the back of the truck.

We planned on a 3500-foot runway plowed out of the hard-packed desert floor. Technically the DC3 could land in 2500 feet, but why take a chance? We did have the room in the large desert.

My only real concern was having the aircraft caught on the ground in a sandstorm. We would have to only fly when the weather looked good and always take it back to Alice Springs to hangar it, even if it caused extra flights.

I hired a three-man flight crew on a short-term basis to man the aircraft.

It was impossible to keep an expedition this large a secret from the press. The expedition members and equipment were being staged in Alice Springs. It took two weeks to bring it all together.

During that time, I responded to multiple interview requests. They all went about the same.

"Your Grace, why are you doing this?"

"I have bought a large amount of land in the desert, but without water, it will be worthless."

"No one else has found water before. Why will you be different?"

"No one else has assembled a team of experts with the proper equipment before, so I have hope."

"How much land have you bought? Is it as large as your Queensland station, and aren't you biting off more than you can handle, trying to develop two large stations at once?"

"This is a long-term project. The station may never become viable if I don't find water. If not, I will have a lot of sand to sell."

I had to repeat that about a dozen times. Again no one inquired as to why that exact area. If they had, I would tell them the land and soil looked the best to take a chance on if we could irrigate it.

The land we were testing for water was twenty miles before the Reef. Most aquifers were large. If one were there, it would probably extend to the Reef. If not, we could run a pipeline to it.

The object was to try to find water, but most of all, establish a trail to the area. I had come to believe the experts when they told me how difficult this country could be to travel in.

One enterprising reporter asked to ride along in my Land Rover and send daily reports via short-wave radio. I told the cute young lady she was welcome to accompany me.

We had to add an extra tent to accommodate her. I thought about offering to share mine but thought better of it. As I got to know her better, it was a good thing I didn't. She wasn't my type. She wasn't any man's type, but she was a good traveling companion. She and one of the jillaroos hit it off and became close friends.

After all the rushing around gathering everything needed, the day finally arrived. We left early in the morning hoping to make fifty miles the first day.

The first twenty of it would be on the Lasseter trail, which I thought was appropriate.

We were only short two jackaroos who were in jail in Alice Springs for getting drunk and busting up a bar. I refused to bail them out or wait anymore. If they could catch up with us, fine; if not, no great loss.

We planned on making the two hundred miles in six days. Fifty miles the first day, then thirty miles a day for the next five. We can all dream, can't we?

We made it to the cutoff to go cross-country with no problems. We were accompanied by reporters racing alongside us mounted on the back of local motorcycles they had hired. They were taking pictures and trying to interview people on the fly.

I refused every one of them. I didn't want to help the idiots kill themselves.

Ten miles down the road the predictable happened. A motorcycle tipped, spilling driver and rider. Being in the lead car, we almost ran over them, but I was able to stop in time and hoped the truck behind me was paying attention. They were.

In our convoy planning, we had allowed plenty of spacing between vehicles for sudden stops.

Lucky for the motorcycle people they only had road rash. It still delayed us for an hour while our two-person medical crew, an intern and a nurse, took care of them.

The other reporters asked why I didn't load them in one of my Land Rovers and take them back to Alice Springs. I didn't even know how to answer them.

Both the wrecked guys were up and walking around, and their bike was still working, so I mounted us all up again, and we motored on.

Joan, the lady reporter who was with me, asked me why I hadn't helped them back to Alice Springs. All I did was point out the two idiots were still running up and down the column trying to get interviews. There was no helping that type.

Chapter 31

Not only were there reporters riding next to our column, but there was also a parade of private vehicles behind us. It would later be reported as a forty-mile-long convoy.

When we reached the turn-off, there was a nasty surprise waiting. One of our advance scouts was there. He had come back on a motorcycle to give a warning.

The advance column had run into trouble five miles down the track we were going to follow. It seemed that sand had shifted and filled a couple of deep wadis.

The wadis had been noted on the map I had made on my driving trip. They were deep, about ten feet wide, and one hundred yards across. The edges were worn down so you could drive down into them, make the crossing, then drive out the other side.

Now they were filled with sand. If you didn't know better, it looked like a flat stretch that could be driven across. An easy way to lose a vehicle and its crew.

Warned, we approached the area slowly. There now was a sign erected with an arrow pointing south. There was also another motorcycle rider to direct us. The advance crew had scouted out a safe crossing place. They had gone north and south to find a safe crossing. South was the closest at five miles.

We made the detour and then doubled back to the original trail. It put an extra ten miles on the day, but by having scouts out, we saved many hours and prevented a potential disaster.

We made the rest of the day with no further breaks in the trail. Since it was spring, we had longer daylight and took advantage of it. We made the planned campsite, arriving two hours later than planned.

The advance group had almost the entire camp set up and a fire started for dinner. We helped them finish setting up tents and digging latrines.

Everyone was still in good spirits. They were telling each other tales of what they had spotted on the road. Joan was taking notes for her nightly call-in.

According to my crew, they had seen Nannup tigers, bunyips, Tasmanian tigers, Yarmayhawho, and hoop snakes. My favorite was the Tasmanian tiger, and I didn't believe they saw a Yarmayhawho; they were only found in coastal areas.

I didn't believe any of them. Though between us we had a hundred or more cameras, no pictures were taken. A hoop snake would have been cool.

After dinner, maintenance had to be pulled on the vehicles. All fluids were measured, fuel topped up, and items like fan belts checked. One MK5 had used an extra quart of oil so we came out of our first day pretty well.

I listened to Joan's radio call; you would have thought we had done everything but fight off wild Indians that day.

Day two started well. We didn't have any more sand-filled wadis to skirt around. What we had was brand new dunes to transverse. This time we had to make a choice, drive an extra fifty miles to go around or try to go over.

None of the three were mountain high, more like fifteen feet. The slopes weren't that bad, so we decided, I decided, to try one truck. It didn't look like there was any danger of the truck tipping over backward.

All of our drivers were desert-trained, but we had a meeting with all the drivers before attempting the first dune.

Reminders were given that they were to go straight up, and if they couldn't make it to go straight back down. No attempted turns; it would tip the truck.

They were to keep moving at all costs; over-revving wasn't a concern; keep those wheels turning.

If you had to turn out of a rut, keep your throttle open, or the rut would prevent the turn, or release it too quickly pushing the truck too far, or too quick, or both.

When reaching the top of the dune, let off on the throttle so that the truck would just make it over the top and not get launched into the air. With this large of a truck, it would be a disaster, and deaths could result.

We also let some of the air out of all the tires to give better traction. We had gasoline-powered compressors to fill them on the other side.

The trucks made it over with no problems. The Land Rovers didn't have enough power to get over the dunes, even though the trucks had worn them down. We used the winches to pull them up and over.

The three dunes took up the entire day. We only made five miles. Rather than fight it, I declared a stop. The advance party had scouted out the next day's travel and reported that the terrain was the same as I had originally reported.

Once more I listened to Joan's report. It seemed we had barely made it in a desperate fight for our lives on those mile-high dunes.

I didn't get upset about her exaggerations. It certainly would make anyone else think twice about following us.

Once more maintenance was pulled on all vehicles. All tires were reinflated to the proper road pressure, and we were good to go in the morning.

As we were talking around the campfire, someone asked why we didn't winch a bulldozer up the dune and plow the top off.

Why didn't we? It would have saved hours.

Day three was a complete surprise. We made the miles and didn't have any obstacles to overcome. Eighty-five miles down and one hundred and fifteen to go.

Day four was not so nice. One of the MK5s transmissions failed. After talking to the experts, we unloaded its contents onto other trucks and left it at the side of the road. We would tow it in at a later date.

Despite that, we made our miles only running two hours late. I noticed the camp was quieter that night than it had been; people were getting tired.

Another thing that was affecting morale was the sand, not the sand in the desert but the sand in our clothes. No matter how you dressed, it got into every crack and crevice of your body.

Showers were set up at every stop, but we only had so much water, so everyone was limited to five minutes. We had to station a man or woman at each shower with a stopwatch.

Day five we had advanced warning of a sandstorm coming so we hunkered down. Tents were set in the lee of a wall made from our vehicles. My experts told me the storm was average. I would hate to see what they called a big one.

We spent day six digging out the vehicles. We had to change every filter on every truck, even though they hadn't been turned on. The engine compartments were full of sand.

Since we had air compressors for tire changes, we were able to blow the last of the sand out of the engine compartments after a lot of digging by hand.

We made no miles that day. This was the day we should have been arriving at our main camp. We still had a long way to go.

Day seven was a good day. We made the scheduled miles. That helped everyone's mood.

Once more Joan's report was amazing. We couldn't have survived the storm she reported. I noticed her main source of information was the jillaroo who was her girlfriend.

Once when the jillaroo was telling Joan how bad things were, the jillaroo saw me and winked. That girl deserved a bonus.

Day eight had one breakdown which held us up for an hour, so it could be classified as a good day.

Day nine was more of the same. We did run into another series of dunes. My recommendation for anyone on a serious cross-desert expedition is to take at least one bulldozer with you.

We winched the dozer up to the top of the dune and started pushing sand. The dunes weren't that high like those that could be found in the Great Erg. We were able to knock the top five feet off and drive the trucks and even the Land Rovers right over them.

It shortened our miles for the day and made the trip easier. People's moods were better that evening. As I went from campfire to campfire, carefully staying in the background, I didn't hear any talk of turning back or lynching the expedition leader.

On day twelve we pulled into the final campsite. We were not quite a week late, but we had made it with only the loss of one vehicle and no people.

While the camp was being set up, I had our water supplies checked. We were in good shape, so I declared the end of five-minute showers to many cheers. For the first time, beer was broken out at dinner.

Joan interviewed me after dinner, asking me how this trip compared to others I had taken. I told her it was the journey of a lifetime.

What I didn't say was that compared to East Germany, Siberia, North Korea, and the Chinese invasion of Russia, this one was a breeze. No one took a shot at me.

Chapter 32

We spent the first day setting up tents and digging latrines, then erecting men's and women's tents over the latrines. We established a field kitchen with dining tables. Then a medical station with four beds was set up.

A radio shack was up and running within hours of our arrival.

A crew double-checked the area I had noted as being fit for a runway for aircraft. It was fit. After they leveled the ground for our tent city, they started on the four-thousand-foot runway.

The first borehole for seismic refraction testing for an aquifer was started. Since there had never been any signs of an aquifer, it was deemed that if found, it would be several thousand feet down.

The first event was to drill down five hundred feet and set off dynamite at the bottom of the borehole. From what was known of the geology of the area, there was probably a layer of sand or gravel under a sandstone layer.

The pressure from the explosives would pass through each layer and some of the waves would bounce back. The time it took to bounce back would tell us the depth of the top of the layer. The time it took the EKS wave to deteriorate to zero would tell us the bottom of the layer.

The remaining waves would then bounce off the top of the next layer.

We would be using a rotary rig with a downhole hammer. This used high-pressure air to clean the chips out after every hit. This was slow and expensive but the best method as all others used enormous amounts of water.

An experienced hydrologist could tell us if the layer was groundwater or not. Once we had a series of good bounces we could then drill and see if there was water there. It was a bit dicey, but the oil and gas industry was making it more science than art all the time.

If we thought there was water, we would then drill numerous holes and map the field.

I was able to regurgitate all this to Joan for her nightly report. I had absolutely no idea of the realities of this type of drilling. Come to think of it, I knew nothing about any sort of drilling.

Now that the water operation was set up and running, it was time to get the road system improved for getting in and out of here.

I wanted as much infrastructure as possible in place before the find was announced to the world.

It only took two days for a runway to be roughed out of the desert. A control tower was set up; think of a tent on a high platform. Landing lights were installed, radios set up, VOR in place, and we were good to go.

The first flights in brought water. We were going through it like crazy. One thing I had made clear to all was that no one was to touch a water soak. They were the lifelines for the Aborigines. If we used them, we would take a season's water in a day, leaving them to die.

I was surprised at the number of Australians who didn't care if they used all their water. I did catch two guys filling buckets from a soak. I fired them on the spot and had them on the next flight out.

I made certain everyone in camp knew about it. It even made the national news, where I received mixed reviews for being too harsh or too soft.

After a week we had the first seismic results. There appeared to be water at about the two-thousand-foot level; that is, it appeared. Only by drilling down would we know for certain.

I gave the go-ahead to start a deep well while exploration continued as to how large this potential aquifer was.

As the drilling started, I received bad news from England. Grandmum had passed away. The funeral would be in three days, so I had the DC3 pick me up and fly me to Sydney where the 707 was waiting. We landed in London on the morning of the third day.

She was being buried in the family plot in the Church of England graveyard at Gravesend. Sadly appropriate.

A helicopter was waiting to take me to Gravesend, where I was able to quietly enter the church just as the ceremony started. My family and all of Mum's cousins and their children were there. I always thought of us as a small group, but I had thirty-some relatives present.

I was pleased to see the Queen Mum there with several friends. It was heartbreaking to see Mr. Hamilton silently weeping.

Mum had the British stiff upper lip, but she looked like she would break at any time. The Vicar droned on about how Grandmum was joining her ancestors who had been interred in this graveyard for over five hundred years and would wait with them for judgment day.

For some reason, I could see Grandmum organizing tea parties for all the ladies who were waiting. They would also enjoy scaring the bejesus out of any late-night smoochers.

After the sermon, I followed the pallbearers to the graveyard. I was able to catch up with my family on the way. Then we had to go through throwing dirt on the coffin. It was one of the few times I ever saw my sister Mary without a smile.

After we performed our duty, we moved on. I ended up standing next to the tombstone of Pocahontas. Few people knew she was buried here after coming to England. Toast of the town, she contracted measles and died.

One event shook me to my core. My grandfather, Grandmum's husband, who I barely remembered, had always told Mum that when he died if all was going well, he would push up daisies. The whole churchyard was covered in daisies. Granddad was welcoming Grandmum to her new home.

I didn't even pretend to have a stiff upper lip at that point.

My parents had rooms at a local hotel, so we repaired there after all the handshakes and expressions of sympathy.

My aunts and uncles along with the cousins met us there. We had dinner. I was treated with reserve by them. I don't think they knew what to make of me.

I tried to find out what my cousins were doing these days. The answers were monosyllabic. Mary finally broke things open.

"Come on you guys; it's only Ricky. Just because he's rich and powerful doesn't mean you can't talk to him."

That got a laugh around the table. My cousins and I were sitting separately from the adults so they could have an intelligent conversation.

Once the awkwardness was broken, the questions started. I had to bring them up to date on all my adventures since going into East Germany.

I got on a roll and was telling the entire tale. At one point I stopped for a drink of water and realized the whole restaurant listened to me relating my tale.

I continued. It was too late; in for a penny in for a pound. It would be in the tabloids tomorrow, but I had given up on their stupid stories a long time ago.

Later I joined my parents in their suite, where we finally were able to relax from the day. You could tell Mum was upset because her mum had just died, but at the same time, she'd had a good run of it.

One thing I realized was that even if they had a good run of it, it didn't make it any easier.

I brought them up to date on my Australian project. I told them we were now drilling for water, as we had identified a possible aquifer. If it was water, there would be a lot of it.

I mentioned in passing that I had completed the purchase of all the surrounding land and mineral rights. You never knew who might be listening.

After eating breakfast with the family, I took a helicopter back to Heathrow where my jet was waiting.

Many hours later, we landed in Sydney after a refueling stop in Bombay. From there it was the DC3 back to the camp. When I got off the plane, it all seemed surreal. I had been to England and back in four days. It was like I had never left. I promptly went to my tent and slept for the next fourteen hours.

That worked out well as I woke in time for breakfast. There were many expressions of sympathy and of course, Joan wanted an interview on how I felt about my grandmum dying.

I may have overreacted at that, as I had her flown out of camp.

Once that unpleasantness was passed, I was told that they were down a thousand feet, halfway there.

In the meantime, my camp was turning into a real town. Tents were being replaced with wooden buildings. Each building was prefabricated and had to be flown in. The crew talked of little else. I seemed to be gambling a lot of money on water being down there.

What they didn't know was that I had already won the bet. It was the raking it off the table without getting robbed that was my concern.

Chapter 33

My concern about having my gold robbed wasn't about common ordinary thieves. It was about the Australian politicians. They could easily decide that such immense wealth belonged to the Australian people and that they were the ones who should hand it out.

They could nationalize the Reef's mineral rights. They would then exercise their right to come onto my land and mine it. In the process, they would destroy any value in the station. All in the name of the people.

What I needed were business partners who would give the Australian politicians second thoughts. Notice I didn't say government, I said politicians.

There was so much potential money involved that I didn't have to think small. My first call was to Mr. Norman.

"Hello, Rick. What can I help you with today?"

"I have a gift for Her Majesty."

"What would that be?"

"Shares in a new gold mining venture."

"Gifts like that can end up being costly."

"Not this one. The Crown won't have to invest anything. The gold has been found and proven to be high content and quality ore."

"That sounds too good to be true. What do you benefit from this?"

"The Australian politicians will be reluctant to try to nationalize my find."

"I would hope so. What percentage are you gifting?"

"Five percent."

"How large is the find?"

"The largest ever found. It could actually reduce the price of gold."

"Australia? My god man, have you found Lasseter Reef?"

"Yes."

"Have you incorporated a company yet?"

"Not yet. I have one more phone call to make."

"Tell the empress the queen says 'hello'."

Mr. Norman once again went up in my esteem. He was sharp enough to figure out my next call, and also high enough that he could speak for the queen, even a simple "hello".

I went to lunch, then called Beijing. I was put through to Her Imperial Majesty's chief of staff. Try saying that three times fast.

"Your Grace, how can we help you today?"

"I have a gift for the empress."

"Gifts are always welcome. Would it be a share in your new gold venture?"

"What! How?" I sputtered.

"We obtained some information accidentally when your father hired cutouts to have the gold samples assayed. One of our people was the one to take the sample to the assay office. From there it was simple to trace back to your father, then you in Australia. I hope it is Lasseter Reef that you have found."

"It is. I would like to gift the empress five percent of the new company. She would have no investment requirements."

"I assume this is to prevent the current politicians in power from nationalizing the find."

"Correct."

"You have also gifted the queen, I hope."

There is only one real queen in our world.

'Yes, and I intend to incorporate the company in England. Also, I'm to tell you that the queen says 'hello' to the empress."

"And she says 'hello' back.

"Rick, I must be honest with you. We knew there was a gold find from transporting the samples. We couldn't backtrack to your father."

"Then how did you figure all this out?"

"For other reasons, I called Mr. Norman right after you spoke. He felt free to talk about the gold find as he knew you would be calling us."

It was good to know our security had worked, but not so good to know that I had a blabbermouth friend.

These calls were made from Jackson House in Sydney. There was no way that I could do it from the camp with only a short-wave radio available.

When I hung up, Jeeves was waiting for me. He had a folded message lying on a silver platter.

It was a short-wave message that informed me they had struck the water, clean water, not brackish, and that it had a strong flow rate they were trying to measure.

This find made the station as valuable as the Reef.

The news got out fast. The Sydney paper carried it as a headline. This was a big deal in Australia. One politician was even quoted as saying that consideration should be given to nationalizing the find.

It wouldn't happen as Australian law was firm on that issue. If they nationalized my water, every station on the continent would be at risk. I made a mental note to find out who his opponent was, and if a decent viable candidate, make a large donation.

When I got to the camp, there was a geyser coming out of the ground. The water was pushing up to fifty feet in the air. People were still dancing under the fountain to cool off.

A crew was getting ready to cap the well off.

I asked if they had any idea how much water was down there, and I was told a bunch. When I asked how strong the flow rate was, the answer was a total surprise.

"To have this strong of a flow from two thousand feet, there has to be a hydrocarbon reservoir pushing on it."

"Let me get this straight, hydrocarbon reservoir; does that mean there is oil or gas in the area?"

"You got it. You just became rich."

I let that one go. It is a good thing I have brought the queen and empress in on this. The wolves would be after me.

The news of the water find had traveled at the speed of sound. This news would be at the speed of light. I made a call to the Sydney newspaper office and got through to an editor.

As I thought, he was already aware of the find. Someone from the site had let the cat out of the bag.

I brought him up to date on what I knew, which wasn't that much. I made certain to tell him that I had filed for and obtained the mineral rights for my property. Also, minerals, oil, and gas would be extracted by Jackson Minerals, which was incorporated in England.

He started laughing at that. "You shut that old so and so down."

He then named the politician who wanted to nationalize the water.

"I intend to pay fair taxes and royalties on my finds, but I'm not giving them away to someone who knows better than me on how to spend my money."

"Right. He is one of the few card-carrying Communists left in our parliament."

"Do you have any idea who would run against him?"

"There is a bright young lady in the Conservatives who lives in that district. She would be a good replacement."

"Do you think a Conservative could win in that district? I mean, they have been electing a Communist."

"He hasn't stood for election; he was appointed to an empty seat last year as part of a trade for votes. I don't think he could win."

He gave me the lady's name and I called Jackson House and asked Jean Ferguson to write a fifty-thousand-pound check to the young lady's campaign fund.

Jean pointed out that if I did that, every politician in the country would be knocking on my door.

I told her to buy a stronger door.

My next call was relayed through the short-wave radio to my office in England. I told them I needed a new company formed immediately. I was to own sixty-five percent, the queen five percent, the empress five percent, and my parents twenty-five percent.

I had intended to do it when I had a chance. Now the company needed to be formed at once.

After taking care of the immediate business, I had a conference with my hydrologists. They recommended that I bring in some oil and gas experts to explore and develop the field. This was beyond their expertise.

I made a mental note to give them large bonuses for their work so far. I hope I can remember all these mental notes.

Their advice was sound. I decided to head back to Sydney where I could place some private phone calls. My first was to the only oil people I knew, the Ewings in Texas. It was no surprise they had learned of a large find in Australia. They didn't know I was involved.

When I explained the story, JR told me they would be delighted to be involved. I told him that sounded good but didn't make any commitments. I had been told that dealing with JR was like dealing with the Devil; you'd better have a long spoon.

He did recommend a Dallas-based company to explore the field. Since I wanted to know who I was getting involved with, I decided to visit their offices in Dallas before I finalized any deals with them. It would be one more long flight, but since the Devil had recommended them, I had better be certain!

Not that I thought JR was the Devil. He had certainly been nice to me when I stayed at his ranch during the National Rodeo championships.

Chapter 34

I called the oil exploration company in Dallas and explained what we had found. They were interested in the project. As a preliminary, they agreed to send an expert out to review all our findings to see if it was worth pursuing.

In the meantime, exploration for water would continue. It would take weeks to drill test wells to confirm the size of the aquifer.

I sat in on a review of the proposed boreholes. Fortunately, they didn't come close to the Reef. Acting as though I was concerned about costs, I made it clear that no deviations from this drilling plan were allowed without my specific approval.

In the meantime, events were moving forward in the space program. NASA had taken the first pictures of the dark side of the moon and done a fly-by of Venus.

A geosynchronous satellite had been launched by NASA.

JE Space Enterprises now had a ring of satellites in place around the earth and was selling the rights to bounce signals off them for greater radio and TV coverage. Few people could pick up the signals, but there was a growing industry in satellite dishes. I wish I had thought of those.

They were also being used to take pictures of specified ground targets.

We had drawn the line at taking any pictures of known military bases of any nation or any places designated by the government of the country in question.

Governments quickly placed their major buildings like the White House or Windsor Castle off-limits. They only had to pay one thousand dollars per site to cover the paperwork and satellite programming costs. We made a pretty penny on that.

Between drilling for water in the desert and watching roads being built on the Jackson Station in Queensland, there wasn't much for me to do.

I decided to fly to Dallas and meet with the oil exploration people. If nothing else, it would get my lazy flight crew off Bondi Beach.

When our flight left Australia, it was with a tanned healthy-looking crew. They moaned and groaned about going back to work, but that only lasted a few minutes.

I think it was like kids going back to school after summer vacation.

I had a new series of books with me to study on this trip. I had to get up to speed on the oil industry. It took five books, starting with exploration and ending with finished products and all in between. These books were starter books, and I expected them to lead me to many others.

Being back in school would have been easier. At least schools had a planned curriculum that covered the subjects. I had to choose my own and hope I chose the right books to study.

I spent the flight starting with oil exploration. If nothing else, I began to get an appreciation for the term, "wildcatters". It seems you got better odds in Las Vegas than in the oil fields.

The oil exploration company had made arrangements for a hotel suite at the Adolphus Hotel in downtown Dallas, not far from their offices. They also had a limo waiting at the private aviation terminal.

I had been picked up at the base of the stairs and wheeled up to the aircraft, so my arrival seemed to be unheralded. I appreciated this more and more as time went by.

From casually traveling the world unnoticed, I went to having my trips followed closely by business types wanting to know what deals I was involved in and probably spy agencies from all over the world wanting to know everything.

Papa-rats-eyes, as Mary would say, followed me closely for the scandal rags.

I had been told that Mr. Hoover had my file updated regularly. It seems he couldn't figure out if I was a good guy or a bad guy.

After a good night's rest at the Adolphus, I had breakfast in my suite with a representative of Dallas Oil.

It didn't take long, about one egg over easy, to establish that I would be the wildcatter taking all the risks, while they provided technical expertise at fixed rates.

That worked for me. Oil would be the icing on the cake, not the real reason for me being in Western Australia. By paying for services, they would have no claims on any other finds.

After their being a service provider was made clear, their representative presented me with a contract to send to my lawyers to review.

Since I was traveling light as normal, I didn't have a lawyer in my baggage. Poor Harold happened to come out of his room about that time, so I asked him to get this sent off by mail to my home office in LA for review.

The Dallas Oil representative came up with an alternative suggestion. He told me there was a new service that made deliveries overnight. FreightEx will have it at my desk in LA tomorrow.

We could drop it off at Dallas Oil's front desk, and it would be taken care of. Harold took it all in stride.

The representative, John Wagner, and I walked the half block to his offices. They were in a modern glass and marble-fronted building. I guess in the oil industry you had to keep up a good front in a business that went from riches to bust overnight.

At the front lobby, a big deal was made of me signing the guest register. I started to sign it Richard Jackson but was asked to include my titles.

What they got was Colonel the Duke of Hong Kong, Richard Jackson, GC, KG, KCVO, LoH, GBM, OGD, HC, 1959 Junior Bull Riding Champion of North America, winner of the Grand Slam of golf.

I had to explain each of the honors. I think the bull riding impressed them the most. John Wagner told me he had been in the stands on the night of my wild ride. He had never seen anything like it before or since.

I told him if I had my way, he never would again.

All this took up an extra five minutes in the lobby. As we went to the elevator, I saw a guy come in the front door whose clothes and demeanor screamed reporter.

Someone had ratted me out, probably at the hotel. Hotels were famous for tipping the press off. They wanted the publicity of a famous person staying there while keeping up the pretense of privacy for their guests.

We met in the boardroom. By count, there were eight men there. The chairman of the board, the president and CEO, plus a host of vice presidents. There was one lowly director there. He was Director of Field Operations. It didn't take long to figure out he was the guy I needed to see; all the rest were window-dressing.

I had to give it to them; they had done their homework. They had a large map of the area around the water drilling base camp. They had a roughed-out plan of first test shots to try to establish what was creating the high water pressure at the aquifer.

From there they had a series of ever-expanding boreholes to home in on the potential oil or gas site. From the looks of it, they were prepared to drill as far away as South America, if needed. At my expense of course.

After the dog and pony show, I and my escort went to Director Bob Springfield's office. There we got down to a more realistic look at what should be done.

I was impressed with Bob's low-key approach to the project. His bookshelf behind him contained several of the books that I had been reading on the plane.

When I mentioned that, it kicked off an interesting discussion on which books I should be reading. After twenty minutes of this, my escort excused himself and told Bob to call him when we were done.

I did ask Bob if he would be coming out to look the project over. He let me know he wouldn't miss it for the world. This had the potential to be one of the biggest finds in modern history, or maybe the biggest bust.

We had lunch served in the board room. I was given the obligatory tour of the offices. They looked like most other offices I had ever seen. I was roped into an autograph and picture-taking session with the bigwigs.

The wheels were a little put off when I insisted that anyone working in the office could have my picture and autograph. It may have honked them off a little, but it ensured that the clerical staff would pay attention to my stuff.

I was invited to dinner at the Petroleum Club of Dallas that evening. They had me leave by a side door as there was now a TV van parked in front of their office. We walked down an alley and entered the hotel through a service entrance.

Chapter 35

Harold was waiting in the suite. He had a man with him who I found out was a tailor. My measurements were being taken to keep on file at this wonderful new store that Harold had found, Neiman Marcus.

The tailor didn't seem impressed by me but carried on about the fact that Mary was my sister. They carried her Princess line and were going to have a special edition dress made for Christmas. He was all atwitter that Mary would be coming to Dallas for the announcement in November.

He described the dress in great detail. Talk about over the top! It was a tasteless display of wealth if you asked me. I wondered what it would do to Mary's image. I made a note to call her and Mum to talk about it.

The dress sounded horrid to me, all the hand-sewn pearls. It reminded me of the story of how the tsar of Russia's family was hard to kill because they had so many gems sewn into their clothes.

I must say the Petroleum Club of Dallas was nice. It was better looking than the British club that I now have membership in. Whites was impeccably kept, but the furniture looked dated. Maybe that was because some of it had been there for the better part of two hundred years.

The service was as attentive and as discreet as at Whites. I wonder if they ironed the creases out of the newspaper they left at your door and replaced all of your banknotes while you slept with brand-new ones.

The first time that happened, I didn't know what to think. I had only stayed there one night and wasn't certain I would again. It seemed creepy to me.

The dinner went well as these events usually do. The table talk revolved around the Aggies and the Longhorns. This was old and tested ground as there were graduates of both schools present.

The only false note of the evening came when JR Ewing stopped by our table.

"Duke Richard, it is so good to see you again. Are these people taking care of you?"

"Yes, sir. Your advice to contact them has been good advice so far. I appreciate your being willing to help me as it has been at least four years since we conversed."

This reply did a couple of things. It let Dallas Oil know that they were still on trial and that JR wasn't the bosom buddy he tried to play.

It didn't faze him at all as he shook hands all around and left.

There was an awkward silence at the table. I broke it when I looked at the dessert spoon in my hand and wondered out loud, "I hope this spoon is long enough for that Devil."

That brought a laugh, and we continued our conversation and had a nice dinner. I managed to avoid taking sides in the great football debate.

The next morning, Dallas Oil continued to work for my business as they had a limo pick me up at the hotel to return me to Love Field.

Traffic was crazy as usual on a business morning. The driver was smooth and kept us moving at a safe pace. That didn't stop one idiot trying to make it through a light that had already changed to red.

The car, a 1955 Chevrolet Bel Air station wagon, broadsided us in almost the exact middle of the limo. Since it was a stretch limo, the driver and I both got thrown around but were not hurt. The driver might have had a concussion from hitting his head on the side window.

The car had come from our right, so it hit the passenger side. I exited on the driver's side. My driver was still sitting behind the steering wheel. I helped him out, and a quick check of his eyes showed both irises to be the same size and opened normally.

I then ran around the front of the limo to check the other driver. When I got there, a man who identified himself as a doctor told me that the lone occupant of the car was dead. He hadn't been wearing a seatbelt and had been thrown forward into the steering wheel.

The contents in the back of the station wagon had come forward and would have broken his neck if he had still been alive.

The doctor, whose name I missed, told me he had witnessed the whole thing as he was stopped at the light that had been run. There was no question that the driver had run a full-on red light at a major intersection.

It didn't take the police, ambulance, and firetruck long to show up. The body was covered with a blanket and the policeman called for backup.

Then the policeman asked who was in the two vehicles. Since the station wagon guy was dead, that only left the driver and me.

The driver was still standing there stunned. I bet he did have a concussion or the mother of all headaches at least from hitting the side window.

That only left me, the doctor, and two other self-identified witnesses for him to interview.

He asked me, "Sir, may I see some identification?"

I was traveling on my US diplomatic passport which had all my titles in it. I never did understand that as the US didn't hand out titles. I think a starstruck person in the State Department exceeded their authority.

When he read it, I thought he whispered, "Oh shit," but it was quiet enough that I wasn't certain. If he hadn't said it, he should have.

He went back to his patrol car and sent off another message. I imagine it was to his higher-ups telling them there was about to be a mess at this intersection.

Since he had already radioed in a fatality, the news trucks were starting to show up.

After his latest radio call, he handed a sheet of paper to each of the witnesses and asked them to write down where they had been when the accident occurred and what color the light was when the station wagon went through.

The policeman, Officer Hayes, came back to me and asked me to write my statement.

"What should I call you, My Lord, or something?"

"Try Richard. This is America; we don't have titles."

He looked befuddled for a moment, "Oh yeah, you have dual citizenship. Well, that makes things easier for my paperwork. You are just Richard Jackson, a normal American citizen, and not Lord High Mucky Muck."

"That title sounds good to me. I'll ask for it the next time they dump one on me."

Traffic had backed up everywhere by now, so he spent time getting it to flow again with the help of the firemen.

The ambulance people had removed the body from the wreck and pulled his ID. In the meantime, other patrol cars were showing up. There must have been a dozen or more.

They had traffic moving again in short order, although it was very slow as people rubbernecked.

Soon a TV van pulled up and started to raise its antenna. A police commander came over to me. He had all sorts of gold braid on his uniform, so I assume he was a commander.

"Your Grace, could we ask you to sit in an unmarked car? If the press realizes you are here, we will never get this thing unwound."

"I will be glad to. Better yet, could I get a ride to the airport? My plane is about to leave."

I didn't tell him the plane only left when I said so.

"Have you written out your statement yet?"

"No."

"Finish that up and you can go. In the meantime, please do it in this car."

I was glad to get out of the hot sun in Dallas. Even though it was October, it still was in the high eighties or low nineties.

As I was getting into the car, I heard a shout.

"Hey, Commander, you got to look at this."

I followed the commander over to the guy standing by the station wagon. I guess I was rubbernecking as much as everyone.

The guy had the duffle bags that had been in the back of the car open. They were full of rifles, pistols, and enough ammunition to start a war.

The commander, who had been handed the dead guy's wallet, wondered out loud, "What were you up to Lee Harvey Oswald?"

We didn't know, but sort of an answer came. Another patrolman, who had radioed in the dead man's ID to get a background check, reported that Oswald had both Secret Service and FBI notices out on him. Any suspicious activity was to be reported.

My driver was taken to the hospital for a checkup, the body was removed, and tow trucks appeared to clear the wreckage. I looked around to see where he was going at such a high rate of speed. All I could see was a sign that said, "Red Wing Airport—two miles."

I finished my statement and was driven to Love Field, where I boarded my aircraft and got the heck out of Dallas.

Chapter 36

From Dallas, we flew to Beijing. My home office had forwarded a message from Empress Ping that she needed to talk to me, and would I please come to Beijing at my earliest convenience?

She was always polite in her communication, but this was even politer than normal. I sent a telegram back to my office telling them to relay the fact I was flying in from Dallas.

The flight was long but not boring, as I had several new books on oil exploration to go through. I loved to learn new things. Especially those that might make me money.

Two naps and three meals later, we were landing in Beijing. Since we were expected, the Chinese Air Force and air traffic control paved the way for a smooth entry and landing.

From there it was an easy ride in a limo to the Forbidden City. While it was an easy ride, I tensed up at every intersection.

Once at the palace, I was taken immediately to see the empress. This was extremely unusual. I normally was given time to rest, eat, and change clothes.

"Rick, I'm so glad you could come at once. It is still October, and we didn't want to miss your birthday."

I went blank for a moment; my birthday had been two weeks ago, and I hadn't even given it any thought. I was now twenty years old, no longer a teenager.

"Thank you, but what do you have in mind, and who is this we?"

"The 'We' are all of your friends and family, and as for what is your birthday present, we all chipped in and bought you a ride."

"It must be some out-of-this-world ride."

When I said that I was thinking Lamborghini or something like that.

"It is. We are sending you into orbit."

That stopped me cold. I had been told that I was too tall to ever fit properly in one of the capsules in use, so I would never get up there.

"We had a new capsule built to accommodate you. Instead of four people, it can only take three, but you will be one of them."

Since the capsules were reusable, I had just been given a ticket to space.

"When can I go?"

Not that I was excited or anything.

"Now if you want to. The space center is holding a launch for you right now. You do know that you haven't been checked out for any space walking, so you will have to stay in the capsule."

That was a mild disappointment, but I now knew there would be other opportunities.

I was taken back to the airport where the 707 was refueled and ready to go. The stinkers in the flight crew had been in on it all along.

When we got to the launch facility, I was raring to go at once. They slowed me down. They insisted on silly little things like checking to see if the spacesuit I would wear inside the capsule fit right.

I was to understand that under no circumstances was I to try to take over the controls of the rocket at any point in the flight. I solemnly swore I wouldn't, with my fingers crossed behind my back. I remembered having to take over during an inflight emergency once before.

A quick physical to ensure I didn't have an ear infection or the like, and I was good to go. Well, that was after being sung Happy Birthday to by my immediate family who had flown in. There were also cards and well-wishes from all over the world.

I had been sent thousands of cards, but only the most important were displayed for me. One caught my eye because it was from a Nina Chaplin. I didn't recognize the name. I did recognize the handwriting. It appears that Nina Monroe, my old girlfriend, was now married.

Mary and my brothers were there. The boys wanted to know when they could go up. I told them it was up to Mum and Dad; I would provide them with a free ride when they had permission.

Mary wanted to know about her ride. I told her it was the same but that we would have to negotiate a price. It was a rare thing for me to be able to open a negotiation with her; she usually beat me to it.

The little minx laughed at me and told me, "I knew you would grow up someday and learn how to do a deal."

She's my sister Mary.

"Hey, Mary, I was in Dallas a couple of days ago and a tailor from Neiman Marcus was describing a dress that is going to be their special edition of your Princess collection for Christmas this year."

"Yeah, it's going to be so neat."

"What he described sounded horrid to me."

"How could those clean-cut lines with an accompanying set of pearls be horrid?"

"I think you better have it checked out; it sounds like they have added half a ton of gems to it."

Mum got involved at this point. "We have a no-change clause in our contract with them. You bet we will check it out."

I hope for their sake the tailor had exaggerated about all the gems. That wasn't my worry. I was going into space.

The next morning, I was taken to my ride. The pilot in command was none other than Jerri Cobb. When I mentioned that I felt honored, she told me a lot of women not only honored me, but they worshipped the ground I walked on. If I wanted twenty or more children, all I had to do was give the word.

I told her I would have to take a pass on that. Having two brothers and one sister was all I could take. If I had that many kids, I would go crazy, and worst of all, with my luck they would be all girls.

She had met Mary and agreed that could be a fate worse than death. I asked her how she had interacted with her. It turned out she had interacted to the tune of fifty-three dollars playing gin.

"Then she turned around and offered to loan it back to me at interest!"

"That's Mary. On the outside an innocent little girl, on the inside a shark."

"She wants a ride into space next year to push Girl Scout cookies. I told her not on my spacecraft. She would sell me so many we would be overweight and not make orbit."

I think that is what they call kidding on the square.

When I went out to the launch pad in the morning, I saw a glorious sight: a rocket and capsule had been painted with my coat of arms. They would burn off in the journey, but it was wonderful to look at. Many a picture was taken, and I saw TV cameras rolling.

This birthday present gave a new meaning to light the candle.

The launch occurred on schedule. A herd of elephants sat on my chest the whole way to orbit. I grunted as I had been taught in my brief training. It did help as I didn't blackout.

On Jerri's advice, I ate a very light breakfast. I'm glad I followed it as my stomach lurched when we went weightless. Fortunately, that was the only lurch it gave. It would have been embarrassing to puke. As Jerri put it, if I puked, I cleaned it up.

The view was almost impossible to describe. I had heard the term "big blue marble" but didn't appreciate it until just now. We live on a wonderful and beautiful planet.

Looking out a viewport on the other side of the capsule, I saw what they called the Big Black. No twinkling stars here, there was no atmosphere to give the effect. They were unrelenting pinpoints of light.

They were numbered beyond counting but gave no relief from the stark coldness of space. I had thought looking down into the depths of the ocean was scary; this was positively frightening. Not that I would ever admit it to anyone.

"Rick, isn't that blackness the most frightening thing you have ever seen?"

"It certainly is, Jerri."

"Believe it or not, you get used to it. Just like any other familiar scene, your mind learns to ignore it."

"The sooner the better."

"At least you didn't scream and curl up in a ball."

"Have people done that?"

"Some of the most macho among us. They go down on the next flight and never come back up."

"I'm glad I didn't eighty-six myself."

"We all are. Without your support, this wouldn't be happening. Now that you are up here, there are some things I want to show you."

It took us about four hours to catch up with the latest version of our space station. I called it the latest version because it kept growing with the interlocking capsules we sent up.

It took a while to make the connection between our capsule and the docking station. Since this capsule would be going down, it was left in place. Those that were brought up with supplies were unloaded and then moved into position to add to the station.

I was in space!

Chapter 37

I was given a tour of the space station. They now had so many capsules attached that each of the ten Space Ladies aboard had their personal room for the week they spent in orbit.

Each room had four lockers so that each woman could leave her belongings in it until her next rotation.

They worked while there, and they worked hard. They were assembling the station plus the long-term moon orbiting station. I gazed out at the enormous collection of capsules, steel beams, metal crates of supplies, and fittings for inside the moon orbiting station, and who knew what else we had launched into orbit for the mission.

For sending this stuff to the moon to build a space station there, we had already done the heavy lifting.

A command capsule was to be the front end of our moon vessel. It would be attached to a spine. Empty, the spine looked like a huge tail. When containers were attached along the spine it would look more like a space train.

Rockets at the end of the spine would push the vehicle along. Since the earth's gravity had been overcome, it wouldn't take anywhere near that force to cause our train to coast to the moon.

There was no intention of traveling under continuous drive. A gentle nudge would get it moving and then a nudge from the front rockets would slow it into orbit. There were smaller side rockets on each end to give small course corrections.

In theory, the train would coast forever if not caught by the gravity of the moon, but even in space, there were small objects that caused friction and would bring it to a stop, a long, long way from here.

If nothing else, the solar winds would blow our ship off course. We were even playing with the idea of solar sails. Now that would be a sight to see, a three-masted spaceship.

This was probably one of the largest projects ever undertaken by man. It rivaled the Great Wall and the pyramids. An international project like no other.

It all came together at the launch center, where we were now doing twenty launches a week. It had been predicted that one in twenty-five would fail. We had one in one hundred fails and were working on improving that.

We had adopted lessons learned on submarines and were following the same procedures as Newport News Shipbuilding. Each weld was given a serial number and inspected multiple times by different inspectors, and the results were recorded.

Incentives were based on safety and 100% inspection results, not the speed of construction.

It was sexist, but we found that women with children were the best inspectors. We told them to act as if their children would be on the rocket.

We also took a leaf out of the parachute riggers handbook. The inspectors would go up on a random flight to orbit.

Draconian, maybe, but we hadn't had any failures. We were unmerciful with our suppliers. A rejection of the product resulted in a complete audit of their quality system. If it was found to be lacking, they were disqualified and had to start the qualification process all over.

It only took the disqualification of one major American aerospace company to drive the message home. I was glad not to own stock in their company.

We worked with a group called the International Organization for Standardization to develop a quality system standard. We accelerated their plans by years.

Their first effort was a logistical nightmare. They took the twenty major elements of a quality system and had them as separate entities instead of merging them into a smooth system.

I turned Drs. Deming and Juran loose on them and that got fixed quickly. I say I, but it wasn't me; it was my high-level instructions, but it was the work of a whole team that didn't even report directly to me. This project was too large for one person to comprehend what was occurring.

Multi-disciplinary team meetings were going on constantly to make certain each group had the same goal.

The whole process came together at the launch site where rockets were built and mated with capsules shipped in from the US. They were shipped using my shipping line of course.

We now had three rocket assembly buildings in use and planned two more.

The biggest headache was fuel. We had enough liquid oxygen and hydrazine to blow us off the face of the earth. Since we had a desert to work with, we had miles of separation, but this led to miles of pipeline.

Again, redundancy of inspections was a necessity. Dr. Deming kept tweaking us that if we built it right, we wouldn't need inspectors. He didn't have an answer for what building right consisted of, so we kept inspecting.

Having a theory is good, but you don't bet your life on your theory being correct until it is proven.

I was jarred out of my reverie by Jerri Cobb telling me that it was time for lunch, space style. Lunch proved to be food in a paste form squeezed out of tubes. Yuck.

When I was shown the toilets they used and how they worked, I was glad I didn't have to go. It made me even more determined to have a large enough station at a Lagrange point where we could give it enough spin to have artificial gravity through centrifugal force.

That reminded me of another test I had had to take in the hurried two days before my launch. The centrifuge to see if I could stand the forces generated at launch.

It made me come close to blacking out, but I didn't, only a little grey. I was told that I exceeded the qualifications to be a fighter pilot. It was a shame I was too big to fit in the cockpit of most of them.

All too soon my time in orbit was up. They presented me with International Astronaut wings that I could wear on my military uniform, as well as a patch for my left shoulder. It identified me as being in the first astronaut squadron, the Apollos.

NASA, who was getting pricklier about us all the time, even criticized us for using Apollo, as they had planned to use it on future moon missions, maybe as soon as 1969.

The ride back down was bumpy, bumpy as all get out. I thought the capsule was going to fly apart or even melt from the heat, but we landed okay. The landing was even softer than any parachute landing I had made.

I was as pumped up over my trip as any free-falling I had done. I was ready to go again. Reality broke in when I realized that I would be launching for the fun of the ride, not to do any real work. Well, boo!

I had to give our documentary crew an interview, but it was fun. They were on my side and not trying to get a hostile reaction from me. When they asked me what the next step would be, my answer was simple, "The moon."

I sent profuse thank you notes to my parents, the empress, the queen, and the US president for their part in making this trip possible. All of them played a role in my birthday present.

I kind of felt bad about how JFK's NASA program was getting kicked around by us. I wish I could do something nice for him.

From the launch center, I made a trip to Hong Kong. I hadn't checked in there for a while, so I thought I had better make myself seen once more.

I wouldn't be making any public appearances. I would be doing a Sunday morning interview on a news program. It was getting harder for me to be out in public without being surrounded by bodyguards.

It wasn't so much protection from people who wanted to harm me; it was to keep fans away. It only took my tie being ripped from my neck at one stop to make me a believer.

When questioned at the police station, the fan told them he only wanted a souvenir. He hadn't planned to sell it. The next day that tie was advertised for sale in newspapers in seven different countries showing pictures of seven different ties, none matching the one I wore.

Mary even approached me about having a Richard Jackson line of neckties. I thought about it but decided it wasn't for me.

I did notice that my little sister wasn't so little anymore. At nine years she was five feet tall. This put her above the ninety-seventh percentile of all girls. This was model height. Not only that, she was graceful. Her pediatrician attributed that to her active lifestyle of riding in horse jumping shows.

I attributed it to her having to run for her life from brothers who had just been scammed. I had never been able to tickle her until she peed her pants, but I still had hope.

Chapter 38

The interview with the Sunday morning news people included questions about my recent space ride. They wanted to know if I intended to allow other people to go up as a commercial venture.

I told them there had been no talk of it, but it was worth considering. Maybe we could auction off seats. Then issue astronaut wings with a serial number.

I should have kept my big mouth shut; within days bids were flowing in, the highest a million dollars. Since there was no clearing office for this, they had sent them to my offices in China, England, and the US.

Since it would impact them the most, I called Jerri Cobb and asked her opinion. She thought it would work, especially if I paid a bonus to all the tour guides. We settled on ten thousand dollars per tourist, the Space Ladies to divide it among themselves.

She was to set up an office at the launch site to accept telegrammed bids. Once the winner of an auction was announced, funds would be deposited in an account set up at the US office.

Since we were doing multiple launches, we could handle five tourists a week. When Mum and Mary found out, they immediately got into the act by setting up an apparel store at the launch site. You could only purchase stuff at the store, no mail or telephone orders.

This had everything from T-shirts that said, "My grandpa went up in space, and all I got was this lousy t-shirt," to some pretty nice stuff. I think Mary took great delight in making certain there was a line of neckties involved.

Once the store was opened for sale, we were all surprised when most customers were employees of the space center. We found out later there was a huge secondary market. Hey, I'm all for free enterprise.

The auction and store all developed over the next several months.

Business in Hong Kong was booming, yet inflation hadn't set in yet, so everyone's standard of living was on the rise. Now how to keep it that way? Our GDP increased twenty-five percent. The government was plowing money back into the infrastructure as fast as it could.

They were also working with my computer division to install a network that would allow home and office computers to talk to each other.

The first time I heard one of those modems connect, I thought a cat was being killed. They were optimistic that when people could send messages and access information from their homes or offices, the web, as they called it, would grow quickly.

Hong Kong was the beta site for this effort, but the early results indicated it would spread fast.

Our desktop computers for home and office were selling everywhere. The challenge now was to get the software translated into many different spoken languages.

IBM had noticed a dip in typewriter sales already. The computers didn't require all the maintenance that the IBM electric typewriters did, and the software made it easier to do corrections.

I spent a couple of nights at Jackson House Asia. Boris was there, and he now had a live-in girlfriend. He had achieved his ambition in life, a girlfriend, Natasha, and all he could eat.

He had put on at least thirty pounds and was trying for more. Soon he would be as wide as he was tall. They made an interesting couple, she was tall and thin, him short and fat. They were happy, so all was right with the world.

We did have a problem with our space capsules. On an unmanned flight, there was a fire on board the cabin. If it had been a manned flight, we would have lost everyone on board. All the contents of the capsule were revisited and made fireproof, and a fire suppression system was installed.

This delayed flights for two weeks but didn't impact the overall program. We shared the information with NASA, and they thanked us. They would have had the same problem.

Surprisingly, it didn't slow down the auctions at all. Seats were still going for over a million dollars. We even turned down one family's request for all four of them to go up in the same capsule. We didn't want to risk losing every member of the family at once.

They finally agreed on a father-son, mother-daughter ride. I was told that there was a huge family argument about who would go first and get the lower-numbered wings. The ladies won. I could have predicted that from the start.

One other comment about the wings. The Space Ladies had wings one through fifty; I had wing set fifty-one. A Space Lady who commanded a mission rated two stars at the top of her wings, mission workers one star, and tourists none.

This allowed later Space Ladies to have a star and gave them more prestige than passengers. I felt lucky to be given one star, even though I had done no work in space.

Jerri Cobb had three stars as overall mission commander.

It was these details that drove us crazy. Building rockets was now a production issue and not rocket science.

The rocket science that was going on was trying to build a spaceplane that would take off from the ground under its self-contained power, not rocket-assisted, fly to orbit, and return to the ground.

It would take several types of engines on the same plane to achieve this.

The science section of our company was looking at scramjets. They had certain advantages. They didn't have to carry oxygen, had no rotating parts which made manufacturing easier with less chance of failure, and had higher specific impulse (the momentum per unit of propellant) than rockets.

This all sounded good, but a scramjet has to be moving at Mach 4 before it will ignite. Then one would only go up to Mach 6 or 7. After that, a solid rocket could boost it to Mach 25 to reach high orbit.

Another objection was the high cost of flight-testing ground facilities that would have to be developed.

We had performed a large amount of experimental work on scramjets in cryogenic facilities, direct-connect tests, or burners, each of which simulated one aspect of the engine operation. Other facilities could control air impurities, heated storage facilities, arc facilities, and various types of shock tunnels each having limitations that prevented perfect simulation of scramjet operations.

We could use turbojets to get the beast off the ground, booster rockets to reach Mach 4, and another set of booster rockets to reach Mach 25.

After a project review and fifty million dollars, I killed the project. Not because of cost concerns, but with a ground takeoff, booster launch, scramjet engine firing, and another booster launch to high orbit, what could go wrong?

I remembered the issues with my original hairdryer. Now multiply those by some large number. We would continue to light the candle.

The scientist who had a vested interest in this screamed and moaned. He tried to go behind my back to my board of directors, who laughed at them.

I was even sued! He claimed that my refusal to fund the project was causing irreparable harm to the human race. I thought that was an interesting way to put it.

Unfortunately, he couldn't find a court that would hear their case. It appeared no court claimed jurisdiction over the human race.

The guy who sued me was eventually hired by NASA. They thought scramjets might be the way to go.

Another budget black hole.

While in Hong Kong, I had to attend a ball given by the governor-general. I appeared in my dress uniform wearing all my medals, with my astronaut wings taking pride of place.

My dinner companion turned out to be May-ling. Since she was going to school in Hong Kong, it would have been a tremendous faux pas not to invite her.

She and I had a nice conversation. At her request I described my space flight; it was very exciting. Then at my request, she updated me on how her schooling was going; very well thank you. If it sounds like we were cool and polite with each other, you got the tone of the communication.

For some reason, neither of us felt like opening up to each other. The fact that we were being avidly watched by over a hundred people may have had something to do with it.

We danced after dinner. While I held her close, she whispered in my ear, "I miss you, Rick. I wish it could be, but it can't."

My response was, "I miss you too, and don't understand why we can't be together."

The dance ended, and I never got an answer to my question. I was summoned to meet some important people. Why they were thought important I didn't know.

After making my manners I looked for May-ling, but she had left.

Chapter 39

The next morning, I boarded my flight back to Australia. I hadn't been able to contact May-ling, even though I had called and left several messages.

When we landed in Australia, the news was about water. The aquifer under my station had proved out.

It was the biggest news in Australia since the end of World War II. This would open up the interior of the country. The experts classified it as one of the biggest finds ever.

A land rush had started in the backcountry. It didn't take long for it to come out that the boundaries of the aquifer were within my one-hundred-square-mile station.

The next big revelation was when speculators tried to file oil, gas, water, and mineral claims on my land. I had those all tied up. People were claiming it was unfair. That I had to have inside knowledge.

How I could have had that wasn't explained. I was after the gold; the oil and water were lucky finds. The gold also, for that matter.

The Australian parliament got involved. They wanted to hold hearings on the matter. I was even subpoenaed the morning after I landed.

I was eating breakfast when Jeeves summoned me to the front door. He informed me that two apparent gentlemen had some legal papers they wanted to serve me.

I could have run for it but didn't bother. I could have used the escape tunnel or hidden in the room tucked away there. That reminded me that I hadn't looked for a similar room in the tunnel at Jackson House Asia.

Mary had checked Jackson House California and there wasn't one. I guess Talmadge didn't feel as threatened there.

At least the summons was for tomorrow, so I flew up to Canberra to be in place for the nine o'clock hearing. I wasn't too worried about events. I suspected what they thought would be an easy win would turn out to be a nightmare for them.

It didn't take long to get to Canberra, so I even did something completely different for myself. I called the largest TV station and asked to be interviewed.

It was part of a chain that Dad owned. I wanted the home-court advantage. The liberals thought they had it. They would soon learn differently.

In the interview, I explained that I wanted a large station in the middle of the continent because I suspected there had to be some resources there. I took a gamble and bought a large swath of land. In the scheme of things, it wasn't much money for me.

It was one of the few times I publicly threw my wealth around.

"I paid three hundred thousand pounds or so for that land. It had been classified as worthless by the same people who have summoned me. When you have multi-billions of pounds, that isn't much money to take a fling with."

"Your Grace, what about the water find; did you have any idea that it existed?"

"None. Hope, yes; knowledge, no. The water exploration didn't start in any fashion until after I owned the land and mineral rights. That can be verified by the people who sold me the drilling equipment and all the other gear needed for exploration."

"What do you expect in the hearings tomorrow?"

"A lot of whining about it isn't fair that I own all this, and that I should be sharing. They have talked about nationalizing it once; they will probably try again."

"What's to stop them?"

"I don't want to ruin the surprise; you will have to wait and see with everyone else."

"Thank you, Your Grace."

"You're welcome, Brian."

The next morning amid many camera flashes, I entered the Australian Parliament building, or as it was titled, the Provisional Parliament Building. It was built in 1927 and intended for use fifty years or less. They had better get on the stick.

The most interesting part of the House of Representatives Hall was the Speaker's Chair.

The royal coat of arms over the chair is carved in oak from timber originally built into Westminster Hall in 1399. The hinged flaps of the armrests are of oak from Nelson's flagship *HMS Victory*, in the Battle of Trafalger.

That chair was historic. I didn't think much of the current occupant. A hearing like this would have been normally held in a conference room, but the entire house wanted to be present, and the gallery was taken up by the Senate. A few reporters found their way in.

I sat on one of the long benches up at the front. To make a point, I wore my formal dress with all honors, and that included my sword. They would get the point soon enough.

They made a big deal of swearing me to tell the whole truth, and nothing but the truth, so help me God.

Then before any questions were put to me, each member of the majority party spent five minutes each explaining over and over why I was a low life. The conservative minority passed on their opportunity to call me names. They didn't defend me either. This was a no-lose for them.

This took over an hour. I don't think I impressed them when I yawned. Later, that picture made the newspapers, even Dad's.

Finally, they asked me questions. Even those questions had five minutes of speeches. The first question was, "Do you think it is right that you selfishly hold all that land and the water beneath it for your personal benefit?"

"I believe I have met every Australian law and statutory requirement."

"But do you think it is fair?"

"It must be because it was your party that passed these laws and your government that established the statutory requirements."

I learned later this was being broadcast on Australian TV and that I was getting cheers in the pubs.

"We never expected anyone to take such gross advantage of our fair and equitable laws. We will need to change them."

"Even though that isn't a question, I will grant you that is your right. However, I suspect there are legal concerns about retroactivity in the application of those laws. I'm certain your High Court will have an opinion."

"How will you answer if I tell you we will nationalize your property for the good of the Australian people."

"I and my shareholders would be upset."

"Who are your shareholders of record?"

Thank you, Lord.

"I'm the majority shareholder, and my parents have a large interest."

I deliberately slowed my speaking down to give him a chance to interrupt me. Which he did.

"We don't care a fig about you and your parents."

"May I finish with the shareholders?"

"Go on."

"Also holding large personal positions in the company are the Empress Ping of the Middle Kingdom, commonly known as China, and Queen Elizabeth of the United Kingdom, also known as the Queen of Australia. "

All hell broke loose. It took over fifteen minutes to bring order back to the chamber. After hammering his gavel so hard I thought the Speaker would break it, he got enough quiet to declare the hearing closed.

While the hubbub continued in the hall, I got up and walked out.

Later that night I watched interviews in a pub, wanting to know about the hearings.

As one guy put it, "The hearings were crooks and now cactus; the duke's performance was dux."

I have no idea what he meant. I received a phone call from the head of the conservatives. He danced around and finally came out and asked for my support in the next round of elections. I told him I would give him the same support as he provided me today. He told me he was sorry that I felt that way. I told him I wasn't sorry I felt that way and hung up.

The next morning, I boarded the DC3 and flew out to the new, new station to see what was going on. I needed a name for it. Jackson Station was already taken. I had a thought but wanted to pass it by Mum first.

Things at the base camp were fair dinkum as the Aussies would say. I understood that much. I still didn't know what the guy in the pub said.

I had a chance to find out when someone mentioned they had heard the pub interviews on the radio.

It turns out that "crook" meant sick or bad off, "cactus" meant dead, and "dux" was first in class. So, the hearings were bad and dead in the water, and my performance was first class. Why didn't he say that? Don't they speak English here? Fortunately, my brain caught up with my mouth before I could say anything.

A blow-off valve had been installed to stop the free flow of water. Now it was flowing into our water tanks. Everyone now could take showers as long as they wanted.

The other important projects were well underway. A highway was being constructed to connect to the Lasseter Road and the oil explorers were still setting off charges to map the area.

Chapter 40

One of the actions taken by parliament in trying to nationalize my mineral holdings was to file suit in the Supreme Court of Western Australia. After it came out that Queen Elizabeth was a shareholder in my company, they did what most courts would have done.

They kicked it upstairs to the High Court of Australia on the grounds that in trying to revoke my mineral rights, any court determination would affect all of Australia. The High Court needed to decide the constitutionality of that step.

This would normally take years to wind its way through court dockets. It took a week for the Supreme Court to throw it over the fence to the High Court.

The High Court, being no fools, knew a political hand grenade when they saw it and passed it on to the Privy Council of the United Kingdom. They based their decision that it was not a constitutional matter, but a matter of law passed by parliament. In this they were correct.

The only surprise is that it only took them a week to make this decision. Now the Privy Council has a Judicial Committee. Their job is to make legal recommendations to the reigning monarch, who always took their recommendation.

The only thing I knew about the council was that John Profumo resigned amid a great sex scandal last June.

The Judicial Council of the United Kingdom was now in the position of deciding if the Australian government could by fiat change their laws to confiscate Her Majesty's property.

Think "Off with their heads." At least they may have been thinking that as they ruled that Australia couldn't change their laws retroactively to seize private property, even if it was for the good of the people.

It would be okay in matters of war, but that was it. Since I wasn't at war with Australia, they couldn't seize my property.

There was also the minor matter that the United Kingdom didn't want to go to war with the Middle Kingdom over the property; after all, it was only water and possibly some oil.

One month after we had confirmed the water and the size of the aquifer, I had firm mineral, water, and oil rights over my land.

There had been several phone calls between the queen and empress, who seemed to be taking delight in turning the government systems against themselves.

The empress, while extremely strong, was not all-powerful, and the queen had that pesky parliament to deal with, so they were enjoying this. To them, it was a game.

I had a decision to make. When to start the gold operation? It wasn't on any timetable, so I decided to let it sit for a while.

I left the operation in Western Australia and returned to Jackson Station in Queensland. The roads had been put in, a dirt airfield put in that would take the DC3, and concrete was being poured for a real landing strip that the 707 or any other aircraft could use.

An agreement had already been signed with the Royal Australian Air Force that they could use it as an emergency strip and even base planes there at need. Since we were near the edge of Queensland, I didn't see that happening.

Fencing was being put up around the entire station. It would take several years to complete, but it had to start sometime.

Small pastures were fenced in for the livestock that we were currently running. Old buildings were being torn down and new ones were being put up for the current residents.

I was pleased to see the little girl Mary's age playing in front of a new house. She waved and gave me a big smile as we drove by on one of my many tours.

The Fergusons had been to Spain and liked what they saw of the operations that I had instituted there. Of course, Ron Ferguson had several ideas of how to improve the Spanish *estancia* and brought back some good ones for this station.

In the middle of all this, I was asked to attend the premier of the movie, *Escape from Siberia*.

Since I had money vested in the movie, I decided to attend, even though I had no real part in the movie.

This required a flight back to the States. I wish there were some sort of rewards program for miles flown. Of course, since it was my airline, I would owe them to myself.

The flight crew didn't even complain about being pulled off Bondi Beach, where they now owned a beach house.

I hadn't known it, but they and my 707 had a part in the movie. They were paid and the plane was rented, and I didn't even know it.

Harold even had a minor scene clucking over the clothes I was wearing when I came out of the Soviet Union.

Because of this, they were all going to walk the red carpet.

The flight across the Pacific was different on this trip. I couldn't get any service at all; they were all wrapped up in what they were going to wear.

When I complained, I was told to hush up. They had heard that my minor appearance had been cut and that I wasn't even in the movie, while they were.

How the mighty have fallen. Rather than get upset, I chose to take it all in good fun. It was that, or pout for the twenty-hour flight.

It turned out to be a fun-filled flight as I got into the spirit and taught them how to walk the red carpet—don't sway too much, just a hint. Then how to do an interview that didn't make them sound like a Barbie doll.

I think my swaying walk down the aisle of the airplane was the best. And no, I didn't wear a dress or makeup, and they didn't have any high heels that would fit me.

We landed a day before the premiere, so they had an opportunity to rest. On the day of the premier, all the stewardesses were taken to the studio to have their hair and make-up done. The guys in the flight crew were wearing their formal flight uniforms.

The guys and the ladies were paired up to walk together. I hadn't had time to round up a partner, so I got stuck with a studio starlet. Warner Brothers owed Twentieth Century on a deal, so I escorted a new actress who was starting to make a name for herself.

Ann-Margret was an interesting study. When not in public, she was shy and reserved. When she made an appearance, she bubbled over. I thought she probably would do well in acting.

She had been told that I knew Elvis, and she wanted to know everything she could about him. I thought I had better keep some bail money aside for Elvis if she ever ran into him.

The walk down the carpet was old hat to me, and Ann knew her way around, so it went well for us. The only time it got weird was when I was asked about something the guy playing me said.

He told them that I hadn't killed those guys in the boxcar scene, which was only put in for dramatic effect.

I told them that he had it wrong. I had taken them down hard. It was funny later in the newspapers. Now who would you believe, the actor who played the part in the movie or the guy who was there?

It was split!

The Russians helped me out for once. They issued a warrant for me for murder in the first degree. I don't think I will be going to Russia in the near future or any future, for that matter.

My flight crew had their moment in the sun. They had several interviews about how it was to fly the Duke of Hong Kong around the world.

Thank goodness they didn't tell how bad I was at gin rummy. Harold declined interview requests, claiming that he had ironing to do.

After that, it was back to Australia the long way. I wanted to stop in England to make certain the Roman dig was going as planned. It got away from me once, not again.

Everything was fine and David reported that it was now progressing better than ever. They now had a clearer look at what life was like during the end of the Roman period in England.

They even found a hint that there was a king in the west country named Arthur. This would be the first evidence that King Arthur existed.

The layover in England proved worthwhile, as the queen requested for me to come to Windsor Castle, where she was currently in residence. Her flag was flying over the castle when I arrived, so she couldn't plead that she had to step out.

She wanted an update on Australia. She told me that she was concerned about how the Aborigines had been treated, and if there was anything I could do to better their conditions, please do so.

For political reasons, she couldn't take a public stand, but she felt that England had created a great injustice. She told me that if there were schools or hospitals to be built on the new station for the Aborigines, I could expense it out of her share.

Elizabeth I was known as Elizabeth the Great.

Will this Elizabeth be known as Elizabeth the Greater?

Chapter 41

"Once more unto the breach, dear friends," was what the flight back to Australia felt like. To the flight crew, it was a job; when the flight was done their work was over. For me, the work had just begun.

I racked up more flight hours. I really had to get certified on this aircraft type.

I did manage to think about the new desert station, as I was beginning to think of it. There had to be a road network that included oil, gold, and arable land.

The only problem was that the only site that I knew for certain was the goldfield. I was still reluctant to reveal its presence to the world.

I thought it would be best to have security plans in place before starting. How to arrange that security without bringing the gold discovery out into the open was the question.

Then there was the equipment needed to mine the gold. It would start as a surface mining operation. I pictured it as blasting the quartz, scooping it up with excavators and bulldozers, and loading it into large dump trucks to haul to the crusher plant.

I had read up somewhat on the next steps. After being crushed, the residual would be sent through a trommel, then a wash plant and shaker operation to separate the gold from the quartz.

Lots of water would be required, so water pumps and compressors would have to be in place. The water could be recycled, but it would require a large holding pond.

Once the gold was separated, it still wasn't refined enough, so it would be taken to the gold room, which was a glorified mechanical gold panning operation.

Since the samples indicated a high amount of gold, it would be smelted on-site and flown to Sydney, where the Australian government would get its share and the rest go into a bank.

This is how I thought it would go on the flight. I wondered what the reality would be. I needed to find gold mining experts for professional direction.

The more I thought about it, the more I realized the less I knew. Maybe I would be better off hiring a mining company to operate the mine rather than trying to reinvent the wheel. Better yet, buy a mining company so I retained complete control.

Now to find a mining company for sale. Excellent staff was the first consideration. Equipment could be purchased. It was the knowledge that I needed.

As far as security was concerned, I thought I needed to take another taxi ride to Uluru.

When we landed, I spent several days at Jackson House Australia. The Ferguson ladies had done a bang-up job of putting the place in order. Jeeves had finished the job.

It seemed weird at first having staff to cater to every whim, but it didn't take more than a couple of days to get used to it. I now even had a resident personal secretary.

One of my first phone calls was to the governor-general's office to inquire if they knew of any expert mining companies for sale.

I should have called the prime minister's office, but due to my recent experiences with them, I didn't want to further upset them with knowledge of possible gold. They would freak out.

There would be leaks in the governor-general's office, but that couldn't be helped. I even tried a little misdirection by mentioning Jackson Station had gold, and I wanted to have exploration started.

I didn't think it would fool anyone, but it was worth a try. If nothing else, it might damage the credibility of the leaker.

I received a return call the next day. There was a reputable outfit that had fallen on hard times. They had the knowledge I was looking for.

A legal battle over a gold field they had been working for another party had them sitting idle for two years, and they were at wit's end. They were locked in as a company, so they had to wait for the legal battles to be resolved. They would be breaking and gone before the court cases were finished.

I contacted the owner who agreed to meet me. She looked like what I thought a gold miner in Australia should look like—weathered from the sun with a brilliant smile and eyes that lit up the world.

It seems her father had died the year before, and she was trying to keep the company together. She introduced herself as Sheila Armstrong. It never occurred to me to make a Sheila joke.

She was about my age. With her looks, it was hard to tell. I explained in general terms what I was looking for. She had to be desperate but still had her pride, so I asked her if the company was for sale, or if was she going to try to stick it out.

"There is no way that we will make it past the next pay period."

"What are your plans?"

"Pay everyone to date and send the equipment to auction."

"Could we incorporate a new company, sell the equipment to them, and hire the current staff?"

"Yes, but why would you do that?"

"I have a proven find that I want to have some control over. I would own the majority of the mining company. You would have twenty percent, and I would be a silent partner in its operations."

"How certain are you of the find?"

I was prepared for that question and handed her the assay reports.

"Bloody hell, you found Lasseter Reef!"

"How can you tell that?"

"The quartz content; the Reef would be the only place that had that much quartz."

"Are you willing to join my new corporation?"

"Where do I sign? This is a dream come true. I get to keep providing jobs for people who are like family to me, work on the largest gold find ever, and oh yes, get bloody rich."

Did I mention that she swore a lot? She and Mum would get along.

I had decided for my lawyer's office to start the paperwork, so we drove over there and signed our portions. I even had money transferred to her company account to ensure payroll could be met. She had been planning to pay them out of her personal funds.

I found out that Sheila was thirty years old, so no romance here, but better yet, I think I had found a new friend. In my new world, having true friends is rated very highly.

As we went about the tasks of forming a new company, I did ask her about security. She told me that roving patrols and a small reaction force worked in Australia.

She told me that the blackfellas made the best security people. They liked to rove anyway, so it wasn't even like work for them.

I was concerned at first that she might be discriminating against them, but found out even the Aborigines called themselves blackfellas, and white men, whitefellas. The term Abo was falling out of general use as it had been used to denigrate the Aborigines.

I had to be certain that I over-hired, as they would go on extended walkabouts with no notice. They wouldn't expect payment for this period, so the only extra cost would be the initial training. Training an Australian Aboriginal to rove around and patrol an area was like hauling coal to Newcastle.

I could see that there was a lot of history that I didn't begin to understand and that I had to navigate this minefield carefully. I wanted to help, not hurt, and most of all not be seen as a modern slave master. I needed expert guidance, or I could make things worse for all concerned.

Based on those considerations, I flew to Uluru and found my original taxi driver. I explained to him who I was and what potential impact I could have on this part of his world.

I needed guidance on what to do, other than removing all white men from the continent.

"Oh no, boss. Only Whitefellas use taxis. I wouldn't have a job."

"So, you don't mind the white man's world?"

"I could live the old life, but my wife wants the new life. She likes shopping, washing machines, and all that stuff."

"Schools for our kids help and having health care is good, though we need a hospital here. I saw one once when I went to Sydney. They would save lives out here."

"That's the sort of direction I need. As my operation on the desert station and oil field grows, I will need people. I think your people would be a great asset, but I want to do it in a way that works for you, not just the Whitefella."

Now they have me saying it.

"I will take you to meet with our elders. They will help. I know they want to do better but don't know how. This may be what is needed.

Chapter 42

It took several days, but I was led out into the desert and met with the elders of Tony's group. His name wasn't Tony, but he told me to call him that. I couldn't begin to pronounce his real one.

The Aboriginal groups in Australia are not tribes like the American Indians. They are a group of people who live in the same territory. They might all speak the same language, and they might not.

I just accepted they were a group with common issues and goals who lived on the territory covered by the desert station.

Why the land was not considered theirs was beyond me. It didn't seem to concern them, so I shrugged my shoulders and proceeded.

I explained that with the newly discovered water and possible oil wells, the queen of the United Kingdom had instructed me to see to the needs of their people. I had to add this didn't include shipping the Whitefella out. They thought that was hilarious.

They had many reasons to be bitter but didn't exhibit it to me. To them, it appeared like a force of nature, something to be endured.

When the laughter stopped, I was told that jobs would be nice, if they recognized the cultural needs of their people.

I explained that I would need to hire many people to run the station and the oil wells.

"What about the gold?"

"What gold?"

"The large gold reef that Lasseter found. We have known about it for thousands of years. We don't need gold and fear the shiny snake that the gold lives in."

"To get the gold, we would have to crush the Reef or shiny snake into many small pieces."

"That would be good."

"Then add many employees to operate the equipment to crush the snake and separate the gold."

"How many people?"

"More than you probably have. I have also been told that I should hire enough to keep the station working while some go walkabout."

"That would be good."

"I would also build houses, schools, and hospitals for your people."

"The women will like that. One more thing, some of us have more wives than one. I have ten. The white men don't like that."

"What happens in your house stays in your house. I'm sorry to hear that you have to bear such a burden."

This brought a smile.

"One needs many wives to show status. All women are not good. Some days I wish I had no status."

"As I said, you have my sorrow for you. Maybe with the new station, status can be shown in other ways."

"How?"

"To start with, you three will be my advisors on native issues. This will give you high pay and better houses."

"Will I have to keep all my wives?"

"What happens in your house stays in your house, as long as it is not a crime of violence."

"You are wise for your age. Your queen has done well in sending you."

"Thank you."

It was so complicated that I didn't even want to try to explain all the ins and outs of the matter.

Tony my taxi driver had sat with us. I turned to him and told him, "You are my official driver at the station."

"Yes, boss."

That took care of the Aboriginal issues for now. I'm sure there will be more in the future.

Checking back at Jackson Station, I found that schools, a library, and a hospital had been started. They were expected to be completed early in the new year, so things were proceeding nicely.

One item that hadn't been settled on was the main house at Jackson Station. While being the residence of the station manager and his family, it would also be the site where events would be hosted.

I thought of using the Talmadge house design but realized it would be out of place in that landscape. In a moment of sheer brilliance, I called the Fergusons and dumped it all on them. I set a budget of one million pounds and turned them loose.

Ron called me back after the call and used several nasty words about me. The ladies would drive him nuts. I told him that was why I was paying him the big bucks.

He did update me that the near pastures were set up and the cattle were settling in fine. The operation was easy to run as it had been rebuilt using all the lessons he had learned in his forty years of managing large stations.

He mentioned that many tourists were making the station a stop on their drives and that one young lady was making a fortune selling authentic Aboriginal didgeridoos.

They were all made in China, but she had the blackfellas peel off the label and then blow in them once, and they were now authentic. He didn't name the girl, but I think I had met her. I made a mental note of never letting her and Mary meet.

I did take the time to give Sheila Armstrong a tour of the Reef. It was all sand-covered as usual. This time, there were three feet of sand covering the quartz.

We talked about how she would set up the operation. When I mentioned that I would like to hire as many Aboriginals as possible, she had no problem with that. It was my profits.

When I explained that the mining company would be working for the station company and had as part-owners Queen Elizabeth and Empress Ping, she was speechless for a short minute, a New York minute, about twenty seconds.

"Sheila, that brings to mind something I have been meaning to tell you. You have moved a lot of people and equipment on my word."

"And your money."

"And my money, but more importantly you have given me your trust. I have arranged for a two percent ownership in the station for you."

This time she was speechless for a real minute.

Once she found her voice and quit hugging me so hard that I thought she had cracked a rib, we made a rough plan for the roads in and out of the goldfield. We agreed that there should be limited admission from other areas of the station.

She and I met with the engineers in Sydney and explained where we wanted some new roads built. We didn't offer why, and they didn't ask, but you could tell it was killing them.

Almost as an afterthought, I mentioned to Sheila that it was a shame we wouldn't be able to do anything with all that crushed quartz.

She straightened me out quickly. This was high-grade almost pure quartz. We would be selling it to India, where they used it for flat glass. I had a "duh" moment when she explained that flat glass is what they used in windows.

The next large event was when word came in that the potential oil field had been mapped, and the first well was being drilled. The lead exploration engineer told me there wasn't a question of oil: it was a question of how much and what grade.

The word got out to the news media, so I had to give a press conference to announce the find. I was asked if I was now going to give in and turn it over to the government for the good of the people.

Where do they get these reporters?

"No, I'm going to pay taxes and let them use that money for the good of the Australian people."

"So, you think you are wiser than the government?"

"Demonstrably so. I have the oil and they don't."

I could have worded that better, as it made front pages all over the world.

"They could send in the troops."

"You do know who you would be stealing from?"

"The Brits wouldn't do anything."

"Want to bet against China? The Russians did and lost Siberia."

Other reporters shouted the idiot down before he could start another world war. I never saw anything under his byline again.

When I explained the potential size and production of the oil field, it left the reporters mute for half a New York minute. I think New Yorkers have their timing down pretty well.

"Don't get too excited. It will take several years to develop the field. We will have to start construction on a pipeline to move the oil to the coast near a large port."

That threw the cat amongst the pigeons once more. Now it was which city would benefit, which land would it cross, and would it endanger the stations it crossed?

I ended the press conference at that point because I had no useful answers to provide. I'm sure the government would come up with some "help".

I decided to return to the States while things were being organized at the gold and oil fields. We had managed to keep a lid on the gold, but it was due to blow off soon.

Chapter 43

The time had come for me to keep another promise. I had to fly to Dallas to be with the family when Mary's new Princess Collection was unveiled at Neiman Marcus. It would be interesting how their special dress would now look since Mary had found out what they had been planning.

It was a cheap flight. I only lost twenty-seven dollars to the sharks playing gin. Was I getting better, or had I just been lucky? Probably lucky.

My reading lists were getting longer all the time. I thought I understood economics, but then another question would come up that I had to find the answer to. This time it was, what if the world's gold supply doubled in one year?

The price for gold as a commodity such as electroplating circuit boards would go down. But then gold was seen as a reserve against hard or dangerous times. Scarcity or excess of gold didn't seem to be an issue. The price would be set by fear, not by availability.

Then there were governments wanting to keep bullion as a reserve for the same reasons.

If the price of gold stayed up because of fear, then gold as a commodity would go down. It gave me a headache thinking about it. What if the annual production quadrupled or went up eightfold?

None of the books I was reading had a clear-cut answer. I think no one knew what would happen if an element valued for its scarcity wasn't as scarce anymore.

That got me from Sydney to Dallas, where my family was waiting at the hotel. We had an entire floor reserved for Mary's circus. I remember my circus fondly; it was a much simpler world.

Hers were her models, makeup people, hairdressers, dressmakers, camera crew, set-up people, and who knew what. Maybe she even had a clown.

That was probably my job.

Out of all the madness we managed to have a family dinner in our suite. Denny was still smarting by having an ear clipped by Dad. Something about one of the models. That boy was heading for trouble.

I asked about the special dress at Neiman Marcus. I was thanked for bringing it to her and Mum's attention. I was shown a picture of the dress and the diamond tiara that went with it. It was the tiara that made the outfit over the top in Neiman Marcus style.

I had to compliment them on the clean lines and simplicity of the dress. It was classic and looked like what a Disney princess would wear. Walt was getting his mileage out of the princess theme. I wondered how long it would last.

Mary asked me to relay a message to Myra. I asked who Myra was.

"She is a girl in Australia who is selling Aboriginal gear. Tell her I have found a better price on didgeridoos, and they are made in Australia."

The world is coming to a sad end.

"I will tell her. How did you get in contact with her?"

"She sent me a letter telling me how she scammed you about being hungry. We have been good friends ever since."

The end will be ugly.

I shot Mum a look and told her it was urgent we talked after dinner. We did, but Mum was of no help. She thought it was great that Mary had a friend her age with similar talents.

I guess the saving grace is that they are half a world apart.

The next morning, we were all up early and went to the Neiman Marcus flagship store. They had it done up for the start of the Christmas season. It was as good as anything I had seen in New York.

Just before the show started, we were joined by President Kennedy and his wife Jackie. They were in town on a campaign stop.

They had been going to ride with Governor Connally, but the Secret Service people talked him into changing his plans at the last minute.

They were nervous about him riding in an open limo. He didn't think it would be a problem but yielded to them. They had been picking up rumors about something big happening in Dallas. They didn't want to take any chances.

The big dress reveal had just occurred and the "Princess" was crowned by Princess Mary who had to stand on a footstool to place the tiara on the model's head.

The oohs and awes were interrupted by the Secret Service almost dragging the president out of the room.

Jackie was left standing there so I took her by the arm, and we went out the same door the president had exited through. It was easy to find him because he was in a room down the hall. He was surrounded three deep by agents.

Jackie was allowed into the room, but I had to stay outside. I asked one of the agents guarding the door if he was allowed to say what was going on.

He looked at his partner who nodded okay.

"Governor John Connally has been shot while riding in the motorcade. The president was scheduled to be with him."

"Do we know his condition?"

"Not certain, but it appears he will live."

"Did they get the shooter?"

"Some guy on a grassy knoll that overlooked the parade route."

"Wouldn't that have been..." I started to ask but from the look that passed the agent's face, I decided not to ask.

I was summoned into the room by an agent. The president wanted to speak to me.

"Rick, once again I seem to be in your family's debt."

"I don't see how."

"Your sister Mary had an event going on that allowed me to divert. Connally understood not wanting to miss a major donor's event."

"Happenstance, sir, just happenstance."

I saw the look on an agent's face. I think the Jackson family will be under a microscope soon. Oh well, that must have happened a hundred times as we rose in prominence.

"Also, thank you for bringing Jackie back here; these clowns left her."

I could also see the look on several agents' faces. These were to protect the president at all costs, not the first lady. Where were her agents? That was their problem to sort out.

I bowed out of the room and went back to the showroom. In the best of traditions, the show was going on, but when I walked back into the room all eyes turned to me. Better now than later.

"Ladies and gentlemen, the president and his wife are fine. They were removed by the Secret Service in an excess of caution. Governor John Connally has been shot, but not fatally. That is all I know."

That certainly resulted in an explosion of noise. I had just ended the show as people got up to leave. I had forgotten these were the elites of Texas. One way or the other, they might be affected by events.

The only one who didn't seem phased was JR Ewing.

"Shot but not fatally? Someone won't be getting a full paycheck."

At that, he turned and walked away. Nah, it couldn't be.

Mary was excited. This would give her Neiman Marcus show worldwide publicity. I asked her if she cared that a man got shot.

"He didn't die, did he?"

I gave her a long look. Nah, it couldn't be.

At least I knew Mum wasn't involved. She would have been the one on the grassy knoll, and she had been here with us all the time. What strange family and friends I have.

I was introduced to the model who was still wearing the special dress and tiara. That was when I found out that I was her escort to a dinner being held here in the store. She was real eye candy on my arm. It was a shame that her head appeared to be stuffed with cotton candy.

I did my duty and escaped after she talked about a group called the Chippendales for the whole meal. They may turn her on but didn't sound like a group I would like to meet.

I also thought that we had to be careful about having her around Mary. The young lady may be a financial shark, but she was innocent in all other things.

As I said good night to the model whose name I was making a point not to remember, Mary approached me.

"I'm sorry Rick. We had to pair her with someone. Did she go on and on about the Chippendales?"

"She did."

"I don't see why anyone would get so excited about chipmunks; she can't even get Alvin's name right."

"Yeah, she is a little dense."

"Not only that, she talks about the show they put on. I don't think anyone would want to see a naked chipmunk."

"You do every time you see one outdoors."

"But I don't get funny looking when I talk about them."

"I think we need to get you to Mum so we can leave."

I needed to clue Mum in, so she could keep Mary from going to one of their shows!

Chapter 44

After Dallas, we headed back to LA. It was time for another board meeting of Jackson Enterprises. I tried to wiggle out of it but for some reason, they insisted the chairman of the board be there.

We had to have pristine records if we ever decided to take the company public. I didn't see any reason to ever do that, but the rest of the board insisted.

My first stop was to see Jim Williamson in his office. We had to plan the agenda for the business meeting. Before we got deep into the weeds, he explained the cash bonus and a portion of the licensing profits were working.

It was started for the computer software division but had become general practice across the entire company.

By putting the licensing profits into a pool that was shared by the staff who had worked on or given direct support, we were making a lot of people well off. None were getting rich, but they weren't hurting either.

A side effect was that we had quality people clamoring to come to work for us. Not only that, our retention rate was the highest in any industry. This in turn reduced training costs for all divisions.

I had thought a lot of people would take the money and run, but I was wrong. We found out that people like to work, especially in a company where they see rewards and a constant professional staff working alongside them.

Poor supervisors couldn't thrive in this atmosphere. Nothing was actively done against them unless they were stupid enough to get fired with cause. Most self-selected out. You had to be extremely incompetent to not realize when you weren't fitting in.

Once again, we talked about the upcoming business meeting. We both agreed that the format we used in the last meeting worked so we would follow it again.

The next week flew by in a flurry of pre-meeting meetings. Unlike our last meeting, I now realize how much work was involved in getting ready for a state of the business meeting.

I avoided involvement in the past, but now I knew that I had to be involved if I was to consider this my business. Silly as it seems, I was starting to enjoy it when things went right.

By the time all the meetings were finished, I pretty well knew the status of the business. This time I didn't have to ask why we had to have the meeting if we now knew the results to be presented.

I told him that I didn't envy publicly held companies and their having to go through this every time they had their annual meeting. We did it so we were comfortable with what was being presented. They did it to build a line of defense and excuses for any shortcomings.

"I'm glad we aren't publicly held."

"Not at this time, but someday it may be in your best interest to go public. This way we will be ready. Also, if the company is ever investigated, we can demonstrate that due diligence was being exercised."

"You told me that before. I'm just getting to hate meetings."

"Unfortunately, a necessary evil."

"It will be interesting to see this new PowerPoints software in use. It has to be better than all those overheads."

"The new chips helped in developing a way to create them quickly and projecting them without all the heat."

The people who were putting the presentations together had a ton of notes to give to the developers for improvements they would like to see.

On the day of the business meeting, once again I was up early and got my run and exercise in. After that a good breakfast and a shower. I wore the same suit, custom-made, by Hart, Shaffner, and

Marx. It was dark blue with the finest red line running vertically. I thought it gave the right impression.

We met in the small conference room for the divisional meetings. We were following the same time allotment as we had for the last meeting.

The agenda allowed an hour each for Jackson Personal Products, Jackson Home Products, and the Entertainment Division. Jackson Transportation was two hours in the afternoon. Then there were two hours for the Space Division.

First up was a review of Personal Products. The meeting room was set up with a sideboard with the usual coffee, tea, orange juice, bagels, and donuts.

I had coffee and my usual crème filled donut even though I had a large breakfast. If we had these meetings too often, I would get fat.

The new markets that we had opened in Brazil, Argentina, Peru, Columbia, and Chile had brought in twelve million this past year. Once more ahead of projections.

It looked solid overall in Africa. Hairdryer sales were starting to pick up in South Africa. Market penetration in Egypt and Southern Rhodesia was finally making projections.

We still couldn't get a foothold in Liberia. Maybe if they had more electrical power it would help. The major source of power was hydroelectric, and every time the plants were up and running, they would have a revolution and shut them down.

Don had talked again to the managing director of the Firestone Plantation. Mr. Dawson was still helpful, but everything was held up by the corruption in the Liberian government which in turn led to another revolution.

The revolutions were not about cleaning up the corruption but that the revolutionaries wanted their turn at the corruption.

We continued to refuse to pay the bribes requested. These were for large cash payments. I still supported our position.

Australia and the New Zealand markets were above projections, which had been ambitious in the first place.

Europe was still spotty. The Mediterranean countries were still slow adopters while the Scandinavians couldn't buy enough dryers and curling irons. We discussed spending more money on advertising in the Mediterranean countries but finally decided not to. A few ads weren't going to change a culture.

The bottom line on the Division was that it was going to earn over thirty million dollars in profit this year, well over the twenty-two million projected.

Mark and Sharon Downing had again flown in for the meeting. It was good to see them. They brought their almost one-year-old daughter with them; this delayed the meeting for half an hour while everyone cooed and awed over her.

She was starting to teeth and was a little cranky. I picked her up and she threw up all over my suit. After my initial urge to throw a tantrum, I put a good face on it. I handed the coat to a secretary and asked that it be sent out to a one-hour dry cleaner.

Fortunately, the shirt and tie missed the mess. It did make me think of Empress Ping being my dry-cleaning lady. That brought a smile to my face, which seemed to relax everyone in the room.

Mark Downing reported, "The purchase of a competitor last year continues to work out nicely. The production facility and its infrastructure have filled the expansion needs. The old workforce continues to find our company much better to work for. Another attempt to unionize their location has failed miserably."

The profit pace had been projected at nine million. Instead, it would be eleven. Mark's sister's wails had given away to sobs. He even relented enough to give her one percent of his share. This enabled him and Sharon to get together with his family once more.

Before lunch, we reviewed the numbers of the Jackson Entertainment Division. The accounting group gave us dry numbers from movies and music.

We took a restroom break before the meeting and refreshed our coffee.

Since I had no new movies out, it was a review of past endeavors. This was from the failed Surfer movie and revenues from *Over the Ohio.* OTO was fantastic. It had set US box office records and had done the same when released overseas.

The big earnings were from the movie, *Escape from Siberia.*

It earned six million dollars in its first week. It was still being argued if I had killed those guys on the train. People were going to the movie and watching the scene to decide what happened!

The cattle drive movie had been delayed once again because of some post-production problems. I wondered if it would ever get released.

On the movie front, it now looked like eighty million dollars, which beat last year's projection of seventy-five million. This was the last year we expected to make much money from movies unless I went back to acting. That wasn't in my plans at the moment.

The music from all songs had been projected at $300,000 but ended up near $200,000. There was hope for American music after all.

Susan Wallace was still doing very well. Mr. Spiller had set me up as a silent partner in her talent agency and was kept informed. Even so, I kept my hands off and would continue to do so unless she called for help. By keeping informed I could step in if her pride stood in the way of asking for help.

It didn't look like she would ever need it. I asked that she be approached to see if she wanted to buy me out. Not that I wanted out, but she might want all the fruits of her labor.

Last year she didn't want to buy me out. This year she did, so the board approved the deal at the agreed-upon price. I was happy about her success.

Chapter 45

After lunch was Jackson Transportation, as it was normally the longest review. It included the production of shipping containers, the Scottish Line, and Narrow Freight.

Once more they were asking for additional financing allowing them to grow even larger. I just thought last year's numbers were large.

Freight Forwarding was doing well after being spun off as a new and separate part of Jackson Enterprises. This was not to be confused with the company I set up independently, FreightEx.

The Scottish Line had added three more ocean-going freighters at forty-five million. Ship prices were still going up. It seems there was some inflation going on, that or the buy-one-get-one-free sale was over. I asked for a look to be taken at ship pricing over the next ten years. Maybe we should be ordering more before prices went up again.

The book value of the company was now well over two billion dollars. This year's profits had been estimated to be three hundred and seventy-five million dollars, but instead, they were four hundred and eighty million.

Putting it all together, I would make almost five hundred and fifty million dollars this year.

Jim Williamson gave the numbers his overseas accounting teams had recaptured for us. There was still no grand theft in under-reporting of royalties on the beer can pull tabs, but the nickels and dimes added up. The group more than paid for itself. We had wondered if we would need them all the time.

We agreed to continue the group permanently. For two years in a row, it had proven its worth. This continued attention to the small details would prevent large thefts.

There were new and brand-new items on the agenda.

The R&D department's breakthroughs on IC chips and their products continued to be a major topic. Licensing had started and we were mentoring several companies in their first production phase. We were encouraged with our choice of licensees as the quality and quantities were meeting expectations.

We thought we would have reduced profits because of our licensing the processes out. Maybe we had all our numbers out of skew because we were making millions more than we had originally estimated.

This money was going directly into the Space Division to support their equally large drain on our treasury.

My three-step improvement process based on what I had learned in the Gulag logging operations was going well.

I refreshed everyone on that process. The forests were not a monolithic growth. There would be one team out identifying large and useful tree lots, then a team would prepare the logging site by cutting brush and making roads. The third team would do the actual logging.

Dad once more thought that was a good idea and that maybe I should be sent back to a Gulag every year to learn new processes. I didn't think he was very funny.

The last item on the agenda of that session was how my idea of an airfreight line working from a hub concept was working. It really wasn't a business item of JE; it was my way of telling them they were all wrong. We had now expanded the operation out of California to everything west of the Mississippi and those customers wanted us to go nationwide.

When I first presented my budget for the operation, all the others were against it. I had taken what they said in stride. Rather than argue, I started a separate company without those naysayers. It wasn't as though I didn't have the money.

The only thing left was for the accountants to tell me if I would have anything left after the tax man took his share. Not only here in the US, but in all the countries we worked in.

Sam Wingate, our corporate attorney, had a tax accountant update me on my earnings and tax position.

I was still in the ninety-one percent marginal tax bracket and the only way I would ever get out of it was for the government to change the tax rates.

My five-million-dollar salary wasn't the real money. That was the company's profits. On those, I would owe over one hundred million dollars. Of course, I would keep three hundred and thirty million.

I once more made a mental note to think about spreading my money around a bit. The US stock market was great, but there were other markets around the world. I had bought a lot of land in Australia and that was proving to add to my too much money headaches. Fortunately, the Space Division was using it like there was no tomorrow.

When it was time to present the status of the Space Division, I was a little nervous. This was the first time that I had to let them know how much money we were burning through.

I decided to get the bad news out of the way first. I told them that I had spent or committed one billion dollars so far on the space program. It didn't surprise them as much as I thought it would.

Dad wanted to know if I was breaking even yet. I told him not yet, but that I was trying my best. For some reason, he didn't laugh at my joke.

I did tell them that the program was generating revenue through the satellites we had put in place. Not enough to support the program, but it helped.

The moon orbiter was about to be launched. I explained that it would house a permanent crew of ten. They would be in charge of missions up and down to the moon.

This was to be a continuing mission so we would never be in the position of leaving any crew on the surface of the moon. This was a risk that NASA was taking. We were in this for the long haul, not bragging rights.

Other than a general concern that I might be spending faster than it was coming in, they were fine with the project.

My next presentation was on my two stations in Australia. Jackson Station in Queensland was well underway and was the model of a standard Australian cattle operation. It would end up being the largest of its type, but there wasn't anything controversial about it.

The Lasseter Station in Western Australia was a different story. This was the first time I had revealed the name of the station. I told everyone it was in honor of the early explorer. After the gold find was announced, that is what everyone would call it anyway. The actual cattle ranch would work under the JE brand.

Everyone present knew about the water and the strong potential for oil. The wealth from this would make up for any shortfalls from the space program.

When I revealed the existence of the gold reef, it set off a hubbub of conversation. I let it run for a few minutes. The common question was how much gold?

I told them it looked like ten thousand metric tons a year. To put this in perspective, the world had been producing a little over two thousand metric tons a year.

Jim Williamson asked, "Won't this depress the price of gold?"

"If it were a pure commodity, it would; however, it is considered to be real money which backs up paper money. All the governments in the world buy gold. They only sell it when they are in financial difficulties. Gold is considered a haven even by governments. So, no, I don't think it will affect the price of gold.

"We can sell our share of the gold on the open world market. Right now, that is about four hundred dollars an ounce. We will sell in China and India where they allow private ownership, especially in the form of simple gold jewelry."

"What about the US market?"

"There is no legal US market. The government forbids anyone from owning gold, other than collectible coins and jewelry. They keep the price they will pay for gold at an artificial low, so few will mine for it in the US.

"I suspect gold operations in Alaska smuggle it to the Canadian Yukon for the better price."

"Is there any movement underway to legalize private ownership in the US?"

"Not that I know of, which is a shame. If people would be allowed to own gold, the price per ounce would go up and the government reserves would be worth more."

"Maybe you should make a pitch to President Kennedy about that."

"I think I will. I can make the point to him that I won't sell the gold to the US at their stupid low price when I can get ten times as much elsewhere. That might change his mind."

The last question was, "How many years until the gold plays out?"

"My mining people tell me it could be good for one hundred years."

Jim Williamson, who had been scribbling on his notepad furiously, told the group, "There are 32,150 troy ounces in a metric ton. At four hundred dollars an ounce, that is 12,860,000 dollars a metric ton."

I replied, "Though we could do ten thousand tons a year, we are going to limit it to two thousand tons a year. That is equal to the current annual production worldwide. I feel that 128 billion dollars a year would destroy the world's economy, so I'm mining for 25 billion and change!"

Jim must have been overwhelmed as he didn't even ask me for a raise.

"Folks, there are many a slip between the cup and the lip. Let's be careful with this information."

There were solemn nods all around the room. I had run these numbers in private, so I'd had several days to get used to them. I still didn't know what to make of this. The only thing I did know was while money meant little to me now, in the future, it would mean less.

Once the meetings were over, at the end of the day numbers were spinning in my head. It is a good thing I took a lot of notes and had copies of the PowerPoints. Everyone agreed that the PowerPoint software was easier to watch than overheads.

Chapter 46

After my corporate board meeting, Mum, Dad, and I had a serious conversation about what to do with The Meadows. With Grandmum gone, there was no reason to keep it as a residence.

We didn't want to sell it outright, as the land had the Roman find attached, and we wanted to keep that independent, especially from the English archaeologist mafia.

We also had the staff and Mr. Hamilton to consider. We finally decided to make it the headquarters for the dig. Not the actual camp site but a place for formal dinners and overnight guests.

Mr. Hamilton would be in charge of it with a lifetime position. In a fit of dryness, we decided to call it life tenure, a swat at the universities.

We would continue to fund the Elizabeth Newman Center, as we were formally naming it. We intended to ask the Queen Mum to be its patroness.

While I was home, we found out that Mary was a math prodigy at the genius level. She always had shown talents in that area, but not until Mum found her working differential equations for fun were we aware of her abilities.

That was when Mum also found out that for a fee she was doing Denny's geometry homework. That didn't end well for either of them.

Mary was given tests to find out her true knowledge levels. Not many kids get promoted from the fourth grade to being a junior at Stanford University. I can't wait to hear those stories. The place will never be the same.

After this fun and games, I headed back to Australia to keep things moving there. The flight was long, and I got a lot of reading done. I was trying to figure out what impact all that gold would have on the world.

It seems like what I had first thought would hold. Governments would absorb the gold to build up their reserves, so there would be no visible change. The paper currency would have strong backing, but we could depend on the politicians to take care of that.

I got another five hours in my logbook as PIC. I should take the qualification rides shortly. I made a definite plan to do that the next time I was in the US. Now that I was twenty, I would be allowed to qualify. I still didn't understand why they wouldn't let a sixteen-year-old fly a jet. They let them drive a car, and that was much more dangerous per mile traveled.

As far as I knew, there weren't any backroad drag strips for jets. Maybe I should check that out.

It was a cheap flight once more. This time I only lost seventeen dollars at the gin. I must be getting better; I know those sharks I flew with wouldn't take it easy.

Harold asked for some time. He wanted to show me the designs for formal uniforms for the astronaut corps. Some were pretty sharp. I wanted to avoid the all-black look that the Nazis used, even if it looked spiffy.

After that, the summer white uniforms of the US Navy looked the best. I recommended those. With the gold astronaut wings, they were glamorous looking. The women's versions had both slacks and skirts. I liked the slacks for some reason.

For winter wear, we stuck with the navy blue jackets. Again, they had the most professional look about them. We did consider the English and other armed forces' looks, but they were either too plain or too pompous. The English were plain which would work, but could you picture an astronaut dressed like a Halberdier of the Pontifical Swiss Guard?

On second thought, I asked Harold to send the Swiss Guard uniform as one of those under consideration. It would be fun to hear what the ladies would say. Harold was eager to do so, more than I thought he would be.

That was worth a few laughs on a long and boring flight. Once in Sydney, I spent several days at Jackson House. My secretary there had things for me.

There was a long list of phone calls that should be returned. He had listed the topic of the call on each one. I was able to either return them or give him an answer to relay back. It was amazing how many phone calls he was able to take care of.

Most of those were social invitations. I had him turn down all invitations to private events. I didn't have time, and I didn't want to be involved in all the social games.

I had avoided them with the upper crust of England and didn't want to get involved in Australia. I didn't want to be a big fish in a small pond. Maybe that was why I didn't want any part of it.

Jeeves came to me in the afternoon with a note on a silver platter in hand. Rather than tell him how silly it looked, I used the letter opener that he had on the platter and opened it.

This was an invitation I should accept. It was the formal opening of the new library section at the University of Sydney. It was the home of the books which Talmadge had left behind. Even though most of them had never had the pages cut, they were a treasure trove.

Harold recommended a conservative suit and tie for the event. Jeeves concurred, so that settled that. It seemed I would never be allowed to pick my clothes again.

That is unless I was out in the field; then I would wear what I damn well pleased.

The event at the library required me to stay an extra day in Sydney, but it proved to be worth it. I was able to make several extra stops. The first was to the engineering offices that were working on Jackson Station.

"Your Grace, we are pleased that you could stop by."

"Please, for the sake of expediency call me Richard, which splits the formality hairs between Ricky and Your Grace."

"Very well, Richard, but in public it will be, 'Your Grace'. It is for our prestige in working for a duke."

"Okay, I can see that.

"Now, down to business, how are things progressing?"

"For all practical purposes, the station is up and running. Its function is to be a cattle ranch. It is doing that right now."

"What about the things that make life bearable for the people on the station?"

"The school was certified this past week by the Queensland educational authority. They were quite impressed with both the faculty and the facility. The curriculum is the standard Australian curriculum, so there were no problems there."

"Did they set up those new computers we sent to the school?"

"Yes, they did. We have already had inquiries from the state education authority about obtaining them for all the schools in Queensland."

"I will look into it."

My immediate thought was that this was a big win. We could afford to give them to the schools because it wouldn't take long for the new users to want to have one at home. We would be growing our market. If it worked in Australia, we would have to consider the rest of the world.

Maybe even set up computer cafes in college and university towns, where students could write and print their papers out. It would be faster and cheaper than a typewriter. It would be fun to see what the local entrepreneurs would do with it.

"It sounds like things are moving along."

"Then there are the longer-term projects underway like the slaughterhouse and beef packing plant. The railroad and the highways are slower, but they will be in place by the end of next year as forecast."

My next stop was to see the prime minister, at his office's request.

I still wasn't happy with the Australian politicians trying to nationalize my find, but business was business, so I let it go.

"Thank you for coming to see me, Your Grace."

I let the "Your Grace" stand; I wasn't that forgiving.

"My pleasure."

Said without gagging, I may add.

"I understand that you are considering a pipeline to a major port if significant oil is struck."

"That is correct."

Make him work for it.

"What ports are you considering?"

"There are several that would serve the purpose. No decision has been made."

"Would you be open to suggestions?"

Now, was I going to continue the feud or try to make peace?

"Rather than go back and forth on this, why don't you have one of your departments conduct a study and give recommendations? I'm willing to go along with what they recommend."

It was Christmas and Boxing Day rolled into one for him. Political plums everywhere.

"That is extremely thoughtful of you, Your Grace. I'm glad to see that you recognize that the Australian government can see what is best for the Australian people."

"As long as the government keeps their hand out of my pocket, it is up to the people to decide how much they will let the government take out of their pockets."

He looked like he was sucking on a lemon! What fun.

Chapter 47

The prime minister knew to quit while he was ahead. He had control of where the pipeline would go and its political patronage.

I made it clear the pipeline would be built by a company other than JE. We would be a major investor to get it started, but shares would be offered to the public.

Once more you could see the pound signs in his eyes, as he could tip off his friends and donors about a major investment that would give returns.

For me, it would have the government on my side removing obstacles generated by regulatory requirements. I also planned to sell off my shares over time to recoup my investment. Let the Aussies have the headaches of an ongoing project.

With that, I moved on to my next appointment, a suit fitting for the library dedication. Harold and I were resisting the move to what was called the Mod look, or Modern look. Neither was I going to let my hair grow long, even though it was driving my hairdryer sales up.

The library dedication was a quiet affair. All the highbrows were present. I wouldn't have looked out of place in a more modern cut suit, but I was happy with my business-like look.

The wide ties they were now wearing were almost a joke. We had gone from one-inch-wide ties like Frank Sinatra wore to four-inch ties similar to the Beatles'. Ringo had a lot to answer for. Wait till I see him next.

Most of the people were pleasant, and we exchanged a few polite remarks. One guy seemed to have it in for me.

"Your Grace, by any chance have you read any of these books?"

"Only those with pictures."

This brought a few laughs from those standing near us.

"As one would expect."

"Have you read the one you are holding?"

"Of course, I have."

"Strange, I notice the pages haven't even been cut."

"I mean that I have read another copy."

"I'm sorry that you can't explain yourself clearly."

I had been to several of these types of events at Oxford and had learned not to take any hostages. One could say anything as long as you were polite and oblique about it. If you could cause the other person to ask what you meant, it was a clear win.

"I thought I explained myself very clearly."

"I don't think so as I had to ask what you were trying to say."

"Maybe you are slow on the uptake."

Now I had him. He was on his way to using invective.

"You are probably right; I'm not used to people who can't express themselves in a clear and mannered fashion."

"I'll give you clear and mannered!"

"You may start at any time."

Now he was starting to lose his temper. I couldn't let it go that far or I would look bad. I took a step closer to him, putting myself inside his personal space. It also had me looking down from my six foot five inches to his five foot four inches or so.

"I think you are trying to bully me!"

"Heaven forbid. Why would I do that? I think the shoe is on the other foot. You approached me asking if I had read a book. Your tone was one such as I couldn't read."

I leaned close to him and whispered, "Give it a rest."

He looked at me and the people listening avidly to the exchange and realized that this wasn't going like he thought it would.

"I'm sorry you misconstrued my statements, Your Grace. I will leave now."

He walked towards the door. One of the doormen, read guards, relieved him of the book he was walking out with.

"Who was that person?" I asked.

"He's one of the Twickenham crowds. They think he was the greatest who ever lived and hate anyone who doesn't agree with them. Your reputation from Oxford precedes you."

The speaker, a very interesting young lady, caught my attention. She was an attractive brunet with pronounced features, two of them.

I needlessly introduced myself. Lady Anne Hobson did the same. I offered to fetch her a glass of the champagne being offered. She accepted and accompanied me as I made my rounds talking to those present and accepting their lauds for the donation.

As the evening wound down, I asked her if she wanted to continue. She did. We went to a dance club until the early hours. When I escorted her to her door, she asked me, "In or out?"

Truly a Hobson's choice.

The next morning after my walk of shame, I left for Lasseter Station.

My taxi driver was waiting for me at the Lasseter airfield. It was still a dirt strip, but the land next to it was being graded to build a permanent runway.

I told him he was just the man I wanted to see.

"Why's that, Boss?"

"We need to start a heavy equipment operators' school for the blackfellas."

"You're going to announce the Reef soon then?"

"Soon, but I need a few things in place first. The rough road has been laid out. Now we have to pave it to match the rest of the roadwork we have on the station. Then we need to fence the area in and start patrols."

"That will take some time."

"Less than you may think. We will use equipment to drive the fence posts and tractors to tension the fence. This won't be the normal fencing operation. I want to have a ten-mile by twenty-mile area fenced around the Reef."

"The materials are on order and will be delivered next week. By Christmas, I want things ready to go, which means fences up and roads in. We will also need to start on permanent structures at the mine site.

"I know this is going to take a lot of work and a lot of people. Pass the word we will pay top wages for the effort. The best workers will be kept on for the long term. As I promised the elders, I will over-hire so traditions can be kept. There will be schools and medical help on site."

"Who is going to do that for you, Boss?"

"You are."

"But I can't do all that myself."

"The mining company will be here shortly to stake things out. It has been arranged for them to help you get set up."

"Taxi drivers don't make much money."

"Will fifty thousand pounds a year help?"

"Just call me the big note man!"

"It will take time. Start by getting the word out that we are hiring. The mining company will be bringing in all the equipment and showing how it is used, but it will be hard work.

"When they start showing up, keep good records of who is working. We will pay cash every week even during training."

"Boss, that may not be a good idea. All the men will get drunk."

"That is why we will ask them to bring their wife to get paid."

"You are a mean boss!"

"Whatever it takes to get the job done."

After talking to Tony and getting him comfortable with his new job, I went to the water exploration crew. I guess the exploring part was done. Now they were in the process of drilling wells and capping them.

We discussed how the water would be distributed around the station. They were puzzled as to why I wanted water piped over to a spot on the map. I didn't explain why that spot. It was to be the retention pond for the mine. I called it a stock pond, and they accepted that.

If a true stockman had been around, he would have questioned why I wanted water in a place that never could support livestock of any sort, including camels.

Having set that in motion, my next and last stop of the day was the oil exploration group. They were close to the trap where they thought they would strike oil. They had to go through a layer of sandstone, then shale. They had identified where the trap would lay above the reservoir layer, so they thought they had a good chance. The field seemed to be a large one.

It was encouraging, but until we knew, it wasn't worth getting excited about. I don't think they understood how I could be so blasé about the whole thing. They didn't know what I knew. The oil was almost an afterthought.

After the crown's share and taxes, I was still looking at over fourteen billion US dollars a year. How would I spend it?

After my last meeting, I flew back to Sydney on the DC3 on its last supply flight of the night. I had to hurry if I was going to make it in time to clean up and get ready for my dinner date. I would hate to miss my choice.

Chapter 48

The next morning, I said goodbye to Lady Anne, who was on her way back to England. We made no concrete plans to see each other again. Beyond the physical attraction, we didn't have much in common.

She envisioned a quiet life with a house and attached garden, two children, and a dog to take walkies. My life never would approach that, well, maybe the children and the dog.

Another cheerful goodbye hug and we moved on with our lives.

I flew back to Lasseter Station on the morning run of the DC3 to the main airfield. The place was a beehive of activity when we landed. Tony was waiting for me as I had radioed ahead.

He drove me over to the goldfield. On the way, he updated me on the last two days of activity. He had spread the word that work was available for any Aborigine who wanted it. Cash on the barrel head.

Sheila Armstrong was now onsite and with her help, he now knew what he had to do. She had brought in a convoy of fencing and mining equipment, along with materials like fence posts and fencing.

She had a surveying team out marking the fence line. There were already men putting in the first fence posts and stretching the fencing. As he told me what was all going on, I realized how poor of a job I had done in preparing him for what needed to be done.

"Tony, I'm sorry I gave you such poor initial instructions and support to get started."

"No worries, Boss. That's why you hired Mizz Armstrong and her people. They know what to do."

"Is she easy to work with?"

"She is one fine Sheila."

I had to think that one through. Did Tony just make a joke?

"That she is."

"I might ask her to be my second wife."

"I wouldn't do that Tony; that's not how whitefellas do it. One man, one woman at a time."

"I know that, but how do you show your status?"

"By what you do, and I guess by the material goods you have accumulated. We have a saying, 'He who dies with the most toys, wins.' It is meant to be a joke but has a grain of truth."

"Do you have many toys?"

"I have money. I can buy any toy I want."

"So, you are high status among your people?"

"From that point of view, I have the highest status of all people."

"Good. Your status means I have high status. Now I won't have to take a second wife. One mother-in-law is one too many."

I had never considered the downside of polygamy. Having multiple wives to keep happy would be hard, and multiple mothers-in-laws a nightmare.

That was an educational drive to the goldfield.

When we got to the goldfield, Sheila Armstrong had a command tent set up and crews busy all over the place.

You could tell she was in her element. In the tent was a large table with a detailed map of the area laid out. On it were flat paper cutouts with drawings of what was to go there.

She called them templates. They could be moved around if it was found something wouldn't fit when the land was walked.

She had moved the airport runway three times this morning as the surveyors told her of problems encountered. Now they had a four-thousand-foot strip staked out and bulldozers were already leveling the area.

The trommel, wash plant, and associated equipment were being hauled into place.

"Sheila, I'm impressed; you are further along than I ever envisioned."

"You don't make money sitting around. By the way, we have a security station set up, and they are holding the reporters and the curious back by the main station road. They saw my convoy come through and know something is up."

"I knew that we couldn't keep the lid on this for long. I was hoping to be further along with security such as the fencing, but I guess I will have to announce the find."

"You know you have a new name up here?"

"I'm afraid to ask."

"We have blackfellas, whitefellas, and now goldfella working here."

I groaned. That sounded like a villain in a bad James Bond movie.

I decided to get it over with. I had Tony drive me out to the main road where a group of ten guards was blocking access. They had chosen a cut through a dune, which made it easy to control.

There was a small crowd trying to get in. There must have been five reporters and ten busybodies waiting.

Rather than be mobbed, I stood on the hood of one of the blocking vehicles.

"May I have your attention?"

Not certain why I asked, everyone was looking at the idiot standing on the hot hood of a car in the Australian Outback.

"I'm Richard Jackson. I can see you are curious about what is going on back here. I would like to announce that I have found and am starting to work Lasseter's Reef."

That set the cat amongst the pigeons. Questions were being shouted left and right.

"If you have press credentials, I will give a short tour of the area. Those of you who are just curious can follow us in, and you will be allowed to drive around the main road and back, so you can say you have been here. This is the last time the general public will have access."

It was allowing this or having my name blackened from the start. There was no doubt it would go downhill from here, but I might as well start on a high note.

Tony and I led the parade the ten miles back to the worksite. He let me off at the headquarters tent and led the curious ones on a driving tour. I instructed him to allow them to collect a piece of quartz from the Reef, so they would have something to show for their efforts.

I took the reporters in and showed them the map of what was being done. Sheila had done us proud, as she had Cokes on ice for everyone. We sat in a semicircle on folding chairs while I gave the story.

I started with my flight to Uluru and my accidental find. This led to a bunch of questions, as it came out that I had bought the land and mineral rights before I suspected water and oil.

One of them commented that I had pulled a horseshoe out of my behind. I didn't disagree. The next questions centered around my fight to avoid nationalization by the Australian government.

My giving a portion of the company to the queen of England and the empress of China suddenly made sense.

There had to be a socialist in the group.

"Do you think it is fair that you are taking Australian resources from the hard-working Australian man?"

"I'm following all the rules that your Australian government has set up. Even they have conceded that what I'm doing is fair and legal under Australian law. Even the original hardworking Australian Aboriginals agree with what is going on."

I'm not going to repeat what was said next. The reporter who was so concerned about fairness revealed himself as the racist that he was. The other reporters couldn't distance themselves from him fast enough.

That worked out fortunately for me, as their stories would prevent me from being unfair. I emphasized that the government would get a share of the gold right off the top and that I would then have to pay taxes on my share.

I didn't go into the projected amounts, as that would have put unfairness right back on the table.

After the show and tell in the tent, we went out to the Reef. Today it was buried in several feet of sand. Sheila had a bulldozer brought over and a swath cleared.

The quartz sparkled in the sun. Mr. Lasseter had to either be smiling or cursing in his grave. I know his descendants would feel that he had been vindicated. I made a mental note to invite them out for a tour, and maybe have some sort of monument erected at the entrance.

I decided that I should be out of Australia when the news hit, so I arranged a flight out as soon as the reporters were finished. We had no phone lines and didn't offer the use of our radios, so they had to go back to the main camp to call in the story. That would give me a head start on getting out of the country.

I hadn't been to China in a while to check up on my businesses there. Things like the bank in Guangzhou didn't make the JE business meeting. I had to figure out why that hadn't happened. I hoped it was only a communication issue rather than fraud or theft. In China, it could be anything.

Chapter 49

I flew back to China that evening. My assistant at Jackson House had called ahead and made all the arrangements. This was helpful, and I wondered if I should have a traveling secretary with me all the time.

That or one at each of the Jackson Houses. Or even one with me to coordinate with one at each residence. I was starting to get comfortable with the idea that money in itself has little meaning to me. The one thing that limited me was time.

I should be working on high-level decisions on all my programs rather than lining up limos and airplane schedules. Even whenever I had some time available, it would be better used for studies or downtime.

If nothing else, my time with Lady Anne taught me that it was nice to take a day off just for me.

The arrangements in Beijing went like clockwork. No Chinese fighters threatened us. Transportation was waiting at the airport and my rooms at the Forbidden City were ready for me.

I even had an appointment set with the empress the next morning.

She was happy to see me from the reception that I was given. Thinking about five percent of twenty-five billion would make most people smile. That didn't count any oil revenue or profits from the station when it was up and running.

"Richard, I'm so glad to see you! These are exciting times, which are much better than interesting times."

"Yes, they are. The space program is now assured."

"You are correct but that isn't the most exciting thing for China."

"What is?"

"Our population pressure is about to be relieved. Even though it is winter in Siberia, a great migration is being assembled. Villages, towns, and cities with too many people are sending settlement groups in the spring.

"I have declared that each group shall be self-contained with all the elements they need to be successful. There will be farmers, teachers, medical staff, and members of every occupation required for success in each group."

"Every group will have these?"

"Each group will have representatives of those occupations. Depending on the size of the group, one person may fill several functions. For example, not every small village needs a librarian, so we might have an elementary teacher with librarian knowledge wearing two hats.

"The critical occupations like tractor repairmen and blacksmiths will be in each group."

"That reminds me of a city I learned about in my Ohio history class. The town of Leipsic, Ohio was founded to relieve pressure in Wurttemberg in what is now Germany.

"All of the farms in the area had been subdivided many times to support multiple children. It finally got to the point that any new subdivisions wouldn't support a family.

"A local priest found himself in the same predicament. The parish had more priests than needed. Rather than be shipped to Africa or some other wild place, he organized a mass migration to America. This was in the 1840s.

"Instead of subdividing the farms, the head of each family was convinced to contribute to the purchase of land in Ohio for their youngest family members.

"They also were careful to select a representative of each occupation needed in a new settlement. So, they were able to found the town of Leipsic with surrounding farms with few problems. By the time of the American Civil War, they had factories in place to support the war effort.

"The town was so self-sufficient that local schools didn't teach in English until the 1920s. That was at the insistence of the Ohio Board of Education."

The empress broke in with, "That is exactly what we are hoping for here, but language won't be a problem. We were on the verge of having to limit the number of children in a family. Now we are safe for at least another fifty years."

"If the Chinese economy continues to grow, the birthrate will drop as people realize they don't need children to support them in their old age."

She said, "Yes, but our demographers are predicting that will cause trouble in Europe and the US. Their birth rates are heading down below the replacement rate. To support their economies, they will have to bring other groups in."

Continuing, she added, "Depending on which groups they are, the culture and work ethic may be lost, which will doom the countries to a lower standard of living. I'm determined not to have that happen in China."

She was passionate in saying, "The Middle Kingdom will once again be the center of the world because of the lack of foresight of the current world powers."

I made a mental note to speak to President Kennedy and Queen Elizabeth about this. I loved all the countries involved and didn't want any of them to fall by the wayside.

The empress and I discussed the current state of the space program. We were nearly ready to launch a permanent station to orbit the moon. This station would be the base station for the exploration and development of the moon.

We had lunch together. After lunch, I went to my Chinese business headquarters to check up on my Chinese investments. This included an update on the Bank of Guangzhou.

I could have gone directly to the bank itself but thought it was wiser to find out what was going on before I arrived. If things were bad, I didn't want to end up as a hostage.

My office was expecting me. As normal, the Chinese tended to overdo it. The entire office staff was lined up in the lobby of the building and bowed to me as I entered.

I was getting used to being an important person, but this went way beyond what I expected or wanted.

I stopped and returned the group bow, then yelled, "Now take a tea or coffee break on me; then back to work!"

The older staff stood confused; the younger ones acted as though they had been given an extra recess at school. I bet that is the last time they will line up like this, well, unless the kids get their way.

I was escorted to the board room. They had a presentation packet ready for me. I leafed through it and didn't find one reference to the Bank of Guangzhou.

I held up my hand. We will get to this presentation after I learn the state of the Bank of Guangzhou.

There was an embarrassed silence. The chairman finally broke it. "I thought you knew. There is no longer a Bank of Guangzhou."

"What!"

"We changed the name to the Noble House, as it has become the largest trading company in China. The bank is now represented in every province of the country."

"Why haven't I received any financial reports?"

"When you founded the bank, you made it clear that all the profits were to be spent back into the Chinese economy to improve the infrastructure."

"So I did. I didn't realize it would go this far. How large is the company now?"

"The value of Noble House in American dollars is over two billion and growing. To keep investing in the infrastructure, we are now investing in a hydroelectric dam on the Yangtze River at Three Gorges. It will generate electricity and control flooding. Every decade we lose millions of lives along the river, so this will be a blessing."

"This is embarrassing that I didn't know this, but I bet if I had read all of the reports you have sent, I would know this."

He didn't say anything, he just gave me a slight bow.

"Please continue this process. If it gets hard to invest money in China, I would take a look at Africa. There must be a lot of raw materials there, which exploited, would help those countries out."

"We will investigate opportunities."

I got out of there as quickly and politely as I could. Talk about not knowing what was going on. It was completely unacceptable. I was not only embarrassed, but I was also furious with myself for allowing this to happen.

I stayed in my rooms at the Forbidden palace that night, without any company. I gave a lot of thought about what I had going on in the world. It was too much for one person to control. I had to break things up.

I kept running into this and every time I thought I had it under control, things would grow, and I would be out of control once more. Maybe it was time to split off some of the Jackson Enterprise Divisions, settle for the income, and let control go. Heck, I had already let control go.

The next day when the time zones were right, I placed a call to my parents. They had always been my best counselors.

When I explained my nasty or wonderful discovery about the Bank of Guangzhou, they were understanding. It seems they had already figured out that events were outpacing me, and I had to let something go. The question was what?

Chapter 50

Now that I knew what happened to my bank and somehow gained a new title, Taipan, I was off to the space center to see what I really cared about.

A lot of what I had done was fun, like the movies; some not so fun, like singing; others, just because. They were now all stepping stones for outer space.

I was going to establish mankind in this solar system. Einstein had condemned us from the stars. I would take us as far as we could go, then look for a new key to the future.

The launch center was a beehive of activity. They were now up to a launch a day. Every day a new prediction of our coming disaster was made by NASA. What they didn't seem to understand was that we had taken it from experimental prototypes to a mature manufactured product.

All it took was time and money, lots of money. I had to get the gold mine producing soon or I would run out. That in itself was mindboggling.

When I arrived, I was met by the entire launch center management. They had a briefing prepared for me. Normally I would have been impatient about this, but something important seemed to be up, so I held my comments.

"Your Grace, we know how you hate long meetings and useless announcements so I will, as the Americans say, cut to the chase. We are ready to launch the moon orbiter."

Whoo-hoo!

Now I wanted all the details. This was the best briefing that I could have had. The only better would be when they told me they were landing on the moon and that I was welcome to come along.

Maybe I was dreaming of the last, but this was real progress.

"When is the orbiter leaving Earth orbit to head to the moon?"

"As soon as you give the order."

"Let's do it now."

Of course, it wasn't that simple. It would take two days to set everything up. Maybe if I had told them I was coming in advance, they could have made it happen, but this was still great.

The orbiter was loaded with supplies and the ten crew members were in place. All Space Ladies, I might add.

The rockets which would launch them were now being attached to the orbiter's frame. Two escape vehicles, each of which could carry all ten astronauts, were in place.

The last was very important to me. There was no way this was going to be a death or glory flight like NASA was planning.

One thing that was conspicuous in not being present was a moon lander. That would be later after we had the orbiter in a lunar orbit. Then we would ship two landers to the orbiter. Again, there were two for redundancy.

We hadn't announced our flight program, but these things always get out. Some people had made fun of us for having two of everything. When asked, I reminded them that Chris Columbus had three ships.

Most of the delay was in coordinating news coverage. Three media people were invited to witness the launch, one each from China, the UK, and the US.

China and the UK were easy. They had state-owned broadcasting, so it was easy to decide who went. The US was a different story. All three networks wanted a representative on board.

I was sorry that the Dumont network had folded, as I loved Captain Video and His Video Rangers. I had desperately wanted to win the spaceship that was in their contest, but it wasn't to be.

In a box somewhere, probably the back of my closet at Jackson House California, was my flying saucer ring, a "secret seal" ring, electronic goggles, a secret ray gun, a rocket ship key chain, my decoder, and my membership card, along with a set of 12 plastic spacemen.

That show, along with Tom Corbett, Space Cadet, had started my journey to the stars.

I'm still aggravated with Einstein. I even wrote him a letter asking him to revisit his theories, but he never replied. I was eleven or so at the time.

I came up with a simple solution for the US network problem. We needed money for the program. They had money, so we auctioned off the seat. CBS won and sent their new anchorman Walter Cronkite.

It took them three days to show up with all their equipment. Somehow each of the networks thought they could bring a crew of up to ten people with them. Why you would need a makeup person in space I never would understand.

Once they realized that we would be providing the equipment and technicians, we got it sorted out. I only had to call Empress Ping to have her tell Chinese Broadcasting they were limited to the reporter. The rest got the message after that.

I don't think the makeup girl was that thrilled about going anyway.

Once they were safely in orbit, we were ready to send the orbiter to the moon. It wasn't a spectacular launch like those from the ground. The boosters fired, and the orbiter moved away as stately as a Spanish galleon. That meant slow and cumbersome. It reminded me of my grandmum and her friends when they were out for a walk. Slow and steady but majestic in their progress.

The trip would take two weeks. They would be under boost for two days, coast for ten days, and then have the reverse boosters fire for two days to bring them into orbit around the moon.

The reporters all told me that it was anticlimactic, but they made up drama for the launch. Listening to them, the orbiter had blasted off to the moon in a fiery spectacle.

Jerri Cobb had been interviewed before boarding the launcher. She told me as she boarded that she might never come back after those interviews.

I went up to orbit to see the launch. There was no way I would miss this important moment. If I could have gone with them I would, but I was told in no uncertain terms that wasn't going to happen. My mum was the one elected to tell me. These guys don't play fair.

The reporters were given a complete tour of the space station in orbit around the Earth. They were even given chocolate chip space cookies prepared in orbit.

I had to ask how they did the dishes in orbit. The answer was they didn't. The dirty dishes were sent back down to earth to be washed and returned. This was similar to laundry being shipped from California to Hawaii and then returned in the gold rush days, so it was not a big surprise, but still.

The TV pictures broadcast from space demonstrated our private enterprise program was far ahead of the US government space program. So far, they had people circle the earth.

We had people staying up for days at a time. Now we were on our way to the moon. Their schedule was to do that in another six years if all went well.

You would have thought that Congress would have defunded the program, but they didn't. I attributed that to all the pork that was floating around and the hidden hand of the US Military in the background.

I'm certain the military wanted the high ground.

It made me toy with the idea of creating a space cadet program with armed ships but realized that would cause no end of problems. I wasn't ready to start a world war.

For my second trip to orbit, a tiny Roman numeral two was etched on my astronaut wings. I thought I was hot stuff until I saw that Jerri Cobb was up to twenty-seven.

It wouldn't take long, and the Roman numerals would overtake the wings. Something had to be done. Me, a micromanager? Never!

I was interviewed by all of the broadcasters who went up. They each were wearing their new wings. They were given crew wings, rather than tourists' ones. In the future, I would see those wings mounted on a plaque behind every one of them when they were in the air. It ain't bragging if you have done it.

There was one secret on the flight that never made it out. The guy from the BBC couldn't handle weightlessness and threw up all over the place.

I helped clean up the mess and decided that certain foods would be taken off the preflight menu. Better yet, send them up hungry.

For the cleanup, we had these nifty handheld vacuum cleaners that had been invented for this very purpose. They had a battery with a small charge so they could be easily used anywhere. I sent one to our R&D group to see if there would be a market for them.

If there was, we would have to be certain that the inventor or inventors received credit for the invention and participated in the financial rewards.

Another day in the life of Richard Jackson, Space Cadet.

Chapter 51

It was now time to head back to the US. This was Thursday, and Christmas was next Wednesday. I had decided what to buy my family months ago. So, all I had to do was make certain everything was ready.

Nothing radical happened on the flight. I even won five bucks at gin rummy. I figured I was now only out about four hundred dollars. I might get ahead if I played for another ten years or so.

I had over a thousand hours in the 707 so I made an early New Year's Resolution to pass the certification tests. The flight crew had finally broken down and let me practice pulling out of stalls and spins. This was without anyone but the pilot and co-pilot on board.

It was nice to be back at Jackson House. Mum and Dad had it decorated to a fare thee well, Dad the outside and Mum the inside. They had hired professional decorators to put up all the big stuff, but you could see their influence.

Dad had a huge Star of Bethlehem set on top of the tower. It could be seen across most of LA. It had even made the news. Aircraft were using it as a landmark.

Mum had the whole house decorated. The ballroom had a Christmas tree in each corner. The tables were set with dinnerware in a Christmas pattern. There were poppers at every place setting. This did tell me there would be at least one large event. In the spirit of the season, I would escort cheerfully whomever I was assigned.

It seemed every room had a tree decorated. All but one. The library had a tree set up with no decorations. Christmas Eve, the family decorated it with all our ornaments which we had collected over the years. It was our family tree.

My brothers, sister, and I made paper chains for the room and strung popcorn on strings. The angel we had used for as long as I could remember was the topper. This was Christmas as it should be, a family event.

This year I decided to go all out for the family. We had always bought each other small gifts, but this year I went big.

On Christmas morning we sat around in house robes and slippers, drinking hot chocolate and coffee while we opened our presents one by one.

Mary's gift from me was a computer. The box she unwrapped was the size of a shoebox. It didn't contain a computer. It contained a description of the computer I had built for her.

The R&D branch had come up with the ability to run computer chips in parallel. I had them build a computer that had one hundred chips running in parallel. This machine would solve a math problem one hundred times faster than the standard computer we were building with one chip.

The only problem with it was the heat generated. The computer had to be run in a room that approached freezer temperatures, not refrigerators but a freezer.

This took a large supporting infrastructure with lots of electricity available. It took them three months to build it at Stanford, but it was ready in time for Christmas.

Mary about six months ago was found to be bored in all of her classes in the fourth grade. That was why she was always in trouble. Testing showed that she was advanced in all subjects except math. There she was genius level.

That probably explained why I never could out-negotiate her.

At the same time, the computer was being put together, the software people were writing software that worked in areas such as field theory, quantum mechanics, quantum field theory, gravity, supergravity, and general relativity.

I have no idea whatsoever what those areas are about, but Mary had talked about all of those at the last tea party we had.

The software recognized tensors, spinors, and lie groups, in a symbolic view, meaning that it has special commands, and special data types to work with.

Again, no idea.

It was made plain to the people at Stanford the computer was Mary's to use as she wanted when she wanted. If she wanted to share her computer time, it was up to her.

I had bought land next to the university and had the building erected. The staff is employed by the Mary Jackson Institute. There is no way the professors in the math department can take it over. Oxford had taught me some lessons.

The building also had a nice office filled with whiteboards for her to work with. I don't know if she will ever have any scientific breakthroughs, but it wouldn't be from a lack of support.

I had convinced Denny some months ago to take a screen test at Warner Brothers to see if he could do a bit part in a movie. There was no bit part. I wanted to know if he could reasonably appear in a movie.

His screen test came across better than my original one. Denny was now eighteen years old and despite himself, had never got in any major trouble. It wasn't from the lack of trying, especially with the girls.

His present was a major role in a beach movie, *Where the Girls Are*. I was bankrolling it as a B movie. If it broke even, I would be happy. Beach movies are the thing right now, so I thought it would end up profitable.

He would be the surfer boy who lived near the beach, earning a living as an auto-mechanic. He would run into a pretty girl whose boyfriend is a snobbish college boy.

You can figure out where the plot goes from there. Oh yeah, the girl's dad owns a top-ranked Indy racing team that needs a good mechanic, and they all lived happily ever after.

The Beach Boys had agreed to make an appearance in one of the dance scenes, so we touched all the bases. I refused to sing "Rock and Roll Cowboy".

Eddie, who had just turned sixteen, was the hardest and easiest to buy for. He had completed his Eagle just before he turned sixteen, got his driver's license, and discovered girls.

Mum and Dad had bought him a Corvette for Christmas. As my present, I paid for a high-performance driving school course. He could use his new Corvette at this Nevada school. It was set up for him to go there between Christmas and New Year's. My parents thought it was a good idea, as Eddie seemed to have a need for speed.

My brothers and sister were surprised and extremely pleased with their gifts. I had gotten an ugly Christmas sweater, a Tom Corbett Space Cadet t-shirt, and a stuffed hoop snake that could be rolled like a hoop.

I loved them all.

My gift to my parents was something that they had been putting off for years. They had ordered a 707 some years ago but kept selling their place in the production lineup. They had become a standing joke at Boeing.

They had sold their place in line so many times, they had paid for the plane twice over.

I had got with the Boeing people, and unbeknownst to my parents, bought their place in line when it was about to come up. I left my jet with Boeing for them to copy the interior. While mine could be altered by moving compartments in and out, theirs was a permanent build.

It ended up looking nicer than mine. The Boeing people pointed out that the interior of my plane was showing its wear and tear and maybe I should think about a rebuild or even a new aircraft.

I talked it over with my flight crew, and they all advised me to buy a new aircraft. My current one had a lot of hours on the airframe and the engines would need replacement soon, so it wouldn't be that much more to buy a new one and have everything built-in.

I think they just wanted a new toy. I signed with Boeing for a new jet. I had to pay through the nose to get a better place in the production lineup.

My parent's jet would be done up in the Jackson colors with Mum's coat of arms. Mine would be the same except for my insignia.

What worked out neatly was the fact that Mum and Dad had bought me a six-passenger helicopter and had a landing pad installed at the house. On Christmas day, I was able to fly them to Ontario Airport to see their new jet being flown in.

My parents both hugged me tightly. It was a wonderful Christmas.

There was one last Christmas present for me. I got a call from Australia. They had struck oil, a gusher. They estimated it would be one of the largest finds of the century.

The goldfield had been opened up and the first cleanout of the wash plant was performed. There was gold there. Even more than predicted.

After what I had spent on Christmas, I needed that.

Chapter 52

On Boxing Day, we gave out our annual presents to our direct staff and those who provided service, such as the sheriff's department.

Dad always delivered hams for every person who worked at our sheriff's substation. The trashmen had a couple of gift-wrapped bottles of scotch left on top of the bins.

The mailman got an unstamped envelope of cash. It had never been returned because of no postage.

My parents probably took care of several dozen other service providers that I didn't know about.

I had Jeeves contact Mum to see what I should be doing in Australia and Hong Kong. He would take care of that for me. I made it a standing order for all future years.

The internal staff was all awarded a cash bonus. Not that we were trying to encourage tax evasion or anything.

The bonuses depended on position and length of service. Our cook at Jackson House was the first hire, and she received one thousand dollars.

Mr. Hamilton in England was sent a pair of solid gold cuff links. The design was a golden knot. The knot was on both sides of the link, not the type with a flat on one side.

I had wracked my brain about gifts for the queen and the empress. I had gifted them a fortune in partial ownership of Lasseter. I finally settled on a handmade season greetings card. It gets to a point that you can't go any further.

I sent Mr. Norman a greyhound pin with a diamond in its eye.

Boris and Natasha received ten cases of vodka. It just seemed appropriate.

The hardest to buy for was May-ling. What do you buy for a girl who you would love to woo but who had indicated that it wasn't to be? I chickened out and sent her a handmade card.

The Saturday after Christmas, Mum had a charity ball. As I guessed, she requested me, not ordered, to act as an escort at need.

It was a white tie affair, so I had the proper tuxedo to wear. Harold insisted that I wear my miniature medals. Who am I to gainsay my valet?

This included a sash with my knighthood orders. If nothing else, I would stand out.

At first, it looked like I would get off scot-free. At the very end, a lady and her daughter were announced. Yes, Mum had people announced. It gave her charity balls a higher tone than any others in the area.

As people were admitted and their invitations checked, they had to fill out a card as to how they would like to be announced. It was to be Judge So-and-so or Doctor Who. Things like that or even a simple Mr. and Mrs.; nothing frivolous if you please.

They would hand the card to the announcer at the top of the stairs. The acoustics were such that his voice carried. The announcer was a bit actor with a wonderful baritone voice who was hired for the occasion.

The couple then would descend the stairs to the ballroom. Mum, Dad, Denny, and I formed a short receiving line.

When the mother and what I presumed was the daughter were announced, you could see Denny start to quiver. He had eyes on the daughter. Denny had several incidents where irate fathers forbade him to see their daughters again.

There were no children involved, but I think that was more luck than planning.

Mum took charge and told the lady that Denny would be her escort to dinner and that I would escort the daughter. I must say Denny took his defeat gracefully.

That told me he had been in deep trouble recently and was on his best behavior. I hoped he would grow up soon before he messed up his life.

Eddie and Mary weren't attending the dinner. I don't know where Eddie was, probably playing that new game Dragons and Dungeons with his friends. He had told me about it, but it seemed silly to me. I don't think it will catch on.

The young lady, Patricia Strang, was a pleasant companion for the evening. She and her mother were here because her father, an army colonel, was on TDY in Germany. That is Temporary Detached Duty.

Her mother wanted to come to the ball and was actively looking forward to it when her husband received his orders. Patricia agreed to accompany her so her mother wouldn't be alone all evening.

One obvious thing was that this wasn't a setup for her to meet me.

I asked her if she had a boyfriend that she had left at home for the evening. There was no boyfriend. She didn't have time for one as her graduate studies at UCLA in physics were intense.

I asked her what part of physics she was interested in. She told me string theory. Her tone was such that she didn't expect me to have any idea what that was about.

Since Mary, my genius sister was up to her eyebrows in that sort of thing, I had learned enough buzzwords to hold a general conversation.

I thought Patricia, never Patty, was going to spill her drink when I asked her which flavor of quark she preferred as a sundae topping.

"Rick, how do you know enough about physics to be able to make a joke? It is a specialized field, and few people know these things."

"My little sister Mary tells me about it at her tea parties."

"Your little sister?"

"Mary is enrolled at Stanford and is majoring in physics. She hopes to have her undergrad degree by the time she is eleven, and a Ph.D. by fifteen."

"Of course! Your sister is Mary Jackson. I've read about her. I would love to meet her."

"Well turn to your right a little, look up to the balcony, and wave to the little girl with the camera with the huge photographic lens on it."

"What is she doing?"

"Knowing her, she is trying to get pictures to sell to one of the tabloids. We are trying to break her of the habit, but she claims she needs the money."

"Doesn't she get an allowance?"

"Mum and Dad let her keep five hundred dollars a month from her earnings, and the rest goes into a trust fund. She claims that is cruel and unusual punishment because a girl needs her chocolates."

"She has a point, you know."

"Her clothing company payments are over a quarter a million a month. That is a lot of chocolate. She might get cavities if she is allowed to eat all that."

"Wait, your Mary is the Mary of Mary Jackson clothing?"

"Yep."

"Wow, I have to meet her!"

"Let's sneak out of here and go up to her. I'll introduce you."

We sidled our way out of the room and went up to the balcony. Mary was still there.

"Mary, I would like to introduce you to Patricia Strang. She is studying physics at UCLA and loves your clothing line."

That ended my need to escort Patricia to dinner or anywhere else. She and her new best friend Mary headed to the basement where pizza was being served.

Dumb me went to dinner by myself. It took about two minutes for me to realize that it wasn't a good idea. I think the whole room saw me sitting alone and wondered what had happened to my dinner date.

From the looks Mum was giving me, I had to go tell her quietly where Patricia had disappeared to. She had me go tell Mrs. Strang. Both the ladies thought it was funny and were laughing.

This didn't help me at all. The tabloids the next day were speculating on what I had done to have the young lady abandon me.

Insult to injury, I was drafted the next day to accompany Mary and Patricia in a limo up to Stanford so Mary could show off her new computer setup.

They talked about strings, tensors, up, down, strange, and other weird stuff the whole trip. At one point Patricia commented, and Mary started to respond but stopped mid-sentence.

"But if that is true, then cold fusion is possible!"

I had a vague idea of what fusion was but had never heard of cold fusion.

The girls started writing notes and equations on every piece of paper they could find. I had to have the limo pull over at a G. C. Murphy's and buy notebook paper and pencils.

They managed to explain to me what cold fusion was. I realized that if they could make it happen, it would be invaluable out in space and down on Earth for that matter.

What was coming next?

Finished for now.

Back Matter

The next in the series is Book 15 The Lunar Kingdom[1]
Enelsonauthor.com[2]

For information on hiring Janet E. Rupert to edit your fiction project, email:
janeteditorrupert@gmail.com

1. https://www.amazon.com/Richard-Jackson-Saga-Kingdom-Alternate-ebook/dp/ B09SZS38T7

2.   https://www.enelsonauthor.com/

Other books by Ed Nelson

The Richard Jackson Saga *Book 1 The Beginning*
Book 2 Schooldays
Book 3 Hollywood
Book 4 In the Movies
Book 5 Star to Deckhand
Book 6 Surfing Dude
Book 7 Third Time is a Charm
Book 8 Oxford University
Book 9 Cold War
Book 10 Taking Care of Business
Book 11 Interesting Times
Book 12 Escape from Siberia
Book 13 Regicide
Book 14 What's Under, Down Under?
Book 15 The Lunar Kingdom
Book 16 First Steps
In the Richard Jackson World
Mary, Mary
Stand-Alone Story
Ever and Always
Cast in Time Series
Book 1: Baron
Book 2: Baron of the Middle Counties
Book 3: Count
Book 4: Earl
Book 5: Earl of the Marches

Did you love *What's Under? Down Under*? Then you should read *Lunar Kingdom* by Ed Nelson!

Coming-of-age stories don't have to be all teenage angst. They can be fun-filled adventures that become more serious with age. With humor,we follow a young man's coming of age in the late 1950s and early '60s. Starting in the summer before his freshman year, he goes through high school and beyond. He finds wealth as an inventor and fame in Hollywood as he searches for a girlfriend. Wealth and fame prove far easier than girls.The fifteenth book in the series, Lunar Kingdom, has Rick exploring the moon and outer space. Danger, fame and fortune, and adventure seem to be his lot in life. He finally connects with the love of his life. His actions have caused a change in history as we know it. He and Russia have their final confrontation. Then there is the moon and the outer reaches to explore.This tongue-in-cheek saga is all true, give or take a lie or two.

www.ingramcontent.com/pod-product-compliance
Lightning Source LLC
Chambersburg PA
CBHW070317260626
47160CB00003B/868